MRS. JEFFRIES
DEFENDS HER OWN

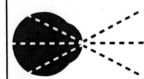

This Large Print Book carries the
Seal of Approval of N.A.V.H.

MRS. JEFFRIES DEFENDS HER OWN

EMILY BRIGHTWELL

WHEELER PUBLISHING

A part of Gale, Cengage Learning

Detroit • New York • San Francisco • New Haven, Conn • Waterville, Maine • London

GALE
CENGAGE Learning®

Copyright © 2012 by Cheryl Arguile.
A Victorian Mystery.
Wheeler Publishing, a part of Gale, Cengage Learning.

Wheeler Publishing Large Print Cozy Mystery.
The text of this Large Print edition is unabridged.
Other aspects of the book may vary from the original edition.
Set in 16 pt. Plantin.

LIBRARY OF CONGRESS CATALOGING-IN-PUBLICATION DATA

Brightwell, Emily.
    Mrs. Jeffries defends her own / by Emily Brightwell. — Large print ed.
        p. cm. — (Wheeler Publishing large print cozy mystery)
    "A Victorian Mystery"—T.p. verso.
    ISBN 978-1-4104-5169-9 (softcover) — ISBN 1-4104-5169-0 (softcover)
    1. Witherspoon, Gerald (Fictitious character)—Fiction. 2. Jeffries, Mrs.
(Fictitious character)—Fiction. 3. Police—Great Britain—Fiction. 4. Women household employees—Fiction. 5. Murder—Investigation—Fiction. 6. Large type books. I. Title.
PS3552.R46443M648 2012
813'.54—dc23   2012026934

Published in 2012 by arrangement with The Berkley Publishing Group, a member of Penguin Group (USA) Inc.

Printed in the United States of America
    1 2 3 4 5   16 15 14 13 12

ED297

MRS. JEFFRIES
DEFENDS HER OWN

CHAPTER 1

"Your excuses are getting tiresome, Jones." Ronald Dearman fixed his disapproving glare upon the hapless clerk standing on the far side of the wide mahogany desk. "If it happens again, you'll get the sack. Is that clear?"

"Yes sir," Daniel Jones said quickly. "I understand, and I'm grateful you're giving me another chance. But my mum was so ill I had to take her to the doctor. She's better now, so it shouldn't happen again."

"See that it doesn't," Dearman snapped. He glanced at the clock on the wall next to the door. "Are you the last one here?"

"Yes, sir," Jones stuttered. "It's past six o'clock, sir, and everyone else has gone."

"Go ahead and leave, then. Just make sure the windows are closed and locked."

"They are, sir." Jones edged toward the door. "Mr. Anson ordered them closed before he left for the factory, and I locked

7

them then." He broke off, wincing as he realized he'd said just the wrong thing.

Dearman's eyes widened. "Mr. Anson ordered," he repeated. "Mr. Anson isn't in a position to be ordering anything around here. I'm in charge of the office, not Henry Anson. Do you hear me, do you understand?"

"Yes, sir, of course, sir." Jones stumbled backward, desperate to get out of the office before Dearman decided to sack him. "I only meant —"

"I know what you meant," Dearman shouted. "And I'm not having it. Neither you nor anyone else in this office is to take any notice of what that upstart says. Now get out of here before I change my mind and you find yourself unemployed."

"Yes, sir, yes, sir." He lunged for the handle, yanked the door open, and flew into the outer office. "Good night, sir," he called over his shoulder.

Dearman didn't bother to reply. He sat up, his body stiffening as an image of Anson's face flashed into his mind. He wished he could sack that one. Anson strutted around like the cock of the walk, safe and secure as the favored one. At that thought, Dearman's heart pounded and his chest tightened. He took a long, deep breath

8

and expelled it slowly. His doctor had warned him about getting upset, said it wasn't good for his blood pressure. Dearman shifted slightly, trying to ease the pressure in his chest; he could hear a faint buzzing in his ears as well. He took another breath and deliberately relaxed the muscles in his shoulders and arms. He was determined to stay calm.

He'd not let Anson win by conveniently dropping dead of a stroke or heart failure; he intended to be here for a good number of years yet. The little sod was going to have to wait a long time before he got this office. Dearman turned his head and focused his gaze on the lamp on his desk. As it was a cold, miserable gray day in March, it had been lighted since the middle of the afternoon. He smiled slightly. His heart had stopped pounding, and the buzzing in his ears was gone. He laughed softly as a gust of rain slammed against the window. Oh yes, he intended to be at Sutcliffe Manufacturing for a long, long time.

His good humor restored, he leaned back in his chair, satisfied that he had his world under control. Even better, he had Daniel Jones, the junior accounting assistant, completely cowed. The man had made the mistake of taking one too many days off. It

9

didn't matter to him that Jones was taking care of his ailing mother; he simply needed to ensure that Jones was completely intimidated. He was a bright lad, perhaps too bright, and that wouldn't do at all. Junior accountants needed to know not to ask too many questions about matters that didn't concern them.

Dearman yawned and stretched his arms toward the ceiling, enjoying the solitude of the quiet, empty office. Other than his annoyance at hearing Henry Anson's name, it had been a good day, especially for a Monday. He'd successfully quelled a minor rebellion amongst the clerks over the time allowed for the midday meal break, bullied Jones into submission, and arranged for a new and less expensive reconciliation accounts clerk.

He frowned suddenly as he heard footsteps in the outer office. "Jones, is that you? I thought you'd left for the day," he called. The footsteps paused and then continued on toward his door.

Dearman straightened his spine and stared at his closed office door. "Who's there? Jones, is that you? Answer me. Who is there?"

But no one replied. Instead, he saw the knob turn, and a second later, the door eased open.

He slumped in relief. "Goodness, it's you. Why didn't you reply when I called out? What's that you're holding?" His voice trailed off as his visitor stepped farther into the room and aimed the gun directly at his forehead.

"No, no, you can't do that." Dearman shoved backward with all his might and tried to throw himself to one side. But he couldn't move faster than a bullet.

The visitor squeezed the trigger, and as planned, the sound of the shot was drowned out by the blast of the horn from the six-fifteen ferry as it passed under the South-wark Bridge.

Ronald Dearman stared in stunned surprise for a brief moment and then flopped forward onto his desk. The murderer moved quickly across the small space, stopping by the body and checking to make sure that Dearman was truly dead before pulling a set of keys out of the deceased's coat pocket. Satisfied that the victim wouldn't live to tell any tales, the assailant blew out the lamp and left the premises, double-checking that both Dearman's office door and the main door were locked tight.

Inspector Nigel Nivens struggled to keep

from smiling as he stood over the corpse of Ronald Dearman, deputy manager of Sutcliffe Manufacturing. The inspector wasn't happy the man had been killed, of course, but he was delighted that for once, he'd been assigned the murder.

"It's about time you got one, sir," Constable Morehead said to Nivens.

"Why wouldn't I get it?" Nivens replied as he studied the position of the body. "It's in my district, and apparently, a mere deputy manager wasn't important enough for the Home Office to insist the case be given to Inspector Gerald Witherspoon."

He spoke freely in front of Morehead; they'd worked together on a number of cases, and Nivens knew that the young constable was ambitious and very much in awe of Nivens' social and political connections. Besides, Morehead was the only constable who liked him enough to have a drink with him. When he stepped into any of the local policeman's pubs near the station, he might as well have been invisible. None of the off-duty constables or detectives would so much as look in his direction. He wasn't well liked and he knew it. He tried not to let it bother him, and for the most part, it didn't. Power was far more useful to him than popularity.

"Well, it's only right that you get it, sir," Morehead agreed. "You've plenty of good collars on your record, and it isn't fair that every important case be given to Inspector Witherspoon. The rest of us need a chance to prove ourselves."

"And prove ourselves we will." Nivens smiled briefly. "I intend to solve this case quickly, and that will lead to others."

"You like solving murders?" Morehead asked.

"Of course not, but you've been around long enough to know that is the way to the top. Catching killers gets one's name in the papers, and that, Constable Morehead, makes the brass sit up and take notice. One of these days, I intend to have Bradford's spot."

"You want to be the commissioner?"

"Naturally, and once I've successfully concluded this investigation, I fully expect to be promoted. I've several reporters who owe me favors, and they'll see to it that my name is prominently mentioned in all the newspaper accounts."

"Inspector Witherspoon has solved dozens of murders and gets his name in the paper all the time, but he's not been promoted." Morehead moved to the far side of the desk so he could get a better look at the body.

13

"That's because he's a fool." Nivens' good humor vanished at the mention of Witherspoon's name.

"I heard he's been offered promotion many times, but he always turns it down," Morehead continued. His attention was on the corpse, and he was oblivious to the fact that he was annoying his superior. "Supposedly, he doesn't need the money and he's happy with his current position. I know the lads all speak well of him."

"I wonder if the lads would think so highly of him if they all knew he had more help than any of us get when he's on a case." Nivens lifted the victim's head to take a closer look at the bullet hole in his forehead. "He'd not have such a high solve rate if it wasn't for his servants. They help him, you know, especially that housekeeper of his, Mrs. Jeffries. She's the sharp one behind his success. You wouldn't think a woman would be able to put two and two together and come up with the correct answer, but she does. Witherspoon's solution rate wouldn't be any better than anyone else's if he didn't have her and the rest of them snooping about on his behalf." Nivens let go of the victim's head and it thumped hard against the desk.

Morehead glanced at the office door and

winced as he noticed it was slightly ajar. "Mrs. Sutcliffe is just outside, sir," he whispered in an attempt to remind his superior to be a bit gentler when handling the victim.

Outside the dead man's office, Fiona Sutcliffe stood frozen in shock. She couldn't believe her ears. For a moment, she panicked, but then she brought herself under control. Stumbling just a bit, she moved to the nearest desk, yanked out a chair, and sat down. She had to think, she had to decide what to do. Just how capable was this Inspector Nivens? From what she'd overheard, he was more concerned with his own ambition than anything else, and that could cause her great difficulties. It wouldn't take long before he found out. There had been too many witnesses, and she was under no illusions that her servants would hold their tongues. But which was the more dangerous course of action? Letting this investigation take its course or going to her for help?

She sat there thinking, going over every possible outcome, while all around her, constables searched the premises of Sutcliffe Manufacturing looking for evidence. She ignored the muffled voices and the shuffling feet as she concentrated on the problem at hand. She wasn't superstitious, but on the other hand, she wasn't one to ignore the hand of providence. Hearing that name after so many years surely meant something.

The door opened and the plainclothes officer stood on the threshold. He was a portly man with dull blond hair, bulbous blue eyes, and a large mustache. He stared at her for a moment, then turned back to the office and said to the constable, "When the police surgeon has the body moved, do a thorough search of this office. I'll start the interviews."

She stared at him cooly as he came toward her, noting with surprise that his blue suit was exactly like one her husband owned, his shirt was pristine white, and his black shoes were shined to perfection. She didn't think policemen earned the sort of money it took to get their clothes tailor made.

"Mrs. Sutcliffe." He stopped in front of her chair and gave a small bow of his head. "I'm Inspector Nigel Nivens. I understand that you found the body."

"You've been misinformed, Inspector," she replied. "It was Mr. Dearman's wife who found him."

"But the first constable on the scene reported that you were here when he arrived," he insisted.

"Of course I was. I accompanied Mrs. Dearman here this morning. We arrived before the office opened for business, and I used my position as the wife of the owner to have the porter unlock the doors. But it was Mrs. Dearman who found him."

"It's been a right miserable day out," the cook, Mrs. Goodge, complained as she picked up the last of the lunch plates and handed them to the maid. "Even Fred hasn't been pesterin' anyone to take him walkies."

Fred, the household's mongrel dog, raised up from his spot by the cooker, gave a desultory wag of his long tail, and then curled back down to sleep. Outside, a chilly spring rain fell steadily against the window-panes over the sink, but the household of Inspector Gerald Witherspoon was warm and cozy.

"I don't know, it's not that bad," Wiggins, the footman, commented. "It's wet, but the streets aren't floodin'."

"Thank goodness for that," the cook exclaimed. "It wouldn't do for Betsy and Smythe's train to be delayed, not if they want to get to their ship on time."

"I wish they weren't going. I'm going to miss them so much," Phyllis muttered as she took the dishes to the sink. "Oh dear, I can't believe I just said that. You're all going to think I'm selfish."

"We'd not think that," Mrs. Jeffries, the housekeeper, said. "We're all going to miss them."

Phyllis smiled broadly. She'd been here less than a year, but it was already home to her. Her face as round as a pie plate, she had dark blonde hair worn in a bun at the nape of her neck and lovely, porcelain skin. She was nineteen and plump as one of Mrs. Goodge's roast chickens. "Don't take any notice of me; I want them to go and have a wonderful time."

"We all do," Mrs. Goodge said. "But I do think takin' a baby all the way to Canada is risky. I don't see why they couldn't have waited until Amanda Belle was a bit older before goin'."

Mrs. Jeffries ducked her head to hide a smile. Amanda Belle wasn't just Smythe and Betsy's infant daughter, she was also the cook's goddaughter. Mrs. Goodge hadn't expected to find a family so late in her life, and she hated that she was going to be away from her "lambkins" for over two months.

"They'll both be right annoyed if we get us a murder while they're gone," Wiggins declared. "Mind you, with the inspector

18

bein' assigned to that special fraud investigation, the victim would need to be important before they'd pull 'im off that."

Inspector Gerald Witherspoon was the most successful homicide detective in the history of the Metropolitan Police Force. He was also rich. He'd been working in the Records Room and living in modest lodgings when he'd inherited a huge house as well as a large fortune from his late aunt, Euphemia Witherspoon. He'd also inherited Wiggins, the brown-haired, apple-cheeked footman, and Smythe, the coachman. He'd hired Mrs. Jeffries, the widow of a Yorkshire policeman, to run the household. She'd arrived a few weeks before the first of the horrible Kensington High Street murders, and before anyone had realized what she was doing, she had encouraged the inspector to ask a few questions on his own and had the rest of them out gathering information as well. Witherspoon had solved the case. Ever since then, the inspector had been given one case after another . . . especially if the victim was rich, famous, or well connected.

"Let's hope we don't get a case," the housekeeper said. "With Betsy and Smythe gone, we'd be spread very thin on the ground."

"Oh, but I think we could manage." Phyllis began pumping the water into the sink. "I mean, there's the four of us, as well as the others. That would be enough."

The housekeeper hid her smile behind her teacup. Phyllis had been very reluctant to take on the task of assisting the inspector with his cases — for the simple reason that their dear inspector had no idea he was getting help. The housemaid had been terrified that if Witherspoon found out they'd been asking questions, she'd lose her position. Mrs. Jeffries had realized the girl had gone through some very tough times before coming to the inspector's household and hadn't insisted the maid do anything that made her uncomfortable. But Phyllis had watched the satisfaction that working for the cause of justice had given the rest of the staff, and on her own had decided she wanted to help. She'd surprised them all by displaying some rather useful skills. Phyllis was an excellent forger.

"Of course we could manage if we had to," the cook complained. "But I agree with Mrs. Jeffries, we'd be spread thin. It takes a lot of effort on all our parts to find what bits and pieces we need to get a case solved."

From upstairs, they heard a knock on the front door.

Phyllis leapt up and started for the back

staircase. "Are you expecting anyone?" she called over her shoulder as she reached the bottom step.

"No, and the inspector didn't mention anyone coming by today, either," Mrs. Jeffries replied. "I've no idea who it could be."

"Perhaps it's a message from Betsy and Smythe sayin' they are comin' home," Mrs. Goodge said hopefully.

Mrs. Jeffries laughed. "They've hardly had time to get to Liverpool to board the ship. Besides, I know that deep down you want Betsy to see her sister."

Betsy's family had been torn apart over the years. But Smythe had located her sister and paid for the woman and her husband to come to England from Canada for Betsy's wedding to Smythe. Unlike most coachmen, Smythe was very, very wealthy. He'd made a fortune in Australia.

The cook sighed. "Of course I want her to see her relatives. But when you get to be my age, you're never sure of how many days you have left."

"Don't say things like that, Mrs. Goodge." Wiggins frowned at her. "You've got plenty of years left."

Wiggins and the cook had grown very close in the years they'd worked together.

"That's nice of you to say, lad, but the truth is I'm old. Luckily, my health is good, so I'll probably last until they get home."

Upstairs, Phyllis opened the door to find a tall, slender woman of late middle age standing on the stoop. She wore an elegant forest green mantle with stylish brass buttons down the front and held a black umbrella over her head. She had brown hair seamed with substantial amounts of gray, done up in a elegant coiffure topped with a hat decorated with pheasant feathers and bands of veiling the same shade as her mantle.

"May I help you, ma'am?" Phyllis asked.

"I'd like to see Mrs. Jeffries," the woman replied. "As it's raining, I'd also like to step inside."

Reacting to the authoritative tone, Phyllis opened the door wider but then stopped. She'd been warned on several occasions not to let strangers in, regardless of how well dressed they were. Their inspector was a well-known policeman who'd sent dozens of criminals to the dock. Phyllis took a deep breath. "I'm sorry, ma'am, you'll have to wait on the stoop. I'll go get Mrs. Jeffries." With that, she slammed the door shut and rushed back down to the kitchen. "There's a strange woman at the front door," she exclaimed. "She's wanting Mrs. Jeffries, but I remember what you told me and I didn't let her inside. I think she's going to be annoyed — she didn't look happy when I told her to wait on the stoop."

Mrs. Jeffries was already on her feet, and Wiggins was right on her heels. They hurried up the stairs. When they reached the hallway, the footman sprinted past her. "Let me open the door," he said. "If you know the woman, we can let her in."

Mrs. Jeffries started to argue and then clamped her mouth shut. He was only doing what she'd instructed him to do. "Yes, that'll be fine."

Both of them stopped to catch their breath when they reached the door. Wiggins looked at her and she nodded. He opened the door.

"I'd like to see Mrs. Jeffries," the woman snapped. "I'm not accustomed to being kept standing in the rain."

Mrs. Jeffries recognized the voice.

"May I have your name, ma'am?" he asked politely.

"It's alright, Wiggins, I know her." Mrs. Jeffries smiled at the footman. "Can you please go downstairs and ask Mrs. Goodge to send up a pot of tea? She was just brewing one when we came up, so it should be ready by now. We'll be in the drawing room."

She turned back to her unexpected guest and held the door wide open. "Do come in, Fiona. I'm sorry you were kept waiting."

"I'd sack my servants if they behaved in such a manner." She collapsed her umbrella and stomped over the threshold into the foyer.

"Then you'd be foolish. Inspector Witherspoon has arrested over thirty murderers, and the staff has standing instructions never to let a stranger into the house," she replied. "A good number of those killers were upper-class, well-dressed women such as yourself. Now, before this goes any further, what do you want?"

Fiona Jeffries Sutcliffe stared at her for a long moment, and then her lean, still-lovely face crumpled in fear. "I want your help."

Mrs. Jeffries wasn't sure she'd heard correctly. "My help," she repeated. "What on earth could I do to help you?"

"Forgive me, Hepzibah, I've no right to comment on how you run this household. But please, don't turn me away. I'm desperate, and I know I've not been much of a sister-in-law, but for David's sake, please don't turn me away."

Mrs. Jeffries stiffened at the mention of her late husband's name. In the blink of an eye, a jumble of thoughts, images, feelings flew through her mind, and one part of her wanted to grab this woman by the elbow, march her out the front door, and tell her to never set foot here again. The two women stood in silence. Mrs. Jeffries stared at the pool of water dripping off the end of Fiona's umbrella onto the floor as her conscience did battle with old resentments and remembered anger. Conscience won. "Of course I won't turn you away," she said softly. "Come along, let's go into the drawing room."

Fiona hesitated. "I know you're the housekeeper here, Hepzibah. I don't want to get you into trouble with your employer. I'm quite prepared to go to your rooms or even the kitchen. We don't have to use the drawing room."

Mrs. Jeffries stared at her sister-in-law for a moment and then laughed at the absurdity of the situation. "That won't be necessary, Fiona. My employer won't mind in the least. Come along, it's this way." She led her down the hall and through the double doors. She took a moment's satisfaction as Fiona stopped and blinked, no doubt surprised by the beautifully decorated drawing room. Waving at the settee, she said, "Please sit down. Tea will be here in a moment. You look like you could use something hot."

"I could use something a bit stronger than tea," Fiona muttered. "But I'll take anything you offer."

"Would you like a sherry?" Mrs. Jeffries stared at her curiously. She'd been so stunned by her sister-in-law's appearance on her doorstep that she'd not really taken a good look at her. Now she saw that Fiona's hazel eyes were wide with fear, her expression haunted, and there was a pale, white ring about her lips, as though she'd suffered a terrible shock.

"Yes I would," Fiona admitted. "I know it's terrible to do such a thing at this time of day, but I'd love a good sherry."

"Then that's what we'll have. From the expression on your face, I imagine I'll need one as well." Mrs. Jeffries hurried to the liquor cupboard, pulled out a bottle of Harvey's Bristol Cream, and grabbed two glasses. She poured both of them a drink.

Just then, the doors opened and Phyllis came in with the tea tray. "Thank you, Phyllis, but you can take that back down to the kitchen. Mrs. Sutcliffe and I are going to have a sherry instead. Tell Mrs. Goodge and Wiggins that I'm sorry to have put them to any trouble."

"Yes, Mrs. Jeffries." Phyllis nodded respectfully and retreated the way she'd come.

As soon as the door had closed, Mrs. Jeffries handed her guest her glass and took a seat across from her. "Now, what's this all about?"

Fiona didn't answer immediately; she took a sip of her sherry and stared off into the distance. "I'm not really sure how to begin," she finally murmured.

Mrs. Jeffries said nothing, she merely waited. She was curious but she was also patient. After all these years, her sister-in-law had suddenly shown up on her doorstep. But knowing Fiona as she did, she was certain there was a reason. She raised her glass to her lips.

"There's been a murder," Fiona began.

Mrs. Jeffries paused for a brief moment and then took a drink. She said nothing, again waiting for her guest to continue. It was a policeman's trick she'd learned from David. Say nothing and let the suspect rush to fill in the quiet space. Not that Fiona was a suspect, but nonetheless, Mrs. Jeffries had found this to be an excellent device in getting additional information out of people.

"Ronald Dearman, the deputy manager of Sutcliffe's, was found shot to death this morning. He was in his office. You should remember him, you've met him before. He was at our wedding."

27

As Fiona had done her best to ignore her relatives on that particular day, Mrs. Jeffries had barely been introduced to anyone. "That was thirty years ago, Fiona," she reminded her. "I've a good memory, but I can't recall this particular person. Are the police certain it was murder and not suicide?"

"It was definitely not suicide." She gave a short, harsh bark of a laugh. "Ronald Dearman was the last person in this world who'd take his own life. He is — or was," she corrected, "married to John's sister, Lucretia."

"Weren't you her paid companion when you met John?" Mrs. Jeffries asked.

Fiona stiffened slightly. "I was, but that was a long time ago and has nothing to do with the matter at hand."

"Are you still close with her?" she pressed.

"No, not for many years, but that has nothing to do with why I'm here now."

"I presume you're here because you need the assistance of my employer, Inspector Witherspoon, in this matter?" Mrs. Jeffries guessed.

Fiona shook her head, raised her glass, drained it, and laid it on the end table by the settee. "No, that's not why I'm here. Oh Lord, this is so hard. I can't believe I'm in this predicament." She closed her eyes, drew a deep breath, and then looked at Mrs. Jeffries. "I know that Inspector Witherspoon is brilliant, but it's your help I need, not his."

Mrs. Jeffries finished off her sherry in one huge gulp. She hadn't expected to hear that. To give herself a moment to think, she grabbed both their glasses, got up, and went to the cabinet. "I think we can both use another one of these," she muttered.

Her mind worked furiously as she poured two more glasses. What on earth should she do? The Fiona she remembered from years ago wasn't the sort of person to avidly follow murders in the press; she'd have died before she did something so common. So how did she know about the inspector's homicide record, and more important, how could she possibly guess that it was Witherspoon's household who could be of help to her? There was only one way to find out.

"I'll be glad to render any assistance possible." She handed Fiona her glass and took her own seat. "But I'm mystified as to what you think I could possibly do."

Fiona gave her a thin smile. "Do you believe in fate? I didn't, not until this morning. Up until then I would have said that intelligent, superior people weave their own destinies by the decisions they make, but

29

Ronald's murder showed me how very wrong I was. Fate or destiny or whatever one likes to name it can come along and turn a life upside down in the blink of an eye. That's what happened to me today."

"You've obviously had a very upsetting experience, one that I'm sure will stay with you for a long time. But that's quite common — murder has a terrible effect on the people around the victim," Mrs. Jeffries said. "That's one of the reasons it is so important that society catches and punishes those that decide to play God and take a human life. But you haven't answered my question. Why did you come to me?"

"Because I overheard the policeman investigating Ronald's murder mention something very interesting. I was standing just outside the door, and the man has a voice that carries quite easily. I'd not been listening all that closely, but then I heard Inspector Witherspoon's name mentioned, and as I knew he was your employer, that caught my attention. Imagine my surprise when I heard him say that Inspector Witherspoon wouldn't have solved any of those murders if it hadn't been for you and the rest of his household servants."

"That's nonsense," Mrs. Jeffries replied. She felt a tremor of apprehension race up her spine. "What's the name of this police-man?"

"It's Nivens, Inspector Nigel Nivens," Fiona replied.

Mrs. Jeffries heart sank as her worst fears were realized. Nivens had been trying to prove that Witherspoon was essentially a fraud since those horrible Kensington High Street murders. He'd only ceased his nasty snooping into the household's activities because he'd found himself beholden to Witherspoon over a little matter of with-holding evidence a few years back. But she'd always known it was too good to last, that one day, he'd reappear in their midst and show his true colors. He was an incom-petent bully who'd only made it up the chain of command because of his family's social status and political connections.

For a brief moment, she was tempted to tell her sister-in-law that it was all a silly mistake and that Nivens was a jealous fool who couldn't accept that another police-man was better at solving crimes. She owed Fiona nothing.

She looked up and studied her guest's face. Fiona was staring at her with an expression of mingled hope and fear. "Fi-ona, perhaps it would be better if —"

Fiona interrupted. "I know that you've no

reason to help me, Hepzibah." Her eyes filled with tears. "I know I've treated you shamefully, and I'm deeply sorry for it."

"It wasn't me you treated shamefully, it was your brother," Mrs. Jeffries snapped. A wave of anger washed over her. "He loved you, but once you 'married up' as the locals in Yorkshire called it, you didn't have much time for him, did you? You knew how much he loved you, you knew how much he cared about you, but you were so hell-bent on moving up in life that you pretended he didn't even exist. You were his baby sister, and he worshipped the very ground you walked on, but did that matter to you? Not in the least."

"Please, Hepzibah, stop."

"No, I won't stop. I've held this inside for years, and now you've the nerve to come here and ask for my help? When I think of all the times David made me send you notes inviting you and your new husband to dinner, I get sick to my stomach. If you could have seen the disappointment in his eyes when you never came. You never once set foot in our house after you married, and that cut him to the quick. For goodness' sake, we weren't half-wits that you needed to be ashamed about. We were both perfectly respectable people. We just didn't happen to be rich."

Fiona was out and out crying now. "Dear God, have pity. Ever since his funeral I've been haunted by how badly I behaved. I didn't mean to push the two of you aside. It simply happened that way, and then when John moved the company to London, I thought I'd have plenty of time to go back to Yorkshire on visits and make it up to him. I thought the two of you would live there forever. I didn't expect him to die so young."

"Fifty-two isn't so young," Mrs. Jeffries said archly. She took another sip from her glass, and then a great sense of weariness came over her. She closed her eyes and an image of David's face flashed into her mind. Her beloved husband had been gone for years now, and in that instant she realized that no matter how hurt he'd been by his sister's behavior, he'd have wanted her to help. Mrs. Jeffries opened her eyes.

Fiona's sobs had subsided into a sniffle. She'd pulled a handkerchief out of her mantle pocket and was dabbing at her eyes. She took a deep breath and got up. "Apparently, my coming here wasn't a good idea. I'm sorry to have bothered you . . ."

"Sit down, Fiona," Mrs. Jeffries ordered. "And while you're at it, take off your wrap. I apologize for not taking it earlier and for losing my temper."

"You have a right to be angry." Fiona sat back in her seat.

"I know I do, but the past is the past and David would want me to do whatever I could to help you. Now, tell me what happened and why you're so very frightened about this man's death."

Fiona began to unbutton her mantle. "Thank you, Hepzibah. I'll never forget this."

"I'm not making any promises, and I'm certainly not admitting that Inspector Nivens was right. Inspector Witherspoon is a very talented detective, and his success isn't necessarily because of me or anyone else in his household. Now, how was Ronald Dearman killed and when? I need details, and don't leave anything out, no matter how insignificant."

"He was shot." She slipped the garment off her shoulder and tossed it over the back of the settee, waving Mrs. Jeffries back to her chair when she started to reach for it.

"I know, you've already told me that. But do you know how many times?"

"How many times?" Fiona looked confused by the question. "Oh, you must mean how many times was he shot. I don't know. I didn't look closely when Lucretia started screaming. It was obvious he was dead, so I pulled her away and sent the porter for the police."

"I'm getting ahead of myself. Tell me in your own words what happened. Start at the beginning, please."

"It began this morning. I'd just finished breakfast and was going downstairs to speak to Cook when I heard this awful banging on the front door. As none of the servants were anywhere in sight, I went to the door myself."

"That's not like you," Mrs. Jeffries said.

"I know, but John is away in Birmingham on business, and for some reason, I suppose because they were making such a racket, I was alarmed. So instead of waiting for the butler, I opened the door myself. Lucretia was standing there. She was upset. She said that Ronald hadn't come home the night before and she wanted John to take her along to the company offices to see if he was there."

"What time was this?"

"About seven fifteen," Fiona smile faintly. "When John's gone, I breakfast very early."

"Why didn't she just wait until the office had opened and go along herself?" Mrs. Jeffries asked.

"The office doesn't open until half past

eight, and she claimed she was too worried to wait. Frankly, I think she wanted to get there before the office opened because she was frightened of what she would find. She didn't want to be humiliated in front of the staff. There have been rumors that Ronald drinks more than he should." Fiona couldn't keep the note of contempt out of her voice.

Mrs. Jeffries glanced at the glass in her hand. "I take it Mr. Dearman had been working late the prior evening?"

Fiona nodded. "That's what Lucretia told me. I told her that John was out of town and I'd no idea where his keys were. To be honest, I wasn't sure what to say. We're not the best of friends, and there's been gossip about their marriage, so I thought it perfectly possible that he'd decided not to come home for reasons of his own. But I could hardly say that. She insisted that we get into the building, so I told her I'd go with her and have the porter let us. She was satisfied with that, and we took a hansom cab to the office."

"Where exactly is the office?" Mrs. Jeffries asked.

"On Queen Street Place by the Southwark Bridge. Lucretia seemed to get more and more nervous as we made our way there — she kept yelling at the driver to hurry. We went into the building, and I told the porter that I needed to get into our suite of offices on the second floor."

"Had the porter let you in on other occasions?" she asked. Their previous cases had taught her to question people carefully about the details.

"He knew who I was. Last week, John had left his spectacles at home and as I was going to be shopping close by, I came in to give them to him. He can see without them, but it does cause a great strain on his eyes."

"So the porter took you right up," Mrs. Jeffries pressed. She wanted to understand the exact sequence of events.

"We had to wait for a few moments," she replied. "It's a large, modern building, and several of the other businesses were already open for the day. When we arrived, the porter was busy helping another gentleman. When it was our turn, I explained what we needed, and then we waited while he went to his kiosk in the back to get the spare keys."

"Did he give you the keys, or did he accompany you?" she asked.

"He accompanied us and unlocked both the outer door and the door to Ronald's office." Fiona closed her eyes and took a deep breath. "I was certain he'd be in the room asleep or drunk, and not wanting to witness a scene, I hung back a bit so that Lucretia could have some privacy. The porter opened the door and stepped back to let her enter. She went in and then I heard her screaming. Both the porter and I raced into the office. That's when we found him. I knew right away that he was dead."

Mrs. Jeffries regarded her curiously. "How did you know?"

"There was blood all over the top of his desk." She swallowed convulsively. "And Lucretia was standing there, holding his head up and . . . I . . . I could see the hole in his forehead. Oh God, it was awful. I wasn't fond of Ronald, but I'll never forget that sight as long as I live."

"What did you do then?"

She grimaced. "I forced Lucretia to let go of him, and then I eased his head back down as gently as I could." She shuddered. "Then I pulled her out of the room and yelled for the porter to fetch the police. After that, everything is a blur. Suddenly there were policemen everywhere. I overheard one of the constables say that it wasn't a suicide as there was no gun near the body so it had to be a murder. Unfortunately, Lucretia heard him as well and started having hysterics."

"What did you do?"

"I took her into John's office and poured her a drink. He keeps a bottle of whiskey in his desk. Then I told her to lie down. I was going to stay with her, but the constable came and said the inspector wished to speak with her. As she was in no condition to speak to anyone, I went and told him that she was incoherent and wouldn't be much use until she calmed down."

"So she was alone in John's office when you went to speak to Nivens?"

Fiona nodded. "Yes, why? Is that important?"

She ignored the question. "Did you go right back to Lucretia?"

She shook her head. "No, I stayed in the outer office. I could see John's office door from where I stood, and I wanted to make sure they left her alone. I'm not fond of Lucretia, but she was in a state. It was when I was standing there that I heard your name so prominently mentioned."

"Do you want my help because you're going to be a suspect?" Mrs. Jeffries watched her carefully as she asked the question.

Fiona smiled briefly. "You always did get right to the point. Yes, that's precisely why I need your help. I imagine it won't take that policeman long to find out the worst."

Downstairs, Phyllis drummed her fingertips on the tabletop as she waited for Mrs. Goodge and Wiggins. She'd brought the tea tray down to find the kitchen empty. She was about to get up to go look for them when she heard Mrs. Goodge's door squeak open just as Wiggins came in from the communal gardens.

"Mrs. Jeffries didn't want tea," she said, keeping her voice low. "She said she and her visitor would have a drink instead."

Mrs. Goodge's eyes narrowed behind the frames of her wire-rimmed glasses. "Are you certain? I've never known Mrs. Jeffries to drink at this time of day. It's barely past lunchtime."

Phyllis nodded eagerly. "She told me herself and bid me bring the tea back downstairs. I've put the pot over there in case anyone wants another cup and put the rest of the things away. But she and her visitor were going to have sherry."

"I wonder if there is something wrong," Mrs. Goodge murmured.

"Maybe she just wants a sherry." Wiggins sat down next to the maid. "The rain 'as let up a bit, but it's still a right miserable day out there and maybe she wanted a quick drink to warm up her guest. I got cold just takin' them bread crumbs out the birds."

"Did she mention the woman's name?"

the cook asked him as she sat down.

Wiggins thought for a second. "I think I 'eard her call her Fiona. That's right, she said, *'Come right in, Fiona.'*"

"Fiona," Mrs. Goodge repeated. "I've never heard her mention anyone by that name. I wonder who she is."

"Well, whoever she is, she's upset Mrs. Jeffries," Phyllis declared.

"Upset her? What on earth do you mean?" Mrs. Goodge was beginning to get a bad feeling about this visitor.

"Because of the way her voice sounded," she explained. "There was a funny note in it when she told me to bring the tea things back. You know what I mean, she was pretending to be cheerful and all like that, but I heard that she didn't sound right, and she'd gone a bit pale as well."

Back upstairs, Mrs. Jeffries stared at her guest. "That's a very odd statement to make, Fiona. What are you talking about? What is the *worst* that it won't take him long to uncover?"

Fiona smiled bitterly. "I meant that it won't take him long to find out that a few days before he was murdered, I had a dreadful argument with Ronald Dearman. As a matter of fact, I threatened to kill him."

CHAPTER 2

"Has the body been moved from its original position?" Dr. Bosworth, police surgeon for the Southwark District, asked the constable standing guard at the door.

The young constable looked embarrassed. "I'm afraid it has, sir. Inspector Nivens ordered us to move him so that he could look around under the desk for a gun. He wanted to rule out suicide."

"But the new procedures are very clear that the body is to remain untouched until the police surgeon arrives," Bosworth said.

The constable threw a quick, nervous glance over his shoulder toward the open door. "We know that, sir, but when Constable Clark mentioned that to the inspector, he got furious and told us to do what we were told. Just so you know, sir, he also had us rifle the victim's pockets. He said he was lookin' for evidence, sir. The other lads and I wanted to leave him alone until you got here. We're all familiar with the new ideas about crime scenes and evidence gatherin', but —" He broke off abruptly as footsteps sounded in the outer office, and a second later, Inspector Nivens stepped into the office.

Nivens frowned at the doctor. "You're finally here, are you? We sent for you hours ago."

"I had to finish a postmortem," Bosworth replied. "And can you explain why you had the body moved about? You know good and well the new procedures are fairly clear that there should be minimal handling of the victim until after my examination."

"Those 'procedures,' as you call them, aren't in any way official as yet," Nivens retorted. "And until they are official, then I'm in charge of this investigation and it shall be run as I see fit. So please, just get on with it."

Dr. Bosworth stared at him. "Alright, I'll get on with it, but I will be noting in my postmortem report that the victim had been moved and that the senior officer didn't think it necessary to study the body in situ or examine the fatal wounds properly."

"It's not my job to examine the wounds, it's yours," Nivens snapped. "And I told the constables to put the body back precisely as we found it."

"That is both irrelevant and impossible. Furthermore, I know for a fact that most senior officers when in charge of a serious case always examine both the fatal wound so that they can get some idea of the weapon used and the murder scene so as to ascertain any number of other details about the crime. As I understand it, this method has helped senior officers such as Inspector Gerald Witherspoon solve all of his assigned homicides."

"The victim was shot," Nivens yelled, his face flushed with rage. "What more do you need to know? No one has proved that any of those so-called modern scientific methods amount to any more than a hill of beans. I'll not have some upstart doctor telling me how to do my job. Your insubordination shall be duly noted in my report to Chief Inspector Barrows." With that, he stalked out of the room.

Bosworth sighed heavily. He was annoyed with himself for losing his temper. But he'd dealt with Nivens on previous occasions and found the man incompetent and odious. He'd also heard gossip that prisoners being brought in by Nivens were frequently covered with fresh cuts and ugly bruises. But complaining about the man wouldn't do any good. Inspector Nigel Nivens kept his position because of family connections and political influence. Bosworth edged in closer to the body and eased the dead man's head back. He studied the wound, paying close attention to both the size and shape of the bullet hole. Still keeping the head tilted up, he looked at the desktop and estimated how much blood was pooled on the blotter.

"I hope the poor fellow died quickly," the constable standing in the doorway muttered.

"He did," Bosworth remarked. "From the angle of the bullet's entry, it went directly into his brain. That, in and of itself, doesn't guarantee a quick death, of course. But from the amount of blood on the desk blotter, he died quickly. Head wounds do bleed heavily, but from the amount there" — he nodded toward the desk blotter — "I'd say his heart had stopped pumping seconds after the bullet hit him."

The constable glanced behind him and then asked, "Can you really tell what kind of weapon was used, sir? I'm not doubting you, sir, I'm not like Inspector Nivens. Most of us rank-and-file lads believe in the new methods, but can you really say what kind of gun was used? That's almost like magic."

Bosworth smiled briefly. "It's not magic,

Constable. It's science. We can't be terribly exact as yet, but we're moving in that direction, and I predict that one day we'll be able to determine not only the size of the weapon used but also the specific type of gun. As to how we do it, it's simple observation." He angled the victim's face so that the constable could get a better view. "The size of the weapon is determined by the size of the bullet hole. As you can see here" — with his other hand he pointed to the entry wound — "this is quite a small hole, so that tells me the weapon was probably either a derringer or perhaps, if the assailant was standing a bit farther back from the desk, an Enfield. But it most definitely wasn't caused by a large pistol or an American six-gun. The difference in sizes is subtle but real."

"And if we know right away what kind of weapon we're looking for," the constable mused, "then we've got one more thing to help us find the culprit. That's right clever, isn't it."

Surprised, Mrs. Jeffries stared at her sister-in-law. "You threatened him? Good gracious, Fiona, that's not like you. Why did you do such a thing?"

"Why does anyone lose control of their tongue?" Fiona replied. "I was angry at him, so angry that I lost my temper and behaved like a common fishwife. What's more, I'm certain there were plenty of people who heard me screaming at him."

"There were others present?"

"Not in the room itself," she replied. "We were in John's study. I'd seen Ronald go into the room, and knowing he wanted to have a word with me, I went in and closed the door so we could speak privately. But as we were in the middle of a dinner party, I'm sure that both the other guests and my servants got an earful."

"What happened? I need to know where and when this incident took place and all the names of the people who were likely to have overheard it. As we've already established, it's hardly in your nature to lose control, so it's imperative you tell me exactly why you had such an outburst."

Fiona looked down at the half-empty sherry glass in her hand. "As to when it happened, it was Saturday. We had a dinner party, and I'd invited Ronald and Lucretia."

"And the other guests?"

"There were only three other guests: Henry Anson and his fiancée, Miss Throckmorton, and Mrs. Meadows. You might remember her, she was Lucretia's best friend, they were at school together."

"I don't remember her," Mrs. Jeffries said. "The only people I recall from those days are you and John. Now, how many servants were likely to have been in the vicinity?"

"Most of them." She took another sip from her glass. "The study is next to the dining room, so any or all of the servants could have been in there clearing things up. We'd finished dinner, and John had taken the other guests upstairs to his little sitting room to show them his latest map. He collects them, you know, especially old ones."

"What was the argument about?"

"I was afraid you were going to ask me that. It's embarrassing, Hepzibah, and not something I wish to talk about." She looked down at the floor.

"I can't help you unless I know the truth," Mrs. Jeffries declared.

"But what if the subject of our argument doesn't have anything to do with his being murdered?" she asked, once again meeting Mrs. Jeffries' gaze.

"How can you possibly know that? Do you know why Dearman was murdered, and if you do, please say so. That will save both me and the police a great deal of time and trouble. The why, Fiona, almost always points to the killer."

"I don't know why he was murdered, but

I do know that my argument with him had nothing to do with it. It was personal, very personal," she insisted. "I'm certain it had nothing to do with his murder. Ronald Dearman was an odious excuse for a human being. He had plenty of enemies, and one of them finally had enough and murdered him. My argument with him was very humiliating. It's not something I care to talk about."

Mrs. Jeffries got to her feet. "Then we have nothing further to discuss. If you feel you're going to be unjustly accused of murder, then I suggest you obtain legal assistance right away. A good solicitor can advise you as to the best course of action."

Fiona said nothing; she merely got to her feet, putting her glass on the side table as she rose.

Mrs. Jeffries saw that her hand trembled, and she tried to harden her heart to the woman's misery, but then an image of her late husband's face flashed through her mind. For a brief, wonderful moment, she saw him clearly. He gazed at her with an expression she knew only too well, and because of the love she saw in his eyes, she knew that despite her sister-in-law's lack of cooperation, she couldn't turn her away. "Wait, sit back down," she ordered.

Fiona froze and then eased back into her seat, staring at her with a desperate but hopeful expression. "I know you must think me a fool, Hepzibah, and I'm not trying to be difficult, but I really don't want say anything about that horrid argument. It involved the most humiliating moment of my life, but I swear to you, it had nothing to do with the murder."

"Alright, then, I'll take your word for it, and I'll not bring the subject up again unless it becomes pertinent to the murder," Mrs. Jeffries replied.

"That won't happen, I promise you."

Mrs. Jeffries regarded her steadily. "As far as I know, you've never lied to me, so I want you to look me in the eye and tell me the truth. Did you kill him?"

Fiona lifted her chin slightly. "I did not."

Inspector Witherspoon sat at his desk studying an open ledger. He scanned the rows of figures carefully, trying to ascertain if the pounds, shillings, and pence listed in their relevant columns seemed reasonable for the alleged expenditure. He was concentrating so hard, he didn't hear Constable Barnes enter the small office. Barnes, an older constable with a ramrod straight posture, a ruddy complexion, and head full of curly iron gray hair, cleared his throat.

Witherspoon looked up over the rim of his spectacles. His thinning brown hair stood up in tufts where he'd run his fingers through it. He grinned broadly when he saw that Barnes carried a small tray with two steaming cups of tea. "Back already, Constable? I thought you were giving a lecture at the Yard this afternoon."

"It's finished, sir," Barnes replied.

"Did it go well?" Witherspoon asked.

"Very well, sir, though the lads were disappointed that you hadn't come." Barnes came farther into the office. He was totally comfortable with the inspector; they'd worked together on so many homicide cases they could almost read one another's minds. He put the tray on the edge of the desk, handed the inspector a mug, and picked up his own.

"You're the expert on confidence tricksters, Constable, not me," Witherspoon said as he took a quick sip.

Barnes sat down on the only other chair in the room. They were in the duty inspector's office at the back of the Ladbroke Road Police Station. The men sipped their tea in companionable silence for a few moments. The rain had begun again and now pelted the two small windows that faced out into the backyard of the station. The muted sounds of policemen talking, feet shuffling, doors squeaking, and, occasionally, a prisoner whining came through the thick oak door.

"I heard a bit of news before I left the Yard," Barnes commented. "There's been a murder in an office building in Queen Street Place just off the Southwark Bridge. Inspector Nivens got the case."

"He's wanted one for a long time," Witherspoon said. "For my part, I'm quite happy to be working on this fraud case. Unlike people, with numbers, if you look at them closely enough, you can tell if they're lying. Who was the victim?"

"A man named Ronald Dearman, he's the deputy manager of Sutcliffe Manufacturing. He was shot in his office yesterday evening."

Witherspoon tried not to be interested, but he couldn't help himself. "Were there any witnesses?"

"Not according to the first reports that came in." Barnes sipped his tea. "But it's early days yet, so they probably hadn't had time to do a proper survey of all the possible witnesses in the area. Let's just hope that Nivens finds the killer quickly. Everyone on the force has worked hard to restore public confidence in the police since those

Ripper murders. It would be a shame if an incompetent officer put us in a bad light again." Barnes kept his tone neutral, but he disliked Nigel Nivens intensely.

"I wouldn't say Inspector Nivens is incompetent." Witherspoon felt duty bound to defend a fellow officer. "He's got a reasonable number of arrests and convictions. His record is no worse than any other officer."

"And it's not any better, either," Barnes muttered. "But you're right, sir, he's not inadequate at his job. I just wish that there was an officer more experienced in murder investigations in charge, that's all."

"I see your point, Constable." Witherspoon put his mug on the desk. "But the Ripper killings were several years ago, and most of the public has forgotten those awful days. I'm sure Inspector Nivens will do the best that he can."

"Hmm," Barnes murmured. "Let's just hope his best is good enough."

"Go home and get some rest, Fiona," Mrs. Jeffries ordered as she escorted her guest to the foyer. "I'll contact you later."

"How will you manage to investigate this matter?" Fiona asked as she pulled on her gloves.

"We have our ways," Mrs. Jeffries replied.

"Don't worry, as I promised, we'll be discreet and your name won't be bandied about by anyone." She pulled open the door. "Oh dear, it's started to rain again. Wait here and I'll have Wiggins go fetch you a hansom."

But Fiona was already moving past her, her umbrella at the ready. "That won't be necessary. I feel like getting a bit of fresh air. I'll get a cab at the corner." She opened the umbrella as she stepped out onto the stoop. Turning, she smiled at Mrs. Jeffries. "I can't tell you how much I appreciate your helping me. I know better than anyone that I've no right to expect anything from you."

"I can't promise that I'll be of much use," she replied. "But I'll do my very best."

"That's good enough for me." Fiona cocked her head to one side and eyed her curiously. "David always did say that you were very clever and that if anyone had a talent for detecting, it was you. I'll wait to hear from you." She turned and hurried down the stairs.

"Good-bye, Fiona." Mrs. Jeffries closed the front door and went downstairs.

Wiggins and Mrs. Goodge were both in the kitchen. The cook was at the worktable rolling out pie dough, and the footman was polishing the brass lamp covers from the second-floor landing. They both looked at her as she entered the room, their expressions openly curious.

"Where's Phyllis?" Mrs. Jeffries asked.

"She's doin' the second-floor rooms," Mrs. Goodge frowned. "Is somethin' wrong?"

"Not precisely wrong," Mrs. Jeffries admitted. "But there is something we need to discuss. I'm glad it's just the two of you here. The lady who was just here, well, she's my sister-in-law and she needs our help." She could tell by their faces that they were surprised — no, surprise was too mild a term; both of them gaped at her in shock.

"You have a sister-in-law?" Mrs. Goodge sputtered. "Here? In London?"

"Well, yes —"

"But you've never mentioned her before," Mrs. Goodge interrupted.

"I don't see her very often," Mrs. Jeffries said defensively. "Oh dear, I'm not explaining this very well."

"I should say not," the cook exclaimed. "We've worked together here for years and you've not seen fit to mention that you had family in London?"

"Cor blimey, Mrs. Jeffries, that don't seem right," Wiggins added. "We've told you about our relatives. Why were you keepin' yours a secret?"

"It wasn't a secret," she explained. "It's just that we're almost estranged . . . oh dear, I don't want you to feel I was deliberately keeping anything from you. That's not it at all." But she could see from the expressions on their faces that was precisely what they were thinking.

"I should hope not," Mrs. Goodge cried. "We've told you things from our lives that we might have preferred to keep to ourselves, because we're close now and we trust each other."

"I trust both of you." She sank down in her chair. "Oh blast, I'm sorry. I see how this must look. I wasn't deliberately keeping silent about the matter because I don't trust the two of you, it's simply that Fiona isn't a part of my life. I've literally not given her a thought in years because every time I did, I'd get angry over the way she treated David. I don't want either of you to be upset about this. I wasn't keeping secrets. I simply had put her so far out of my life that she didn't matter enough to mention."

For a few moments, none of them spoke and Mrs. Jeffries was afraid that she'd not made them understand.

Finally, though, the cook broke the silence. "You said she's your sister-in-law." She picked up her dough and put it in the pie pan. "She's David's younger sister?"

"That's right," Mrs. Jeffries said. "She was the baby of the family. She 'married up' as they say and we didn't see much of her. We used to invite her and her husband to supper, but they never accepted our invitations and that hurt David very much. So it was a bit of a relief when her husband moved his company to London. That was about twelve years ago, just before David passed away. When I came to London, I stopped in to see her, as a courtesy, and it was obvious that the differences in our social status made me an embarrassment to her. As I'd never really known or liked her very much in the first place, I was quite happy to cut her out of my life."

"So that's why you looked so surprised when you saw her on our doorstep?" Wiggins chuckled.

She nodded, relieved that the footman had gotten over his pique. She glanced at the cook. "Honestly, Mrs. Goodge, I wasn't keeping her presence in London a secret. It's simply that I never think about her at all."

"Can't say that I blame you there. Now, what did she want? Why did she come 'ere?"

"She needs our help," Mrs. Jeffries explained. "There's been a murder."

"If you've not seen her in years, then how did she know that you could help her?" Wiggins asked reasonably.

"It's a long explanation and I'd rather tell you when we're all assembled," she replied. "Can you nip over to Knightsbridge and fetch Luty and Hatchet while I go across the communal gardens and see if Lady Cannonberry is available?"

He nodded as he got up and reached for the top of the brass polish tin. "Let me put this lot away . . ."

Mrs. Goodge shooed him toward the coat tree. "Don't bother. Phyllis and I can take care of it. You get a move on. We've got a murder to solve. It's wet outside and it might take you a bit of time to get to Luty's."

"Take a hansom," Mrs. Jeffries ordered. She pointed to the pine sideboard. She always kept cash in the top drawer for incidental expenses.

Wiggins nodded his thanks, helped himself to a few coins, and then snatched his coat off the peg. "Ask Phyllis to take the lamps up to the landin' for me. I'll 'ang 'em later." He slipped on his coat. "They're up too high for her to reach them."

Fred got to his feet, his tail wagged hopefully. "Sorry, old boy." The footman put on his cap and went to the dog. He patted his head. "But I can't take you this time. They won't let you in a hansom cab. Lay back down, boy, and take a rest. We'll go walkies later, I promise." The dog seemed to understand, for he curled back into his spot as the footman hurried toward the back door.

As soon as he was gone, Mrs. Jeffries went to the coat tree herself. "You're not annoyed with me, are you?" she asked the cook as she slipped on her cloak.

"I'm fine. It was just the surprise of findin' out about her. You've only seen her the one time since you've been in London?"

Mrs. Jeffries put on her bonnet. "The first few years I was in London, Fiona invited me to tea at Christmas. I'm not sure why. By then, David was gone, and I'd certainly not made any secret of the fact that I resented the way she'd treated him."

"She probably felt guilty."

She tied the ribbon under her chin. "I expect you're right. She did feel bad, and I'm ashamed to say that I didn't behave in a way that did me credit. I barely spoke and didn't bother to hide the fact that she and her friends bored me stiff. The third time I received an invitation from her, I sent my regrets. I was greatly relieved when I received no further invitations from her. I suspect she felt the same way."

Mrs. Goodge and Phyllis had tea on the table when the others assembled at Upper Edmonton Gardens. Wiggins had slipped upstairs and rehung the lamps on the landing, Phyllis had finished the cleaning, and Mrs. Goodge had written out a list of provisions she needed to comfortably feed her "sources" while they were on the case.

"Nell's bells, I hope we're not late, but it took forever to get shut of everyone," Luty Belle Crookshank exclaimed as she swept into the kitchen. She was an elderly, white-haired American with more money than the Bank of England and a love of bright clothes. Today she wore a brilliant purple mantle and matching hat over a gray and lavender striped day dress. Hatchet, her tall, white-haired butler came in behind her.

"What Madam means is that our luncheon guests stayed longer than we'd hoped." He helped his employer take off her outer garments and hung them on the coat tree.

"Humph, wipe that smirk off yer face, Hatchet. You enjoyed watching me try to get 'em out the door. You already knew what was what." Luty went to the table.

"True." Hatchet grinned broadly as he

60

pulled out her chair. "Wiggins had informed me our services were needed, but I certainly wasn't trying to annoy you, madam."

Luty's late husband was an Englishman, and like so many of that older generation, he'd gone to the New World years earlier to seek his fortune. He'd found it and Luty while prospecting in the mountains of Colorado. After living for a number of years in San Francisco and New York, he'd finally brought her back to his country and a beautiful home in Knightsbridge. Luty had been a witness in one of the inspector's earliest cases. Sharp-eyed and smart, she'd figured out what the household was up to when they were snooping about. Several months after the successful resolution of the case, she came to them seeking help with a problem of her own. After that, both she and her butler, who had a bit of mystery in his own past, had insisted on helping on all the inspector's cases. She and Hatchet argued frequently but were devoted to one another. But when they were "on the hunt," they were highly competitive with each other.

"Sit down and have some tea," Mrs. Jeffries said. "Now that we're all here, I can share the details of what we're going to have to do on this case. This one is different."

"That sounds ominous," Ruth, Lady Cannonberry, said. She was a slender, attractive blonde widow of late middle years. She and Inspector Witherspoon were "special friends." She'd been married to a peer of the realm, but as the daughter of a country vicar, she'd taken Christ's words to "love thy neighbor as thyself" quite seriously. She marched for the rights of woman, fed the hungry, visited the sick, and gave aid and comfort to the oppressed. In other words, compared to other women of her class, she was a radical. However, her affection for Gerald Witherspoon was such that she did avoid engaging in activities that might embarrass him. As someone who believed that all souls were equal in the sight of the Almighty, she insisted the household address her by her Christian name. But she was sensitive to the fact that none of them felt comfortable doing this in front of Inspector Witherspoon and that was fine with her. "What is so very different about this one?"

Mrs. Jeffries wasn't sure how to begin. "Well, to begin with, Inspector Witherspoon doesn't have this case. It's being handled by Inspector Nivens —" She broke off as there was a collective groan. "I know, I know, that isn't good news, but it is nonetheless the fact of the matter."

"Has hell froze over?" Luty demanded. "Why are we gettin' involved in one of *his* cases? Did he ask us for help?"

"No, my sister-in-law did," Mrs. Jeffries replied. She knew why they were upset, and she didn't much blame them. Nivens was an odious toad, and none of them could stand the fellow. For years he'd tried to prove that Witherspoon's household helped with all his cases. That, of course, was absolutely true, but they went to great lengths to ensure their dear inspector was kept completely in the dark about their activities on his behalf.

"Sister-in-law," Ruth repeated. "You have family in London?"

"Let me explain," she replied hastily. "Fiona is my late husband's sister and she does indeed live here, but she's not been a part of my life for so many years that I literally forgot the woman. When she arrived here today, I was stunned. But she came to me because she needs help. She's afraid she's going to be arrested for murder."

"If she ain't been part of your life for years, how did she know to come here and ask you for help?" Luty stared at her skeptically.

"She came to me because of what she

overheard Inspector Nivens saying," Mrs. Jeffries replied. "Fiona heard Nivens complaining to a constable about Inspector Witherspoon, and my name was mentioned specifically. All of you know that Nivens tells anyone who stands still for thirty seconds that he thinks our inspector has help with his cases. But he's done that for years and no one pays any attention to his ranting. But this time, Fiona happened to be standing close by, and when she heard what he said, she decided to come and see me."

"So our activities on the inspector's behalf haven't become general knowledge in London," Hatchet pressed.

"That's correct and I didn't admit, even to Fiona, that what Nivens said was true. I merely said we'd do our best to help her."

"Go on, then, tell us about the murder." Mrs. Goodge frowned impatiently as she glanced at the clock. "Time's gettin' on."

"The victim is a man named Ronald Dearman. He was the deputy manager of Sutcliffe Manufacturing. Fiona's husband owns the company; he's the major shareholder. She and the victim's wife found the body this morning." She told them everything she knew.

When she'd finished, Ruth spoke first. "Sutcliffe, Sutcliffe," she repeated softly.

"I've heard that name before. They're from Yorkshire originally?"

"That's right, from York. That's where Fiona met John Sutcliffe and married him," she said. "She was originally a companion to John's sister, Lucretia."

"Lucretia then married Ronald Dearman, the victim?" Mrs. Goodge was disappointed. She'd spent her life working in the most elegant, wealthy, and exclusive households in England, but she'd never heard of the Yorkshire Sutcliffes nor of any family named Dearman. She had a vast network of former colleagues that extended across the country; add to that the local tradesmen, delivery boys, and rag and bones men here in London, and she could do her fair share in the investigation without leaving the kitchen.

"Yes, she was the one who actually found the body."

"The murder took place at his office," Ruth said. "Do we know exactly when the killing occurred?"

"Fiona said it must have been sometime between six o'clock yesterday evening and eight o'clock this morning. The office closes at six and if he'd been murdered before then, one of the staff would have heard the shot and raised the alarm. But we need to confirm this information. Frankly, I don't think Fiona really knows precisely how the office functions."

"Why did it take Mrs. Dearman so long to raise the alarm?" Hatchet asked. "Surely she must have worried when he didn't come home last night."

"She probably didn't know," Ruth answered. "Oh, I'm sorry, Mrs. Jeffries, I didn't mean to interrupt."

"No, no, don't concern yourself." Mrs. Jeffries knew that Ruth spoke only when she had something important to say. "Go on, what were you going to say?"

"But why wouldn't she 'ave known he 'adn't come in?" Wiggins asked curiously.

"Amongst the upper classes, the husband and wife often don't share a bedroom. If Mrs. Dearman has her own room, she might not have realized until he didn't appear for breakfast that he'd not come home the night before."

"But the servants would 'ave known he wasn't 'ome," Wiggins pointed out. "They probably did the lockin' up at night. Surely they'd 'ave said somethin'."

"Unless they were used to him not coming home," Phyllis said. "One of the girls I used to take my afternoon out with when I first came to London said their household never waited for the master to come home

66

at night before locking up. The wife claimed that if he didn't get home at a reasonable time, his" — she hesitated and then grinned — "floozy could take care of him."

Everyone laughed. "We'll have to find out if Mr. Dearman was in the same situation," Mrs. Jeffries said. "But whatever the reason the alarm wasn't raised when he didn't come home, that bought the killer additional time before the body was discovered."

"What I don't understand is how on earth we're goin' to find out what the police know," Luty complained. "Let's not fool ourselves. A lot of our information about our murders comes directly from Inspector Witherspoon. He talks freely to Mrs. Jeffries, and between that and Constable Barnes tellin' us bits and pieces, we know what's what. There ain't no way this side of Hades that Inspector Nivens is goin' to tell us one darned thing." She fixed her gaze on the housekeeper. "Do you reckon you can suss out who the killer is without the information we get from the police?"

"I don't know," Mrs. Jeffries admitted honestly. "You're right, of course, Inspector Nivens would never in a million years share anything he learned with us."

"And that ain't all," Luty continued.

"With Betsy and Smythe gone, we're short-handed. That's somethin' else we've got to consider."

"Madam, are you suggesting we're not up to the task?" Hatchet folded his arms over his chest and stared hard at his employer.

" 'Course we're up to it," Luty shot back. "I'm just pointin' out that it might not go as fast or as smooth as other times, especially as it seems like Hepzibah and her sister-in-law don't much like each other."

Everyone was used to Luty's blunt manner, but nonetheless, there was a moment of stunned silence. Then Phyllis giggled, and a second later, everyone else, including Mrs. Jeffries, joined in the laughter.

"You're right, Luty," Mrs. Jeffries said. "We don't much like one another, but for my late husband's sake, I'm going to try my best to help her. However, everything you've pointed out is true. This will be a very, very difficult case, and I won't hold it against anyone if they wish to bow out."

Everyone spoke at once.

" 'Course we're not bowin' out," Wiggins cried.

"I should think not," Mrs. Goodge exclaimed.

"Working for justice is what we do," Ruth declared.

"We ain't givin' up just because this one might be harder than the others," Luty said fiercely.

"Really, Mrs. Jeffries, do you think we'd ignore our duty simply because it might be difficult?" Hatchet sniffed disapprovingly.

Everyone fell silent, and then Phyllis said, "At first I was scared to help out because I was afraid of losing my job and I didn't think I could do it. But then I saw that I could. What's more, I realized that what we was really doing wasn't so much as catching the guilty as it was protecting the innocent." She stopped and stared at the faces around the table. "That's what is really important. All of you have kept the police from arresting innocent people just so they could get the murder off the front pages of the newspapers. There've been times in my life when I wish there had been people like you about — times when me and my lot needed someone to protect us and there was no one there. That's why I'll do anything you ask of me, no matter how scared it makes me."

For a moment, the room was quiet except for the faint ticking of the clock. Each and every one of them was deeply touched. The maid had come to them beaten down by life and so grateful to have a roof over her head that she wouldn't say "boo" to a goose.

She was still fearful, but despite that, she was willing to get out in the world and try to help others.

"Thank you, Phyllis." Mrs. Jeffries smiled kindly at her. "We're glad you feel that way, and we all understand how difficult it sometimes is to put the interests of justice over our own survival."

Phyllis shyly returned the smile and reached for her teacup.

"Now, as we're all agreed we want to move forward, there are some very practical matters to consider," Mrs. Jeffries said.

"You're right about that." Mrs. Goodge sighed. "We'll not have anyone inside the police helpin' us."

"Maybe that ain't so." Luty tapped her finger on the tabletop. "Can't we see if Constable Barnes will give us a hand?"

"That's an idea," Mrs. Jeffries replied. "But he's not on the case —"

Luty interrupted. "That don't matter. Barnes has been a copper long enough to know how to finagle the system. Even if he ain't on the case, he can probably pick up enough information to lend us a hand. I'll bet he's bored stiff workin' on that fraud case with the inspector."

Mrs. Jeffries nodded in agreement. "We'll need to get a message to him right away. I'll send him a note this evening and ask him to stop in tomorrow morning."

"I'll take it," Wiggins offered.

"We'll drop you there when we leave here," Luty said. "I'd offer to bring you back, too, but we've got another engagement tonight and as we're on a case now, I don't want to miss a chance to see if we can pick up anythin' useful."

"That's alright, the constable doesn't live far, just across the river, so I can be 'ome in two shakes of a lamb's tail," he replied.

"We'll need names," the cook blurted. "Your sister-in-law will have to give us a list of people who might have hated Ronald Dearman enough to want him dead."

"And we'll need their addresses as well," Phyllis added. "We can't find out about these people unless we know where they live."

"Oh dear, you're right." Mrs. Jeffries glanced at the clock and frowned. "How stupid of me, I shouldn't have let Fiona leave without getting that information. It's too late to go to her house now. The inspector will be home soon."

"What are we goin' to do about that?" Wiggins crossed his arms over his chest. "It's like ya said, he's only workin' on that fraud case now and that means he's spendin' most of 'is time goin' over ledgers and invoices. He's no reason to be stayin' at the station when it's just figures he's dealin' with, so he'll be comin' 'ome early most days."

"He'll want to know where we are if we're not here," Phyllis agreed anxiously. "And I don't want him angry at us."

Gerald Witherspoon was the kindest and most considerate of employers. He'd not been raised in a household filled with servants, and consequently, he actually treated his staff as human beings. However, even the best of masters would wonder what his household was doing if they were never there when he came home.

"I can help with that," Ruth offered. "The inspector and I have been wanting to spend more time together and this is the perfect opportunity. As a matter of fact, we can start right now." She glanced at the housekeeper. "If you'll loan me a piece of paper, I'll leave a note inviting him to an early dinner tomorrow evening."

"But what about your investigatin'?" Luty asked. "Won't that be hard on you if you're keepin' him occupied?"

"I can easily manage," Ruth replied. "Much of my information comes from my women's suffrage club meetings or ladies' luncheons, and he's at work then. In the evenings, if I happen to be invited to a dinner party that might be useful while we're on the hunt, I'll ask Gerald to escort me."

"Can you speak freely if he's with you?" Hatchet asked.

"Of course." She laughed. "People gossip about murder all the time, and as he's not even on the case, he won't be put in any sort of compromising position."

"Excellent," Mrs. Jeffries said. "We've made a good start, and we do have some names to work with. There's our victim, Ronald Dearman. I know he lived in the same neighborhood as Fiona and her husband, but I don't know the street name nor the address."

"What is the Sutcliffe address?" Mrs. Goodge asked.

"Number seventeen, Whipple Road, Mayfair," she said. "We'll meet tomorrow morning at our usual time. The inspector will have gone to the station by then. If all goes as planned, I should have had an opportunity to speak to Constable Barnes and see if he's willing to help us."

"Let's hope I can find out somethin' tonight at the Verlanes' dinner party," Luty said. "I'm sure the killin' will have made the evenin' papers, so there's bound to be some gossip."

"Good," Mrs. Jeffries said. "Let's hope that solving this one won't be as difficult as we feared."

"I'm so glad you were able to come this morning," Mrs. Jeffries said to Constable Barnes as she ushered him down the back hall to the kitchen. "Wiggins said you weren't home when he dropped the note off, so he wasn't sure if you were free this morning."

They stepped into the kitchen, and Mrs. Goodge, who had just put a pot of tea on the table and sat down, looked up and gave him a broad smile. "Good morning, Constable. I see you got Mrs. Jeffries' note."

"I did, but funnily enough, I'd planned on coming by anyway." He smiled at the housekeeper. "I have something to ask you."

Mrs. Jeffries waved him into a chair as she took her own seat. The cook poured out three cups of tea and handed them around. She waited for him to take a sip before she spoke. "Why were you coming to see me?"

Barnes put down his cup. "Did you hear about that murder near the Southwark Bridge? The deputy manager that was shot in his office?"

"We heard about it, but we also heard that

74

the case was given to Inspector Nivens, not our inspector."

"That's the reason I've come. Late yesterday afternoon, I went to the Yard. That's why I wasn't home when young Wiggins called round. Chief Inspector Barrows sent me a message that he wanted to speak to me about a lecture I'd given there that day to new recruits. I was more than a little annoyed seeing as how I'd been there earlier that day and I wondered why he couldn't have spoken to me then. As it turns out, he wasn't there, but that's beside the point —" He broke off and looked down at the tabletop. A dark flush crept up his already ruddy complexion.

Mrs. Jeffries looked at Mrs. Goodge, who shrugged as both women realized the constable was embarrassed.

Barnes took a deep breath, looked up, and said, "I probably shouldn't admit this, but as I waited in his office, I saw that Nivens had already sent over his first report on the murder. The file was sitting on Barrows' desk and as I could hear Barrows out in the hall tearing a strip off some poor lad, I flipped it open and had bit of a read. I didn't get a chance to read the whole thing, but the reason I've come to see you is because I noticed that one of the names listed in the report" — he turned to Mrs. Jeffries — "was given as Mrs. John Sutcliffe, but in parentheses, her full name had been written and it was Fiona Abigail Jeffries Sutcliffe. Then I noticed that the Sutcliffes were from Yorkshire."

"She's my sister-in-law," Mrs. Jeffries said softly. "And that's how we knew that Inspector Nivens had gotten the case. She came to see me yesterday afternoon. She's terrified that she's going to be under suspicion for the murder."

"I see." The constable fingered the handle of his teacup. "Then if she's a suspect, I'm sorry I didn't have a chance to finish reading the report."

"I am, too. I wonder if Inspector Nivens made the connection between the names," she mused.

"I doubt it." Barnes laughed. "Nivens didn't write the report. He never does — he always gets one of the better-educated rank-and-file lads to do it for him. I imagine it was Constable Morehead that did it. He's a grammar school boy, and the gossip is that he's hitched his wagon to Nivens' star."

"Somehow that doesn't surprise me," the housekeeper muttered.

Constable Barnes shifted in his seat. "Mrs. Jeffries, I have to ask this. Your sister-in-law, did she kill him?"

She gave him a wry smile. "She told me she had nothing to do with his murder. Mind you, we're not close and I've had almost no contact with her for years. But I do know this: Fiona Sutcliffe would walk over hot coals in her bare feet rather than do anything that would endanger her position in society, and being arrested as a murderess would most definitely put her beyond the social pale."

CHAPTER 3

Ruth was the last one to arrive for their morning meeting. She rushed in, shedding her cloak as she crossed the room. "I do hope I haven't held us up too much," she apologized as she hung up her damp garment.

"We've only just sat down," the cook said. "The inspector was late getting out the door. But we've had a bit of luck already: Constable Barnes came by and he's going to help us."

"As much as he can," the housekeeper added. "He did warn us that his finding out anything useful might be difficult as he has no official reason to read the reports."

"Like Luty said yesterday, he's been at it long enough to find his way round that," Mrs. Goodge said confidently. "That's the one advantage to gettin' old, you know all the ins and outs."

"Looks like we're gettin' off to fine start,"

Luty said. "I even found out a thing or two myself. But tell us what you heard from Barnes first."

"By chance, he happened to be in Chief Inspector Barrows' office late yesterday afternoon when Nivens sent in his first report on the case," Mrs. Jeffries began.

"Constable Barnes said that Nivens only sent in the report that fast because he's such a bootlicker." Mrs. Goodge repeated the constable's exact words with relish. "The usual practice is for the senior officer to send in progress reports after they've interviewed all the possible witnesses, and that generally takes several days."

"Constable Barnes is of the opinion that Nivens will be sending in reports to Barrows frequently," said Mrs. Jeffries, picking up where Mrs. Goodge had left off. "And that might work to our advantage. I had the distinct impression that Barnes might be able to get a look at them before they reach the chief inspector's desk. But that's not all he told us. He said the police had already determined that the killer committed the murder sometime after the Sutcliffe Manufacturing office emptied out but before the building porter came on duty. Apparently, the porter doesn't come on until half past six and the last employee, a clerk named

Daniel Jones, left the office at six fifteen."

"Were all the other offices empty by then?" Hatchet asked.

"I don't know," she admitted. "It will be necessary for one of us to go to the building itself and take a good look at both the Sutcliffe offices and the rest of the building, including where the porter's desk is and who, if anyone, would likely know the porter's schedule."

"I'll do it," Wiggins said.

"Take care to avoid Nivens," Luty warned. "He's seen you, remember? He knows us all by sight."

"I'll be careful."

"Unfortunately, Constable Barnes was only able to read part of the report before Barrows came into the room, so that's really all he found out." Mrs. Jeffries looked at Luty. "Your turn. What did you find out?"

Luty grinned broadly. "I found out that the Dearmans weren't a happily married couple. My source told me that the gossip was that they fought like cats and dogs. Dearman had a reputation as a bully, but he never had the upper hand with his wife because she's John Sutcliffe's sister and as he worked for Sutcliffe, he had to put up with her. I know it ain't much, half the marriages in London are miserable, but at least we know there ain't goin' to be too many people weepin' over his grave."

"Considering the circumstances, we've made some progress," Mrs. Jeffries said.

"We're going to need more," Ruth murmured.

"We'll get more," Mrs. Jeffries replied. "I'm going to go see Fiona this morning and ask for a more complete list of Dearman's enemies. Apparently, if he was in the office alone, anyone could have gotten in to murder him."

"Was he the one who usually locked up?" Phyllis asked.

"That was the impression I got from Fiona. She said that Dearman often worked quite late." Mrs. Jeffries' brows drew together in thought. "But I'll ask her that specifically when I see her."

"If he was the one who always locked up at night, then that might help us narrow down the suspects," Hatchet mused. "Generally, the only people who would know such a detail would be either the workers at the office or someone close to the victim who knew his comings and goings."

"Or someone who just stood across the road and watched the place," Luty said. "If Dearman was always the last one to leave the office, it wouldn't be long before the

81

killer figured out he was the one who locked up in the evenings. We know the office was locked when the body was discovered, because Mrs. Sutcliffe had to get the porter to let her and Mrs. Dearman into the office."

"Which means that Dearman's keys should have been in his possession," Mrs. Jeffries murmured.

"Can we get Constable Barnes to confirm that?" Hatchet asked. "If they were in his pocket, they'll have been collected into evidence along with anything else that he had on him."

"I'll ask him," she replied. "And I'll ask Fiona who else had keys to the office. If she doesn't know the answer, she can ask her husband. But I think it's important we find out."

Phyllis got to her feet. "If that's it then, I'll be going. I'll try the nearest shops to Whipple Road, and as the Dearmans lived close to the Sutcliffes, maybe I'll catch two birds with one stone."

"While I'm at the Sutcliffe offices, I'll see if I can find a clerk who likes to chat." Wiggins rose from his chair.

"I'll check in with some of my financial sources to see if they know anythin' about Dearman's finances," Luty offered. The elderly American knew everyone important in London. Despite her lack of formal education and her blunt manner, she was regarded as an excellent businesswoman as well as a colorful personality. Bankers, financiers, and aristocrats numbered amongst her friends. She was as comfortable chatting with a countess as she was buying a beggar a meal. "I always say, there's generally two things people get killed over, love or money, and it don't seem like Dearman was loved by anyone."

"I've a meeting of my women's group today," Ruth said. "I'll see what I can find out there. But I do wish we had more names. Oh, Gerald is coming to my house for an early dinner tonight, so if anyone needs to nip out and take care of anything, you'll have a chance."

Mrs. Goodge smiled gratefully at Ruth. "Thank you. Now I can get my baking done for my sources without having to worry about cooking a fancy dinner for the inspector."

"What about our dinner?" Wiggins asked. "Don't we get any supper?"

"Have I ever not fed you?" The cook frowned at him. "But we can eat somethin' simple."

"Anything you cook for us is wonderful,"

Phyllis said quickly. "Are we meeting this afternoon as well?"

"We are indeed," Mrs. Jeffries said. "I need to pass along whatever I've learned from Fiona today, and I want to hear what you've all found out. I'm not certain our usual methods are going to be as useful as in our previous cases."

"Why wouldn't they?" the cook demanded. "The only thing really different is Smythe and Betsy are gone. We've solved the problem of findin' out what the police know. Constable Barnes has agreed to help with that, so we should do just fine."

Mrs. Jeffries didn't want to infect the others with her pessimism, so she said nothing. But she knew that catching this killer wasn't going to be easy. Constable Barnes could find out what was written in the reports, but there were other, more subtle clues they'd lose. Handwriting on a sheet of paper gave only the cold, hard facts; a report couldn't include a policeman's intuition or analyze the way a witness suddenly stiffened when asked certain questions. No, she wasn't going to fool herself; without all the others this was going to be a tough case to crack. Furthermore, one of Smythe's sources was invaluable. Then again, she thought, there was no reason she couldn't

84

contact that person. It might cost a bit, but if it was too expensive, she'd give Fiona the bill. Suddenly cheered, she said, "You're right, we'll find a way. We always do."

Nivens sat in the small morning room of the Sutcliffe house and glared at the housekeeper. "Could you please repeat that," he ordered. He was in a foul mood; the mistress of the house was making him wait, and he wasn't used to waiting for anyone.

"It sounded as if she threatened to kill him." Henrietta Sanger cast a nervous glance toward the hallway. "Please, Inspector, this is very awkward. I'm sure Mrs. Sutcliffe wouldn't approve of you questioning the household without her knowledge."

He smiled coldly. "Frankly, your Mrs. Sutcliffe doesn't have much choice in the matter. We're investigating a murder, and I won't be leaving here until I can speak with her. Are you certain you made it clear that I was waiting to see her?"

"Yes, sir, I did. Now, if you'll excuse me, I've work to do." She got up from the straight-backed chair and started for the door. Henrietta Sanger was a middle-aged woman with graying black hair, blue eyes, and freckles.

"Wait, I'm not through speaking with

you." Nivens leapt up and stepped in front of her, effectively blocking her path. He wasn't having a good day. He wished he'd gone back to the Sutcliffe offices; the clerks there were easily intimidated. But he'd sent half a dozen constables under Constable Morehead's lead and instructed them to interview everyone in the building. If the constable knew what was good for him, he'd better be learning something useful. "Was anyone else likely to have heard Mrs. Sutcliffe threatening to murder Mr. Dearman?"

"I have no idea. You'll have to ask them yourself." She tried to step around him, but he moved quickly, again blocking her path.

"I've not given permission for you to go," he said harshly. "I've not finished interviewing you."

The housekeeper seemed to suddenly find her spine. She straightened up and stared him directly in the eye. "I don't need your permission to do anything. You're not in charge of this household. I've already told you what I *thought* I overheard, and I also said that as the study doors were closed, I can't be sure of anything. I'll thank you to step out of my way, sir. I've work to do."

"Yes, I'm sure you do," Nivens said quickly. He needed this woman to cooperate, and she obviously was no longer cowed by his authority. He'd try another method. "Mrs. Sanger, please, forgive me, I didn't mean to be rude. I'm sure you're very busy, but can we start over? I really do need to ask you a few more questions."

She hesitated. "Alright, get on with it, then."

He gave her a thin smile. "Mr. and Mrs. Dearman were here for dinner Saturday night, is that correct?"

"That's right," she replied. "Mrs. Dearman is Mr. Sutcliffe's sister, and they are often dinner guests."

"Were they the only guests?"

"No, Mr. Anson and his fiancée, Miss Throckmorton, and Mrs. Meadows were also guests that night."

"One thing I don't understand is why Mrs. Sutcliffe was alone with Mr. Dearman in the study," he said. "In other words, where were the other guests?"

"Mr. Sutcliffe had taken them upstairs into his sitting room," she explained. "He wanted to show them a new map he'd acquired from the Royal Geographical Society. Mrs. Sutcliffe had already seen it."

"Didn't Mr. Dearman want to see it as well?" Nivens pressed.

"I don't know. Perhaps he'd already seen it, and I know that he doesn't like to climb stairs. He was always complaining about Mr. Sutcliffe's sitting room being on the third floor of the house," she replied. "As soon as the others had gone, I overheard him tell her he'd like a private word with her. He went into the master's study, and she followed a few moments later."

Nivens nodded in encouragement. "So Mr. Dearman and Mrs. Sutcliffe were alone together in the study. Is that when they started arguing?"

"I've told you, Inspector, I can't be sure they were arguing."

"But you said their voices were raised," he reminded her. "You said you heard her say she was going to kill him."

"No, I told you I wasn't sure what I heard," she snapped. "You barged in here and started asking questions without so much as a by-your-leave, and like a foolish girl, I allowed you to intimidate me until I didn't know what I was saying. All I heard was some raised voices. For all I know they could have been discussing politics and Mrs. Sutcliffe might have been joking that the Conservatives were going to kill the Liberals in the next election."

Nivens knew that wasn't what she'd implied earlier. He didn't understand how witnesses could end up changing their statements so often. It happened to him all the time. Good grief, what was it about these low-class individuals that they couldn't remember from one moment to the next what they'd seen or heard? "Where were you standing when you overheard these voices?" he asked.

She pointed to the hallway. "I was in the drawing room. I'd come up from the kitchen to supervise the clearing up. We used the Wedgewood service for the dinner party, and I wanted to remind the maids to be extra careful. As soon as I'd done that, I closed the dining room door and left them to it. Just then, Mr. Sutcliffe and some of the guests came out of the drawing room and went up the stairs to his sitting room. That's when I heard Mr. Dearman tell Mrs. Sutcliffe he wanted to speak to her privately. As everyone had gone, I took the opportunity to nip into the drawing room and have a look around. I wanted to see whether they needed more coffee, and I wanted to make sure the sherry decanter was filled. Mrs. Dearman is very fond of an after-dinner sherry."

"When did the shouting start?"

"Not long after they went into the study." She glanced at the closed door again. "It was such a surprise it stopped me in my

89

tracks, but as I said, I can't be sure what they were saying. The walls in this house are very thick."

"Did Mrs. Sutcliffe like Mr. Dearman?" He changed tactics, hoping it would help.

"I've no idea." She smiled smugly. "Mrs. Sutcliffe isn't in the habit of telling the servants who she does or doesn't like. Now, if you'll excuse me, I must get back to work."

Nivens knew when he was beaten. "Can you please go and remind Mrs. Sutcliffe that I'm waiting to speak to her?"

Wordlessly, she nodded and left. Nivens struggled to keep his temper in check while he waited. He was determined not to let his emotions get the best of him. If he was going to learn anything useful, he might very well need the cooperation of people like Mrs. Sanger. He desperately wanted to solve this murder, and thus far, he wasn't making much progress. He stalked around the room, noting the elegant rose and green striped upholstery on the French-style furniture and the expensive green and cream satin curtains on the two long, narrow windows. A secretary of mahogany was in one corner, and landscape paintings hung on the pale green walls. He had to be careful here; this kind of wealth usually meant power even if he'd never heard of the family prior to getting the case. Nonetheless, regardless of how much money they had, if anyone in the Sutcliffe family had committed murder, he'd arrest them. As a matter of fact, he rather hoped it would be someone like that, someone rich enough and powerful enough to make sure an arrest got his name prominently mentioned in every newspaper in the city.

Mrs. Sanger stuck her head into the room. "Mrs. Sutcliffe is free now."

"What was keeping her?" he snapped as he hurried toward the door.

"You'll need to ask her that yourself," she replied as she led him out into the hallway.

Constable Morehead stared skeptically at Daniel Jones. They were sitting in Henry Anson's office at Sutcliffe Manufacturing, and thus far, the constable had not found out anything that pointed to the killer. He'd better find out something worthwhile if he wanted to continue working closely with Inspector Nivens. The man was as ambitious as a Tudor courtier and wouldn't tolerate failure. Morehead understood him completely because he was exactly like that himself. He knew that if Nivens failed to solve this murder, he'd be looking for a scapegoat, and Morehead was determined it wouldn't be him. He'd do whatever it took to learn something, anything that might lead to an arrest.

"Are we done yet?" Daniel Jones asked. "I've told you everything I know, and I'd like to get back to work."

Morehead tapped his fingers on the desktop. "Tell me again why you were the last person to leave the office Monday night."

"But I've already told you." Jones sighed. "How many times do we need to go over this?"

"As many times as I say," Morehead snapped. "Now get on with it and tell me again."

"Alright, then. Everyone else had begun packing up at a few minutes to the hour."

"What hour?"

"Six, we finish at six. I've told you that half a dozen times now."

"Don't be impertinent. Just answer my question."

"He's already answered that question," a man's voice said.

Morehead looked up from his notes. A tall, slender man with dark blond hair, blue eyes, and high cheekbones stood in the open doorway. He wore a dark grey suit, white shirt, and black tie. "I've been standing out here for ten minutes, and I've distinctly heard Mr. Jones answer that question a number of times." He nodded at the open notebook on the desktop. "Don't you write things down in that book of yours?"

"Who might you be?" Morehead asked.

"I'm Henry Anson, and in Mr. Sutcliffe's absence, I'm in charge here." He came into the office proper. "And this is my office. Now, can you please explain why you've wasted a good ten minutes asking Mr. Jones the same questions? The constable outside said you wanted to speak to everyone on the staff. But if you keep repeating the same thing over and over, you're going to be here a week."

"It's simple police procedure," Morehead blurted. He'd sized up Anson immediately. He was youngish, probably early thirties, but he carried himself with an unmistakable air of authority. "We often ask witnesses the same question several times. We do it to ensure they've not gotten confused."

"Mr. Jones didn't sound in the least confused."

"I wasn't," Daniel Jones said quickly.

"In that case, you can go," Morehead said to the clerk. Jones got up, gave Anson a respectful nod, and bolted for the door.

"You'll want to interview me, I assume,"

Anson said. He looked pointedly at his chair, which was now occupied by the constable.

"Yes I would. Sorry about commandeering your office, but I was told you were at the manufacturing site." Morehead gathered up his notebook, rose to his feet, and stumbled around the desk before plopping into the hard straight-backed chair that Jones had just vacated.

Anson took his seat and leaned back. "I was, but I'm here now. Go ahead and ask your questions. There's nothing pressing that needs my attention right at the moment, and frankly, the sooner you've finished taking statements, the sooner we can get back to work. This horrible business has upset the staff, and I'd like it over with as quickly as possible."

Morehead opened his notebook, placed it on the edge of the desk, and had his pencil at the ready. "What time did you leave the office on Monday?"

"Five o'clock."

"I thought the office worked until six." He looked up from his scribbling.

"We do, but I had an errand to do, so I left an hour early."

"Where did you go?"

"To the post office on Cannon Street. I

mailed off a parcel."

"That's only a short walk from here," Morehead said. "Why didn't you come back to the office?"

Anson shrugged. "I was tired, so I went home to rest. I had a dinner engagement later that evening at my fiancée's home."

"What time did you leave the post office?"

"Probably about five fifteen," he replied. "I was in no hurry."

"Where are your rooms, sir?"

"On Hart Street off Bloomsbury Square. As I said, I was tired, so I took a hansom cab and I was home about half past five."

"Did anyone see you?"

Anson shook his head. "I've a key to the front door, so I let myself in and went straight up to my quarters. My landlady wasn't there."

"How about the post office?" Morehead said. "Did anyone see you there?"

"Lots of people saw me, but I don't know any of their names." He smiled in amusement. "Constable, am I a suspect?"

"That's not for me to say, sir. These are simply routine questions. But we have heard that you and the victim didn't get along." Morehead was guessing. But based on Daniel Jones' account of Dearman's reaction at the mere mention of Anson's name, he was fairly sure he'd guessed correctly.

"Dearman didn't get along with most of the people who knew him." Anson's amusement faded. "One hates to speak ill of the dead, but he was a disgusting man."

"Disgusting in what way?" Morehead asked. He was finally getting somewhere; once you got suspects admitting how they really felt about the victim, you were half the way toward a conviction. At least, that's what Inspector Nivens always said, and right now, he hoped it was true. He made a mental note to make certain this interview, with his name prominently displayed, was on the first page of the report sent to the Yard. It never hurt to put your name in front of the chief inspector or the superintendent.

"In every way, Constable. He bullied the staff, was rude to the typewriter girl, and went through everyone's desk. He was a brute and a snoop. The only reason he had a position here was because he married into the Sutcliffe family and John Sutcliffe didn't want his sister to starve."

"What do you mean by 'snoop'?" Morehead asked. "Could you explain that a bit further?"

Anson grimaced. "What's to explain? As I've said, he had a habit of going through people's desks, and he was always trying to eavesdrop on personal conversations. It was almost as if the fellow liked to collect information on the off chance it might prove useful. I know he's searched this office" — he waved his hand in an arc and then thumped the desktop — "and I know he's gone through my desk. Just last week I caught him going through John's desk. When I confronted him, he claimed he was looking for an invoice. But that was non-sense. All the invoices are kept in the ac-counts department."

"Did you tell Mr. Sutcliffe about it?"

"I most certainly did," Anson replied.

"And what was his reaction?" Morehead looked up from his notebook again.

Anson's brow furrowed. "That was the odd thing. I expected he'd be furious, but he wasn't. He just said he'd deal with it and for me not to worry about it."

Wiggins stood across the road from the three-story office building and watched people as they went inside. Clerks, type-writer girls, businessmen, and even well-dressed matrons passed through the double doors. So did a lot of police constables. He wasn't worried that he'd run into any policemen that knew him by sight; these coppers were from Nivens' station or the

Yard, so it wasn't likely they'd know he was a member of Inspector Witherspoon's household, but still, it didn't bode well. People tended to hold their tongues when there were police everywhere.

He crossed the road and entered the lobby. The porter's desk was empty, so he hurried toward the corridor, passing the main staircase and heading for the rear of the building and what he hoped were a set of back stairs. He passed the offices of an insurance firm, a shipping company, and a freight line before he came to the end of the hallway. On one side was a service door leading to the mews, and on the other, the back stairs.

Moving quietly, he went up to the second floor. He peeked into the corridor and saw two constables standing at the far end. All the doors up and down the corridor were wide open, and he could hear the low murmur of voices, the clacking of typewriters, and the rustling of footsteps as people tried to go about their business.

He leaned back against the wall and tried to think of his next step. Going out into the hallway wouldn't work — those coppers would be on him like a shot. Blast, he had to see who worked in the Sutcliffe office. This was a big building and if he just hung about downstairs or tried the local pub, he couldn't be sure of finding an actual employee from Dearman's firm.

So he waited, leaning up against the wall and keeping his ear cocked for footsteps heading his way. He could always make a run for it if the police came near his hiding place. Every time he heard voices or feet in the corridor, he stuck his head out, but it was usually just a policeman coming or going. He did spot a couple of clerks, but they moved too quickly for him to get a decent look at their faces. After what seemed an eternity, he heard a nearby church bell chime the hour, and a moment later, footsteps pounded in the hallway as the office emptied for lunch.

He stuck his head in the hall and saw half a dozen neatly dressed clerks, including a typewriter girl, making their way toward the front stairs. One man, however, turned from the herd of people and came toward him.

Wiggins raced down the staircase, making it to the bottom just as the young man came barreling down. The clerk didn't so much as glance his way, but charged the service door, flung it open, and stepped out. Wiggins waited a moment and then followed him.

As Wiggins stepped out, the clerk turned

and glared at him. "Are you following me?"

"Don't be daft." Wiggins forced a laugh. Blast, he should have been more careful; there had just been a murder here, and everyone would be suspicious of strangers hanging about the place. "Why would I be followin' you? It's lunchtime and I'm goin' to get somethin' to eat."

The clerked looked to be about his own age. He had a long, thin face, hazel eyes, and brown hair parted on one side and cut short. "I've never seen you in this building before," he said. "Where do you work?"

Wiggins could easily have bluffed his way through the confrontation and said he worked for the insurance company or the freight lines, but he decided to play it a bit differently. "I work for a newspaper." He shrugged. "And you're right. I was followin' you. I know you work at the Sutcliffe offices upstairs, and I was hopin' I could 'ave a word with you."

"If it's about the murder, you'd be wasting your time. I don't know anything."

"I'll bet you know more than you think you do," Wiggins said. "Come on, help me out 'ere. My editor will have my guts for garters if I come back empty-handed, and the coppers 'ave got that second floor pinched as tight as a bloomin' corset. You're my only hope."

The clerk said nothing for a moment and then he laughed. "Will you buy me a pint? We're not supposed to drink at lunch, but I reckon that with Dearman dead, no one else will much care."

"I'll buy you as many pints as you like," Wiggins replied, delighted that his instincts had been correct. "Lead the way to the nearest pub."

Phyllis stepped into the grocer's shop and smiled politely at the young man behind the counter.

"May I help you, miss?" the clerk asked as she drew closer.

"I'd like a tin of Lyle's Golden Syrup, please," she said. The household actually needed the item as well.

"Yes, miss." He turned and walked down the row of shelves behind the counter till he reached the end, where he stopped.

"And I was hoping you could help me," she continued. "My mistress gave me a message for a household nearby, but I'm afraid I've lost the address."

He pulled the tin off the shelf, came back, and set it in front of her. "Do you recall the name of the household?" he inquired.

Phyllis pretended to think for a moment.

"Uh, let's see, yes, now I remember. The name was Dearman. Mr. and Mrs. Dearman."

He frowned. "I'm sorry, I'm afraid I can't help you. I've never heard of that family. Will there be anything else?"

"No, that'll be all," she replied.

An hour later, she was ready to give up. Apparently, the Dearman and the Sutcliffe households did their shopping elsewhere, because she'd been to every shop on both sides of the road and had learned nothing. Her feet hurt and she was cold. She stood in front of a tea shop debating whether to go in and have a cup to warm herself up, but she wasn't certain she could. She'd only been in such an establishment a few times, and that had only been because she'd been carrying her mistress's packages. But then she remembered what Betsy said. *You've as much right to a good life as anyone else*, the maid had told her. *And if you want something, you need to hold your head up and high and go after it.* Phyllis straightened her spine and went inside.

A dark-coated waiter hurried toward her. "Good day, miss. There's any empty table over there by the window. Will that do you?"

Phyllis smiled serenely. She was glad she'd worn her best cloak and bonnet. "That will do nicely, thank you." She followed him to the table, sat down, and ordered a pot of tea. When he'd gone, she tucked her shopping basket under her chair and sat back. The place was busy and the tables crammed so close together that she could hear snatches of conversations from every direction. She took a deep breath, pleased with herself for having had the courage to come inside. She half listened to the murmurings from the other tables, enjoying the feeling of being part of the bustling life of the city. But then she heard something that caught her attention.

"I'm not surprised that someone murdered him," a young woman said to her companion at the table next to hers.

Phyllis cast a furtive glance in their direction. Both girls wore plain, serviceable cloaks over their dresses, but she could tell by the lavender material of their skirts that the two of them were housemaids. They were probably on their afternoon out. She turned away as the one speaking noticed her looking at them. Luckily, the waiter was bringing her tea, so she smiled at him and nodded her thanks.

"Why ever not?" the other girl asked.

"Because he's a nasty old thing," replied the first girl, who had blonde hair tucked up under a straw bonnet. "I worked in his house for six months, remember? The reason I left was because he was so awful."

"Lots of masters are terrible, but they don't get murdered," the dark-haired girl scoffed. "You're just pretendin' to know more than you do."

Phyllis kept her expression carefully blank as she poured her tea and added milk.

"I'm not," she argued. "I told you when I left there that somethin' terrible was goin' to happen. You remember, I told you straight out that he'd come to a bad end. Even his own wife didn't have much use for him."

Phyllis added two lumps of sugar to her cup.

The dark-haired girl laughed harshly. "All I remember you sayin' was that you were glad to get shut of the place because his yellin' and screamin' made you nervous."

"That's not true. But let's not argue anymore. I want to enjoy my tea. By the way, did you know that Marion is sweet on that lad that works at the pub? I think she's goin' to be leavin' soon and marryin' him. Leastways that's what she's been hintin'."

"Don't believe her," her friend shot back. "Marion thinks that any fellow that so much as gives her a polite smile is wantin' to marry her."

Phyllis sipped her tea and listened as the girls chatted. They didn't discuss the murder again, and she couldn't be sure that the murdered man the blonde girl had mentioned was Ronald Dearman, but she'd not heard of anyone else being murdered in the past few days.

"Hurry up and finish your tea," the dark-haired girl ordered. "I've got to get back. Mrs. Collier has a fit if any of us are late from our afternoon out."

Phyllis waved for the waiter. She paid her bill, grabbed her shopping basket, and left. Once outside, she studied her surroundings carefully, looking for a good hiding place. The best she could see was a recessed spot between two buildings across the street. She glanced over her shoulder and saw the two girls getting up and gathering their things. She darted across the road, dodging a hansom cab and a delivery wagon before stumbling across the pavement and into the nook.

The girls walked out of the tea shop and turned to their left. Phyllis waited for them to move farther down the pavement before she followed after them. She kept well back as they turned off the crowded high street and onto Bruton Street. She trailed them down the road, around the corner, and onto another street until they stopped in front of a tall, redbrick Georgian house. They chatted for a few moments before the dark-haired girl waved good-bye and slipped down the side walkway to the servants' door. The blonde girl started off again, and Phyllis went after her. When the girl turned another corner, Phyllis broke into a run. "Excuse me, miss," she called as she caught up with her. "But could you stop a moment?"

The girl turned and stared at her suspiciously. "Weren't you in the tea shop just now?"

"I was," Phyllis admitted. "And that's why I followed you. I'd like to speak with you."

"What about?"

"About the man you used to work for." She smiled and came closer. "Was his name Ronald Dearman?"

The girl crossed her arms over her chest. "Yeah, how'd you know?"

"Because it's my job to know such things," she declared boldly. Betsy would be so proud of her. "I work for a private inquiry agency, and we've been employed to look into the murder of Ronald Dearman. My name is Millie Barret."

The girl's eyes widened. "A private inquiry agent? But you're a girl, a woman . . ."

"Women are as capable as men in most things," she replied with a shrug. "And we're better than most men when it comes to asking questions. Women notice details. I'll bet that you noticed lots of details in your household that the master of the house didn't see."

The girl smiled. "I suppose you could say that. But I don't see what I can tell you. I've not worked at the Dearman household in six months."

Phyllis thought fast. "True, but you can tell me about his character." She hoped she wasn't wasting her time. What the girl said was true, she probably didn't know anything that was useful to the murder investigation, but at least talking to her was better than showing up at their afternoon meeting empty-handed. "And if you'll pardon my saying so, I couldn't help but overhear the conversation you were having with your friend at the tea shop and you struck me as someone who is very observant and very intelligent. What's your name?"

"Jean Snelling." The girl smiled shyly. "And I don't have to be back for another hour or so, so I guess it wouldn't hurt to have a bit of a chat."

"Thank you." Phyllis smiled in return. "I noticed there was a park with benches just up the street. If it's not too cold for you, we could go there."

"It is cold," Jean said thoughtfully. "Better yet, there's a pub up the road as well. Let's go there and you can buy me a drink for my trouble."

Five minutes later, Phyllis was sitting at a corner table in the Royal Oak Pub and trying her best not to stare wide eyed at her surroundings. There was a large mirror behind the bar and a barman in a clean apron and a decent white shirt. Two customers, both of them middle-aged men in business suits, stood at the counter, and a well-dressed matron with a footman in tow occupied one of the other tables. An elderly gentleman smoking a pipe sat on the bench closest to the door.

"Now, what do you want to know?" Jean asked.

Phyllis turned her attention to her companion. "Anything you can tell me about the Dearmans," she said. She felt incredibly brave — she was in a pub, a real pub. She'd marched right up to the bar and ordered two glasses of gin just as if she'd done it every day of her life.

Jean wrinkled her nose in thought. "There's not much to tell."

"When we were at the tea shop, I overheard you telling your friend that you weren't surprised someone had killed him," she reminded her.

"That's true. He was a right nasty fellow, and I don't think anyone, even his wife, will be sheddin' many tears at his funeral."

"How long did you work there?"

"A year and a half," she replied. "Then I found another position. He was so angry that I was leavin' he didn't want to give me a reference, but Mrs. Dearman was decent and she gave me one. Mind you, she was used to it, they couldn't keep help. People usually left as soon as they could find another place to go. Between the horrid rations they fed us and their fightin', no one wanted to live in that house."

"Mr. and Mrs. Dearman fought a lot."

"Like cats and dogs." Jean grinned. "He hated the fact that she wasn't scared of him."

"What did they argue about?" Phyllis picked up her drink and forced herself to take a sip. The stuff tasted bitter and it took all her willpower not to make a face.

"Mostly money." Jean took another drink. "Mrs. Dearman used to get furious at him over the household expenses. She claimed that he didn't give her enough to run the house properly, and there was some truth to that. He was miserly with food and heat. Mind you, he always said that he'd give her more if she would tell her skinflint brother to increase his salary. That would really set her off."

"How?" Phyllis asked. She forced another sip down her throat.

"You don't look like you're enjoyin' that." Jean nodded toward her drink. "If you don't want it, I'll have it."

Phyllis handed her the gin. "I don't really like to drink."

"I do." She laughed. "And the mistress is gone today, so no one will notice if I come home a bit happy."

"You were telling me about the arguments between Mr. and Mrs. Dearman," Phyllis reminded her.

"Oh, they fought over everything. He even resented her having her friend over for supper."

"What friend?" Phyllis thought she was losing control of this conversation.

"Mrs. Meadows. She and Mrs. Dearman are as thick as thieves," Jean replied. "And Mr. Dearman didn't much like her and didn't bother to hide how he felt about her."

"Why did he dislike her?"

She took another gulp. "He complained that Mrs. Meadows was always stirring things up, and he was right about that. She'd come to the house every afternoon for tea, and the two of them would sit together and complain about their husbands and how if they had it to do over, neither of them would ever get married. By the time Mr. Dearman come home in the evenings, she'd be so riled she'd lay right into him the second he walked in the door. It was always the same thing as well, money."

"But surely Mr. Dearman made a decent salary if he was working for his wife's brother," Phyllis commented.

"Not according to him." Jean laughed. "But every time he brought the subject up, she'd say he wouldn't have a job without her brother and that she'd brought plenty of money to their marriage and all he'd come with was a half-rotted cottage in some ugly village in Essex. Those were her exact words. He'd get furious and stomp out of the house. I think she taunted him on purpose so he'd leave."

"So he got through all the money in her marriage settlement," Phyllis mused.

Jean knocked back the last of the gin and slapped the glass down on the tabletop.

"Would you like another?" Phyllis asked.

"That's very generous of you." Jean picked

up her glass and waved at the barman. "Thanks ever so much."

"Everyone was quite surprised when she took care of him herself," Edwina Hawkins said to Ruth. "But to her credit, she did. She wouldn't have a nurse in the house."

They stood in the cloakroom of the meeting hall where the March meeting of the London Society for Women's Suffrage had concluded fifteen minutes earlier. Ruth had spoken to several women about the murder, and she'd heard an interesting story about Ronald Dearman. Edwina Hawkins had overheard the exchange, and being the gossip that she was, she'd followed her into the cloakroom. Edwina Hawkins lived next door to Antonia Meadows, Lucretia Dearman's friend.

Ruth was in a hurry to get back to Upper Edmonton Gardens, but she didn't want to be rude, so she nodded encouragingly as Edwina rambled on.

"It was sad," Edwina continued. "Thaddeus Meadows wasn't a very nice man, he was barely civil if you happened to see him outside, and he certainly didn't let her spend any money. The poor woman had to account for every penny she spent on the household. They couldn't keep help, you

know. Not that she had much, but he did allow her to have a housemaid and a cook. Now that he's gone, she lets both of them stop work at five every day even though they live in. There's been grumbling in the neighborhood about that — some of my neighbors are afraid that their own servants will be agitating to get off early. But I don't think that's going to be the case. Mrs. Meadows still doesn't pay very well, and that's the reason she's so lenient with their work hours."

"How did he die?" Ruth turned and pulled her cloak off the peg behind her.

"He had pneumonia," Edwina said eagerly. "The doctor had been there and it appeared that he was getting better, but then he took a turn for the worse and died. I felt sorry for Mrs. Meadows, but you know, even now that he's gone, she's still quite thrifty. Her umbrella broke last week and instead of buying a new one, she gave it to one of those door-to-door tinkers to mend. But then again, once you learn economical habits, they die hard, don't they? The tinker brought it back while she was out, so he banged on my door and I took it for her."

"She is lucky to have a kind neighbor like you," Ruth murmured. She was very disappointed.

"Thank you, Lady Cannonberry, but that's not what I mean. She was lucky because if the tinker had been a minute later, I'd not have been home. It was our executive committee meeting at Mrs. Parsons' and you know what a stickler for punctuality she can be, and as it happened, none of my servants were home that afternoon, either. I'd given them the afternoon off because the painters had done the downstairs hall."

CHAPTER 4

"It's called the Nazareth Sugar Cookie," Mrs. Goodge said as she set a plate of fragrant, golden-baked disks next to the teapot. "The recipe is from Pennsylvania." She smiled at Luty as she spoke. "I thought it might be nice for us to try them out."

Wiggins, his expression skeptical, reached for one. He took a bite, chewed, swallowed, and grinned. "Cor blimey, these are good. You can make them for me anytime you want," he said. "Are you goin' to feed them to your sources?"

"I'm not sure. I made these because I had a bit of vanilla I wanted to use up and I thought Luty might enjoy a treat from her homeland."

"Thank you, that's right thoughtful of ya." Luty reached for a cookie.

"But I'm not sure about feedin' them to my sources," the cook continued. "Some people don't like to try new things. I need them to be comfortable and willin' to talk." She took her seat at the table. "I've had no luck today, but I can see that the rest of you seem to be in good spirits."

Mrs. Jeffries helped herself to a cookie. "If no one objects, I'll go first. I had quite an interesting meeting with Fiona. She gave me the names of several people who either disliked Dearman intensely or who'd had substantial problems because of him." She took a quick bite and paused briefly to see if anyone objected. When no one did, she went on. "Umh . . . this is wonderful." She licked her lips. "Rather sweet, but it has a lovely flavor. Apparently, Dearman disliked his wife's friend, Antonia Meadows, resented the other deputy director, Henry Anson, and had sacked at least two people in the past six months. Fiona didn't know the exact date the accounting clerk, James Tremlett, was let go, but it was within the last two weeks."

"What about the other sacking?" Hatchet asked.

"Fiona said it was months ago and the man had immediately gotten another, better paid position, so I doubt he'd have a motive."

"Dearman's own wife didn't much like him, either," Luty pointed out. "We can't forget that."

"We won't," Mrs. Jeffries agreed. "But I didn't have time to speak to Fiona about her. Unfortunately, before I could finish my conversation, the housekeeper announced that Inspector Nivens had arrived. Fiona made him wait quite a while, but I was too anxious about being recognized to concentrate on everything I wanted to ask her."

"He didn't see you, did he?" Ruth asked.

"No, I managed to get out of the house undiscovered, but it was a rather nerve wracking, and again, I must emphasize that we need to be careful," she said.

"Did she decide to tell you why she threatened the victim?" Hatchet asked.

"I'm afraid not. She simply insists that it had nothing to do with the murder and that she didn't kill him," Mrs. Jeffries replied. "She told me that the other deputy director, Henry Anson, loathed Dearman and apparently the feeling was mutual. When Anson was hired, Fiona said that John told her he was grooming the man to take over the company when he retired. Supposedly, he was also going to be easing Dearman out as well; he'd not been happy with the way Dearman was running the office. But in the last few months, John had changed his mind and instead of putting Anson completely in charge, he'd only put him in control of the manufacturing operations. Anson and his fiancée, Amy Throckmorton, were at the dinner party on the Saturday before the murder. According to Fiona, they were barely polite to either of the Dearmans."

"That must have made for a jolly old time," Mrs. Goodge said. "Where does Henry Anson live?"

"On Hart Street, off Bloomsbury Square. Fiona didn't know where his fiancée lives, but as she's only met Ronald Dearman a time or two, she's hardly likely to have murdered him."

"Maybe she thought that Anson was gettin' the short end of the stick," Luty mused. "Some women are real protective of their menfolk. Could be that Anson complained about him to her and she decided to take matters into her own hands."

"That's certainly possible," Mrs. Jeffries said.

"But not real likely," Luty admitted. "Still, let's not let her off the hook so easily. The least we can do is find out where she was when Dearman was murdered."

"I'll see if Constable Barnes can find that out." Mrs. Jeffries eyed the plate of cookies. They were disappearing fast.

"Did your sister-in-law mention if her

husband knew she'd threatened the victim?" Ruth asked.

"I didn't have time to ask. Once I knew Nivens was in the house, all I could think of was getting out without being seen." She glanced at the carriage clock on the pine sideboard. "It's getting late and the inspector will probably be home on time tonight. We'd best get on with this. Who wants to go next?"

"Wait a minute, what about the keys?" Mrs. Goodge asked. "You were going to ask her who had keys to the office. Surely you had time to do that?"

Mrs. Jeffries cringed. "Oh dear, I am getting forgetful. I'm glad you reminded me. I asked her about them as soon as I got there today. There are only three sets of keys to the main door, and they're held by John Sutcliffe, Henry Anson, and Ronald Dearman. Each of these men has a key to his own individual office, but not to the others' offices."

"So Henry Anson and Sutcliffe wouldn't have had the keys to Dearman's private office?" Phyllis murmured. "But we know that that office was locked, because the porter had to unlock it for Mrs. Dearman."

"Which means that the killer must have the keys," Luty declared.

119

"Not necessarily." Hatchet helped himself to a second cookie. "The killer might have left them somewhere on the premises, and the police may have found them."

"We'll have to ask Constable Barnes if he can find out," Mrs. Jeffries said quickly. "Time really is getting on. Who would like to go next?"

"I will," Phyllis announced. "I didn't have any luck with the local merchants, but I found someone that used to work in the Dearman household, and she didn't have a good thing to say about the fellow."

"How long ago did she leave the Dearman household?" Luty grabbed another cookie and took a huge bite.

"Six months ago, so I know she'll not be able to give us anything useful about the murder, but she did know a lot about the household. She says he was a bully and mean as a rabid dog. The servants were terrified of him and no one stayed very long. The only person he didn't bully was his wife, but Jean said they fought all the time, even in front of the servants. The night before Jean left the household, Mr. Dearman threw a carving knife at Mrs. Dearman!" She broke off with a wide grin. "She said the mistress ducked and the knife landed on the floor, but she'd never seen

120

the mistress move that fast."

"Another marriage made in heaven," Mrs. Goodge said wryly.

"Jean says she thinks that it weren't just fighting so they could make up," Phyllis continued as a blush crept up her cheek. "You know what I mean, some couples fight just so they can . . . well, you know."

"What's she talkin' about?" Wiggins asked curiously. "What do you mean, 'make up'? You mean they say they're sorry, right?"

"I'll explain it to you later," Hatchet interjected quickly. "But yes, Phyllis, we know what you're suggesting. Please go on."

"Jean says the squabbling was real and that they genuinely hated each other," she continued. "She once overheard Mrs. Dearman telling her friend, Mrs. Meadows, that she'd only married Ronald to spite her brother and that it was the worst mistake of her life. If she'd not married him, she'd be free and could travel the world and do as she pleased."

"According to what Fiona said, Lucretia Dearman was so concerned about her husband when he didn't come home, she couldn't even wait a half hour for the office to open," Mrs. Jeffries said thoughtfully. "Yet we know from several different sources that the Dearmans' marriage wasn't a happy one."

"Maybe she was just coverin' up," the cook suggested. "Pretendin' to be worried when in reality, she might even be the one that killed him."

"She must have been," Phyllis said. "My source told me that they hated each other and they argued all the time over money. Mrs. Dearman would deliberately rile him up, and then when they were going at it, she'd throw in the fact that she brought a huge marriage settlement to the marriage while all he brought was a rundown old cottage in some ugly village in Essex and that if he was any kind of a man, he'd at least sell it." She told them the rest of what she'd heard from Jean Snelling, taking care to repeat much of it word for word.

"Goodness, Phyllis." Mrs. Jeffries smiled broadly. "You did get an earful."

"Well done, Phyllis." Wiggins laughed. "And you were worried you'd not find out anythin'."

Phyllis blushed in pleasure, ducked her head, and reached for her teacup. "I got lucky today."

"I think we ought to take a real close look at the widow," Luty said. "I bet that she went to get one of the Sutcliffes to let her into the office so she'd have an audience

122

willin' to testify that she was all worried and upset."

"That's possible, but let's not get ahead of ourselves," the housekeeper warned. "We all know what happens when we leap to conclusions too early in a case. Are you finished?" she asked Phyllis, who nodded. Mrs. Jeffries then said, "Who is next?"

"I'll go," Ruth offered. "I heard something about Ronald Dearman. My source told me she'd seen him last week at a dinner party at the Kingston house. After dinner, the room got very warm and stuffy, so she went out onto the side terrace for some fresh air. That part of the terrace has a good view of the street, and she saw Dearman standing under the lamppost on the corner with a woman. They had their heads together, and then she saw him take something out of his inside jacket pocket and hand it to the lady."

"Could she see what it was?" Luty asked.

Ruth shook her head. "Unfortunately, it was too dark. But she was certain the woman wasn't someone from the dinner party because she went back in and had a good look around. All the ladies were present. It was a good ten minutes before Dearman came back into the room."

"If it was that dark, was she sure it was him she saw?" Mrs. Goodge poured herself more tea.

"Because of the lamplight, she could see him clearly, but the woman was wearing a cloak that was pulled forward, covering her face."

"Cor blimey, this is gettin' interestin'," Wiggins declared. "I wish we knew who this mysterious person is."

"We need to find out," the cook muttered. "There must be some way we can learn her identity."

"And we will find out," Mrs. Jeffries said hastily. "But right now, we must get on with the meeting. The inspector has been working regular hours since he's been on the fraud case, and he might even come home early as he has a dinner engagement with Ruth. Now, who would —"

"But that wasn't all I heard," Ruth interrupted.

"Oh, sorry, I didn't mean to cut you off." Mrs. Jeffries smiled apologetically. "Go on, what else did you find out?"

"It's not much, but as we've learned in the past, it's always best to report everything." She told them about being cornered by Edwina Hawkins. "I realize this tidbit isn't even about the murder, but as Antonia Meadows is Mrs. Dearman's friend, I thought I'd pass this along," she concluded.

"So Mrs. Dearman and Mrs. Meadows were both in miserable marriages," Phyllis said. "It puts you right off wanting to get wed, doesn't it?"

"There's plenty of good marriages about," Wiggins protested. He was a romantic, and even though he'd had his heart broken any number of times, he knew there was a wonderful girl out there somewhere waiting to be his wife. "It's just mainly the upper crust that 'as the 'orrid ones. That's 'cause they don't marry for love."

"Yes, yes, I'm sure both of you are making valid points, but we must get on," the housekeeper exclaimed. "Luty, do you have anything to report?"

"Not a danged thing." Luty snorted derisively. "Today's sources were as useless as teats on a bull —" She broke off at Hatchet's gasp of shock and the giggles coming from the others. "Oops, sorry, did I say that out loud?"

"Really, madam," her butler chided. "That sort of language is very coarse."

"I said I was sorry," she shot back. "Sometimes things slip out. But it's true, my sources today were useless. Besides, as everyone else is still snickerin', I don't think any offense was taken."

"Of course no one took offense," Mrs.

Jeffries assured her. She decided not to worry about the inspector. If he came in and found everyone here, she'd simply say they'd stopped in for tea. "And I'm sorry you didn't have much luck today."

"You're not alone, madam," Hatchet complained. "My day wasn't very productive, either."

"I did alright," Wiggins said. "I found a clerk from Sutcliffe's office. He told me that he was the last person out of the office the night Dearman was killed. The windows was closed and locked, but not the front door, so anyone could 'ave come and gone. He said Dearman would 'ave locked up as he left. He was usually the last one to leave. But sometimes Mr. Anson locked up, only he wasn't there that evening."

"What about the porter, wouldn't he have seen who came and went?" Ruth asked.

"Nah, he doesn't come on duty until half past six and his desk is at the front. But the back door is left unlocked until seven. There's an employment office on the third floor that stays open until seven, and the back door is left unlocked so the day laborers can come in and out to get their wages."

"And the other offices in the building, did you find out what time they closed?" Mrs. Jeffries asked.

"The first-floor offices all close either at half past five or at six. The Sutcliffe offices 'ave the entire second floor, and we know they shut at six. Other than the employment agency, all the other offices on the third floor close at half past five or at six."

"So between the hours of five thirty and six thirty, anyone could have walked through the front door without being seen, and even after the porter came on duty, that killer could have come in the back door without being noticed." Mrs. Jeffries drummed her fingers on the tabletop. "That is going to make this very difficult. Did your source say anything else?"

"Only what we've already 'eard, that Dearman was about as popular as a wart. Daniel Jones, he's the clerk I spoke to, said the man liked throwin' 'is weight about, if you get my meaning. He also told me that Henry Anson has had a few run-ins with Dearman. Jones said last week, he'd forgotten 'is change purse in 'is desk so he came back to get it and Henry Anson and Dearman were 'avin' a row."

"Did he hear what it was about?" Mrs. Goodge asked eagerly.

"Afraid not. He said he was in a hurry so he just grabbed the purse and left; all he 'eard was voices raised and Anson screamin' that he'd not put up with it and he'd better watch his tongue if he knew what was good for 'im."

"I don't appreciate you or anyone else barging into my home and bullying my household," John Sutcliffe said.

Nivens looked him directly in the eye, trying to calculate just how much power and influence the man might actually have. Prior to getting this case, he'd never heard of Sutcliffe Manufacturing, but a few discreet inquiries on his part had revealed it was a prosperous concern and that John Sutcliffe was on a first-name basis with half a dozen members of Parliament and one or possibly two cabinet ministers. Nivens was no fool, so he plastered a conciliatory smile on his face and said, "We meant no disrespect to your household, sir. I'm terribly sorry if anyone misinterpreted our actions. But in our defense, we are investigating a murder and we do have to ask disagreeable questions."

Sutcliffe, a tall, gray-haired man with erect bearing and an air of authority, stood by the marble fireplace. His wife sat on the couch, watching Nivens.

"I'm aware of the reason you're here," Sutcliffe snapped. "Ronald Dearman was my sister's husband and one of my most valuable employees. But that doesn't give you leave to browbeat my household. My housekeeper told me that you reduced the downstairs maid to tears and scared the tweeny so badly she had hiccups."

Nivens tried another approach. "Mr. Sutcliffe, I'm sure you understand that in dealing with the lower classes, one has to be stern."

"That's absurd," he shot back. "People are people, and everyone in this household is to be dealt with in a respectful and courteous manner. Do I make myself clear? Otherwise, Inspector, I shall personally go and have a word with the Home Secretary."

Nivens swallowed uneasily. Blast and drat, he hated backing down, but he didn't have a choice. The Home Secretary would love to give this case to that damnable man Witherspoon and his pack of demented helpers. If this rich toff complained that he was a beast and bully, they'd snatch this murder away from him faster than a doxie downed a gin. "That won't be necessary, sir. Now, if you don't mind, I should like to ask you a few questions. If it's convenient, sir."

"Go ahead." Sutcliffe made no move to sit down nor did he offer the inspector a chair. "Ask your questions, I'll be happy to cooperate. I want this killer caught and sent to the gallows."

"I understand you were out of town when the murder occurred?"

"I was in Birmingham on business. I came home as soon as I heard what had happened," he replied.

"Do you know of anyone who might have wanted Mr. Dearman dead?" Nivens asked.

Sutcliffe glanced at his wife, who gave him a wan smile and the briefest of nods. He looked at Nivens. "Ronald Dearman wasn't a particularly nice person, but I don't know of anyone who actually wanted him dead."

"But someone apparently did," Fiona Sutcliffe murmured softly.

"Exactly what did he do at Sutcliffe Manufacturing?" Nivens asked.

"He was the deputy director, and he was in charge of the day-to-day management of the office."

"Just the office or the whole company?"

Sutcliffe sighed. "Just the office. Until last September, he'd been in charge of both the manufacturing sites and the office, but I'd brought in another deputy director to handle the operations of the sites."

"What's his name, sir?"

"Henry Anson. He's very capable. I

130

brought him in to streamline our operations and upgrade our facilities. He came highly recommended."

"How long exactly has Mr. Anson worked for you?"

"Since last September." Sutcliffe moved away from the fireplace and sat down next to his wife. "I spend most of my time meeting with customers and suppliers. I didn't have the time or the expertise to modernize the company. Henry does. He's already put several timesaving processes in place at both the factory sites. Frankly, even if I hadn't been wanting to upgrade our equipment and factories, the business has grown to the point where it's far too much work for one deputy director to handle."

"So Ronald Dearman went from being the only deputy director to sharing the duties."

"That's right."

"Did he see this as a demotion?" Nivens wished he'd asked Morehead to stay with him while he interviewed these two. He was afraid he might forget something pertinent, and the constable, though not likable, did have a remarkable memory. But after his own disastrous attempt at questioning the servants, he'd sent Morehead and another constable downstairs to reinterview them.

"He didn't see it that way because it

131

wasn't a demotion. His salary wasn't decreased, only his level of responsibility," Sutcliffe retorted. "My sister, Mrs. Dearman, had complained that Ronald wasn't feeling well, and I hoped that bringing Henry into the firm might ease Ronald's burden somewhat."

"How did Mr. Dearman feel about losing a good part of his responsibilities?"

Sutcliffe sighed heavily. "Unfortunately, he wasn't happy about it. I suppose it's best that you hear it from me rather than from someone else, but Ronald and Henry didn't get along all that well."

"Ronald accused Henry Anson of stealing his job," Fiona Sutcliffe explained. "He was furious when his duties were curtailed. I suspect he's done his very best to undermine Mr. Anson's efforts."

"Now, now, dear." Sutcliffe patted his wife's hand. "You don't know that for a fact."

"I most certainly do," she said. "Lucretia went on and on about how furious Ronald was over the matter."

Sutcliffe pulled his hand away and frowned at his wife. "You never said anything to me."

"Of course not," she replied. "It's not for me to interfere in your business decisions."

"Mrs. Sutcliffe, did you host a dinner party here Saturday evening?" Nivens asked.

She regarded him warily. "Yes."

"Who were the guests on that occasion?"

"What's that got to do with Ronald's murder?" Sutcliffe looked from his wife to the inspector. "Why are you asking about a dinner party? We have them all the time."

Nivens gave him a brief, mirthless smile. "I'm sure you do, sir, but as it happens, something happened on that particular occasion that may have a direct bearing on Ronald Dearman's murder."

"We had a number of guests to dinner that evening," she said briskly. "Mr. and Mrs. Dearman, Henry Anson and his fiancée, Miss Throckmorton, and Mrs. Meadows."

"Who is Mrs. Meadows?" Nivens asked.

"She's a family friend," John Sutcliffe replied.

"Can you please supply me with Mrs. Meadows' address?" he asked Fiona. She nodded and he pounced. "Did you threaten to murder Mr. Dearman that night?"

"What on earth are you talking about!" Sutcliffe cried. "How dare you ask such a ridiculous quest—"

"Yes, I did threaten him," Fiona interrupted. She looked at her husband. "I'm sorry, John, but this was bound to come out.

It was when you took everyone upstairs to look at your new map. Ronald said he wanted to speak with me, so we went into the study. He made some awful remarks. I lost my temper and lost control of my tongue."

Sutcliffe was staring at her as if he'd never seen her before. "But you never lose your temper."

"But of course I do," she explained gently. "I simply don't do it in front of you. It's actually been quite a strain all these years."

"What was the argument about?" Nivens asked eagerly.

Fiona Sutcliffe stared at him coldly. "That's none of your business, Inspector. But I can assure you it was a personal matter and that I had nothing to do with his murder."

"Where were you at six o'clock Monday evening?"

"You mean where was I when Dearman was murdered?" she replied.

"Now see here, Inspector," Sutcliffe blustered. "I'll not have my wife spoken to as if she's a common criminal."

"It's alright, John," she said quickly. "I'll answer the inspector. I'm sure he already knows I wasn't home."

He did — that had been one of the few

coherent bits of information he'd managed to get out of the housemaid. "That's correct, your maid stated that you left the house at five o'clock that afternoon. Where did you go?"

"I went for a walk."

"How long were you gone?" He already had the answer to that question, but he wanted to see if she was going to lie about it. He'd not liked her refusal to comment on her argument with Dearman.

She smiled skeptically. "It was past seven o'clock when I arrived home, but I'm sure you know that already."

Constable Barnes felt a twinge of guilt as he put the pint of beer down in front of his old friend Eddie Harwood. They'd started out on the force together, but their professional lives had taken very different paths. Harwood's career was ending behind the front counter in the lobby at Scotland Yard.

"How have you been, Eddie?" He slid onto a stool. They were in the White Hart Pub, and the constable had to raise his voice to be heard over the noise. It was a policeman's pub: close enough to Scotland Yard to have plenty of business but far enough away so that the men could relax over a pint or a whiskey. Constables, detectives, and office workers crowded shoulder to shoulder along the bar. All the benches along the wall were full, and there wasn't an empty stool at the any of the tables.

Harwood shrugged. He was the same age as Barnes, but his shoulders were stooped and his thinning hair had more gray than brown. "I'm just waiting to retire. It'll be another two years and then they'll make me spend my days at home. I suppose I can always work in my garden. How about you, looking forward to giving it all up?"

Barnes shook his head. With the passage of the Police Pensions Act of 1890, he, like everyone else who served honorably on the force, was eligible for a lifetime pension. Prior to this act, the assigning of pensions to individual policemen had been discretionary and to Barnes' way of thinking, arbitrary. "Not really. I got lucky. I work closely with Inspector Witherspoon. It keeps it interesting. It's a nice spot to end up."

Eddie grinned broadly. "Thanks to you, I guess you could say I got a nice spot as well."

Barnes shrugged modestly. He was genuinely embarrassed because he was going to ask Eddie for a favor, but he didn't want his old mate thinking he'd helped him get his current assignment for any reason other than friendship. "All I did was mention to Inspector Witherspoon that you should be considered for transfer to the Yard. You served your time on the streets, and you kept getting those ruddy chest colds from being outside."

"You did more than that." Harwood's smile disappeared and his expression sobered. "Your inspector spoke up for me. He had lots of influence because he'd just cracked three tough cases in a row. My sources told me that Witherspoon respects your judgment. If you'd not recommended me to him and he hadn't put in a good word for me, they'd have let me go for medical reasons and I might not have got any pension. You know what the old days were like — if the higher-ups didn't like you, they wouldn't lift a finger to see that you got something for all your years of service."

"Thank goodness it's changed for the better," Barnes said quickly.

"Our generation didn't get much in the way of promotions, did we?" Harwood continued as if Barnes hadn't spoken. "But that's the way of life, isn't it. There's been a lot of progress in the past ten years, so the lads coming in now will have a better crack at moving up in the organization than we did. Oh well, all in all, it isn't a bad way to make a living."

"And we do some good in the world," Barnes pointed out. "That's better than working a line in a factory or digging coal out of the earth."

"True," he agreed. "I like to think I've put some nasty ones behind bars where they belonged and made a bit of difference in this old world. I'm glad you stopped by tonight. It's lonely going home on my own. You knew that Lucy passed away last year."

"I was at her funeral," Barnes reminded him. "And I was real sorry to hear about her passing. Now, I've got —"

"Not as sorry as I was," Harwood interrupted. "She was a good wife and mother. Of course the children are all grown up and out of the house now, I don't see them much, and so I rattle around all on my own. I know my neighbors, of course, but they've got lives of their own, and my brother lives close by, but he's a younger one and works for the Great Eastern —"

"Eddie, I need a favor," Barnes blurted. He cringed inwardly. He'd not meant to be so blunt, but the fellow wasn't letting him get a word in edgewise.

Eddie drew back slightly as if he couldn't decide whether to be offended or not.

"Sorry, I didn't mean to interrupt," Barnes

said quickly. "But I need you to do something for me."

Eddie waved off his apology. "What do you need? If I can help, I will — you know that."

"You know that Inspector Nivens is in charge of the Dearman murder."

He chuckled. "We're takin' odds on how badly he mucks it up. Everyone was surprised that Inspector Witherspoon didn't get it, but the murder was in Nivens' district and he's been agitating for one for donkey's years. Why? Did your guv want it?"

Barnes gave a negative shake of his head. "I've got another interest in the case. A good friend of mine is worried about it and for good reason. There's some innocent people who might be hurt if Nivens messes it up. Which brings me to my favor: Nivens is likely to be sending in a report every day whether he's made any progress or not."

"We've already had two of 'em," Eddie said. "And the poor blighter was only murdered on Monday evening. So what are you wantin' me to do, hold 'em back a bit so you can have a peek before they go upstairs?"

Barnes grinned. "You always were a sharp one. Can you do it without any risk to yourself? I'll not have you doing anything that might lose you your pension."

"Don't you worry about that." He raised his glass and took a quick sip. "I've been around a long time and I can take care of myself. I owe you, Barnes, so you just stop by every day at the end of your shift and you can take a look at those reports."

The inspector was in a cheerful mood when he came home that evening. "The fraud case is quite fascinating." He handed Mrs. Jeffries his bowler.

"Careful, sir, if you become as adept at fraud as you are at murder, you'll never have a moment's peace." She hung up the hat. She knew that Witherspoon was far more comfortable with numbers than with chasing killers.

He laughed, slipped off his coat, and hung it on the peg. "Oh, I don't think there's any danger of that. This one is a fairly straight-forward case, but the evidence must be properly understood. Shall we have a glass of sherry?" He headed down the hall.

"That would be nice, sir." She trailed after him and they went into the study. She went to the cabinet, pulled out a bottle of Harvey's, and poured them each a glass. She handed him his and took her seat opposite him. She wasn't particularly interested in

140

the fraud case, but they'd established this pattern years earlier and she wasn't going to change it now. When Witherspoon did have a murder, it was this evening ritual that made her privy to every little detail of the case. "How much longer do you think you'll be tied up going through ledgers, sir?"

"Another few days. As I said, it's an obvious fraud case, but the ledgers are rather extensive. The fellow kept two sets of books." He frowned. "I think we may need to bring in someone who is more versed in accounting than I am. Honestly, just when I think I understand the books, I find something else that doesn't make sense."

"You're good at numbers, sir," she assured him. "You'll sort it out." She wanted to ask if he'd heard anything about the Dearman murder, but she didn't dare. Thus far, no one outside her circle except for Constable Barnes knew of her connection with Fiona, and she was afraid of asking too many questions. There was some truth to the old adage that it was wise to let sleeping dogs lie.

"I'm doing my best," he replied cheerfully. "Luckily, it's not a crime of violence, so they're giving me sufficient time to make sense of things." He took a sip of sherry. "But I do feel a bit sorry for Constable Barnes. He's at a bit of a loose end. Today he actually volunteered to take the daily reports to the Yard. I told him there was no need to do that, that one of the more junior constables should be assigned that task, but he said he wanted to do it."

"Perhaps he wanted to get out and about," she suggested. Her mind was working furiously, trying to come up with some reason why the constable would want to go to Scotland Yard every day.

"Yes, I can understand that, sometimes the station does get stuffy and, well, not very nice, especially at this time of year when it's too cold to keep all the windows open. But whatever his reason, I hope the lads at the station don't take advantage of his good nature and give him all the drudge work."

"I'm sure that won't happen, sir," she murmured.

"But perhaps I ought to have a word with —"

"Surely the constable can take care of himself," she interrupted. She knew good and well what Barnes was doing, and the last thing they needed was Witherspoon intervening for any reason. "Constable Barnes is a very proud man. He might misunderstand any action you take on his behalf."

Witherspoon's bony face creased in

thought. "You could be right about that, and I have no wish to offend the constable. I value him too much as a friend."

"Perhaps, sir, he enjoys going to the Yard," she suggested. She smiled conspiratorially and leaned toward the inspector. "I suspect, sir, that he volunteered to go today because it gives him an opportunity to see some of his old friends."

Lord Billington's dinner parties were usually so dull that Luty avoided them like the plague. She couldn't remember why she'd accepted the invitation to this one, but now that she was here, she was determined to make the best of it. She smiled at the elderly gentleman sitting on her left. "Howdy, I don't believe we've met. I'm Luty Belle Crookshank."

"I'm Basil Featherstone. How do you do, Mrs. Crookshank?"

"Very well, thank you."

"You're an American?" His face brightened. "I know who you are. You live in Knightsbridge, don't you, and you're a friend of Lady Cannonberry. Goodness, I've been wanting to meet you. Lady Cannonberry has mentioned you a number of times, and now, here we are."

Flattered, Luty took another look at her

companion. Even though he was sitting, she could tell he wasn't much taller than she was, and like her, he was thin, white haired, and well dressed. But his hazel eyes were lively with intelligence, and when he'd walked into the dining room and taken his seat, his step had been sure and steady. "That's nice to hear, Mr. Featherstone. You're acquainted with Lady Cannonberry? How long have you known her?"

"For years. Her late husband and I did a little business together." He picked up his wineglass and took a sip.

"You're a businessman?"

He put the drink down carefully. "Not really. My business with Lord Cannonberry was a simple land transaction. But we moved in the same circles, so I got to know both him and his lovely wife. Actually, these days I don't do much of anything. But I used to be an inventor." He nodded his thanks as a footman put the first course, a fish consommé, in front of him.

"What did you invent, somethin' excitin' like the telephone?" she asked eagerly.

He laughed. "I wish I had, but Mr. Bell beat me to it. No, I invented engineering machines and measuring instruments. Nothing spectacular, just gears and mechanical devices that help in assembling our industrial goods."

"So you know somethin' of the industrial world." She smiled at the footman as he served her soup, then turned back to her dinner companion. "Did you hear about that murder at the Sutcliffe Manufacturin' office?" She asked only out of habit; she didn't think this old boy would have anything useful to share.

"That was dreadful, wasn't it." Basil Featherstone dipped his spoon into the bowl and scooped up the soup. "I don't know what this world is coming to; the streets are dangerous enough, but one ought to be safe from random violence in one's office."

"Random violence," she repeated. "You think someone just went in and killed the feller? That's not what the papers said."

"Really? I've not read the newspaper accounts; I heard about it when I went to my club. I assumed it was a robbery attempt." He tasted the soup and nodded approval.

"I don't think so. From what I read, it seems like someone deliberately wanted Ronald Dearman dead. After all, he was killed just after the office closed, and a casual robber would have been worried that there might be more than one person left on the premises."

"I must say, I'd not thought of it like that. I suppose I shouldn't be surprised that it happened at Sutcliffe's."

Luty wasn't fond of fish consommé, so she reached for her wineglass. "What do you mean?"

"Oh, I shouldn't have said that," he replied. He put the spoon in the bowl and pushed it to one side. "This soup is delicious, but if I eat any more, I'll be too full to eat the remaining courses."

"Me, too," she replied. "Now come on, don't leave me guessin'. What did you mean? Why weren't you surprised that it happened at Sutcliffe's?"

He grinned. "Well, one doesn't like to gossip, but that firm has had their ups and downs over the years."

"Really?" Luty's spirits lifted. "What kind of ups and downs? Now don't clam up on me. Personally, I love to gossip. It's one of the few pleasures left for someone my age."

He laughed out loud. "I was lying. I love to gossip, too."

"What do you know about Sutcliffe Manufacturin'?"

He gave a quick glance toward the lady sitting on his other side, but she was engrossed in a conversation and not paying them any attention. He turned back to Luty and said, "It wasn't all that many years ago that they almost went under. Sutcliffe's was started back in the early 1840s. The original founder was old Horace Sutcliffe. He was a blacksmith that made ball bearings for a local transport company that eventually became a railroad."

"How come you know so much about the company?" she asked curiously.

"Because I'm from York and I tried to do business with them any number of times, but they were never interested in my inventions. But that's by the by. As I was saying, old Horace soon realized that there was more money to be made in industry than in shoeing horses, so he branched out and began making machines for the local manufacturing companies. By the time his grandson took over the company, they were manufacturing specialized equipment for a number of industries. But as the years passed, they fell further and further behind their competitors, many of whom bought my inventions, I might add."

"But they didn't go under," she said. "They prospered. Right?"

"That's right. Out of the blue, Sutcliffe's came out with a gearing mechanism that could be used to run equipment and machines in any kind of industry. It was literally a universal gear. I must admit, I was quite jealous when I finally got a look at one of them. It was a thing of beauty. Small but strong and so adaptable it could be made to run a weaving machine or a metal cutter. I was amazed when I saw it, and frankly, I'd never have guessed that John Sutcliffe had the talent to invent something like that. But I was wrong. His invention not only kept them from bankruptcy, but it's also made them rich."

"How long ago was this?"

"It's been at least thirty years," he replied.

"I thought you said it 'wasn't all that many years ago,' " Luty chided.

"When you get to be my age, that doesn't seem all that long ago," he shot back. "What's always seemed strange to me is that the gear was the only thing that Sutcliffe invented."

"If it made him rich, maybe he was too busy countin' his money to be bothered to do anythin' else," Luty said. "Besides, he had a company to run."

"I suppose you're right." Basil smiled wistfully. "Silly, isn't it. It seems like it happened yesterday."

"You've got a good memory." She noticed that Lady Billington was staring at her untouched food, so she grabbed her spoon and took a taste of the soup. It wasn't bad, but it wasn't good, either.

"I'd like to think so, but the only reason I recall it so clearly is because it was right around that time that John Sutcliffe married." He chuckled. "And believe me, that set tongues wagging. My mother and sisters talked of nothing else for weeks on end."

"How come? Was there any reason he shouldn't have gotten hitched?"

"Oh no, he'd been courting a young lady from one of the most prominent and wealthy families in York." He frowned. "I believe it was one of the Whitley girls . . . yes, that's right, it was the eldest, Antonia. But that's neither here nor there. She wasn't the woman that he took in holy matrimony, and that's what caused the gossip. He married a girl who was the paid companion to his sister. It was very brave of him — that sort of thing simply wasn't done back then, not like today when people are freer to do as they please. It was right after he married that the fortunes of the firm seemed to turn around, so obviously, all the wagging tongues were wrong. That young lady turned out to be his lucky charm."

Chapter 5

"Now you two stop fretting. I'm an old dog and I know all the tricks," Barnes said as he stood up from his seat at Mrs. Goodge's kitchen table. "We need to know what's in Nivens' reports."

"We understand that, Constable." Mrs. Jeffries rose as well. "But you must promise me that if it appears as if anyone is getting suspicious, you'll stop. I'll not have you risking your career or your pension because you're helping us."

Barnes shrugged. "No one is going to get suspicious. Policemen read case reports all the time. Besides, we don't have much choice in the matter. I've got to see them if we want to find out anything useful."

Mrs. Jeffries cringed inwardly. "I feel like such a hypocrite. On the one hand, we're worried you might get into trouble, while on the other, we've asked you not only to read his reports, but also to find out some very specific details."

He laughed. "Don't be silly. I offered to help you. Besides, what you're wanting will be easy to find. Amy Throckmorton's address should be on Henry Anson's interview sheet, and if Dearman's office keys were found, they'll be on the evidence list."

"But do be careful, Constable," Mrs. Goodge said.

"Don't worry, I'll be fine." He glanced toward the staircase. "I'd better get upstairs and see if the inspector is ready to go."

"What are you going to tell him?" Mrs. Jeffries asked. "I mean, you generally only come by to get him when you're on a murder case together."

Barnes started for the back stairs. "I'll tell him that I missed his company. After all, I do have to walk right past the house to get to the station." He glanced back at the two women and grinned. "You two look like you've the weight of world on your shoulders. Stop worrying, I know what I'm doing. I'll see you tomorrow morning."

Mrs. Jeffries said nothing until she heard his footsteps walking overhead. "I don't like this. Honestly, I'm getting a very bad feeling about this."

"Now don't get yourself in a state," Mrs. Goodge warned. She patted Mrs. Jeffries' empty spot on the table. "Sit back down and finish your tea. You can tell me what's wrong. Talkin' is good for the soul, that's what I always say."

Mrs. Jeffries sat down just as Samson, Mrs. Goodge's fat, ill-tempered orange tabby cat, padded down the stairs and over to the cook, who obliged him by moving her chair back so he had room to leap up.

"Uh . . . he weighs a ton," Mrs. Jeffries complained as the animal curled around and settled into her lap. He made himself comfortable, lifted his head, and stared, unblinking, directly at the housekeeper.

"Stop looking at me like that, Samson," she scolded. "You're making me feel even guiltier than I already do."

"What on earth are you on about?" the cook asked as she stroked the animal's broad back. "Samson likes you, and what do you have to feel guilty about?"

"He doesn't like anyone but you." Mrs. Jeffries tore her gaze away from the cat. "And I feel guilty because I've drug everyone into this matter just to help my sister-in-law. What if Constable Barnes does get caught snooping in Nivens' reports. What then? You know good and well that Nivens wouldn't be decent about it. He'd do his best to get the constable sacked, and then he'd not have his pension —"

Mrs. Goodge interrupted. "What Nivens does or doesn't do wouldn't matter one whit. For goodness' sake, Hepzibah, you're makin' a mountain out of a molehill. Do you honestly think the chief inspector is goin' to sack a constable that works hand in glove with the inspector that has solved more murders than anyone in the history of the Metropolitan Police Force?"

"But . . . but . . ."

"There are no buts," she snapped. She shifted her weight, and Samson flicked his tail, got up, and leapt down. He shot both women an angry glare before trotting off to find a quieter place to nap. "For goodness' sake, we weren't born yesterday, you know what's what in this old world, and the men that run the force aren't going to risk losin' their most valuable man. What do you think Inspector Witherspoon would do if they tried to sack Constable Barnes?"

Mrs. Jeffries hadn't considered this aspect of the situation. "He'd probably retire."

"That's right." The cook chuckled. "As far as I can see, Constable Barnes could sit outside Nivens' office readin' the ruddy reports and there would be nothing he could do about it."

Mrs. Jeffries was quiet for a long moment,

and then she shook her head. "You're right, I don't know why I've let myself get in such a state."

"You're in a state because you don't like or trust your sister-in-law."

Mrs. Jeffries went perfectly still. "You're right," she said. "You're absolutely right, and I think that deep down I'm worried that Fiona may have lured me into a mess that will end up hurting all of you."

"That's not goin' to happen." Mrs. Goodge got up and grabbed the teapot. "We're smart and we know how to take care of ourselves. We went into this with our eyes wide open, and we'll get at the truth. It's what we do, and no one except you is worried about how it's goin' to turn out. Now stop your frettin'. I'm going to make more tea. The others will be here soon."

By the time the others began to trail into the kitchen, Mrs. Jeffries was in much better spirits. Come what may, they'd all agreed to help Fiona and they'd do the best they could.

"You're not gonna believe this, but I actually have somethin' to report," Luty exclaimed as she flopped into her chair. "Who'd a thought that I'd hear anythin' useful at Lord Billington's dinner party."

"Then let's take our seats and get started,"

Mrs. Jeffries said. "We've a lot to do today."

Luty waited till they were all in their usual spots before she spoke. "Last night I started chattin' with the fellow I was sittin' next to. I brought up the Dearman murder, and he ended up givin' me an earful." She told them what she'd heard from her dinner companion, making sure she mentioned every detail, and ending with Featherstone's dramatic statement that despite all the wagging tongues and gossip, the woman John Sutcliffe married turned out to be his lucky charm.

"And their marriage did indeed cause tongues to wag," Mrs. Jeffries murmured. "I remember it well. David and I were stunned when we heard the news." She frowned slightly, her expression thoughtful. "As a matter of fact, now that I think of it, David went to see Fiona when he heard the news of their engagement. He was upset about it but wouldn't tell me why, and we hadn't been married very long ourselves, so I didn't want to press him."

"Press him about what?" Phyllis asked.

"About the engagement, about his meeting with his sister." Her brow furrowed as the memories flooded back. "Oh my gracious, he was in a terrible state when he came home that afternoon." Her voice trailed off as the scenes from her past flashed through her mind. The room was quiet save for the faint clip-clop of horses' hooves from the nearby streets.

Finally, Mrs. Goodge said, "Exactly what do you mean by 'a terrible state'?"

"He was so upset he drank half a bottle of whiskey," Mrs. Jeffries said softly. "It was the only time in our married life I saw him drunk. We'd been given the bottle as a wedding present, and I'd stuck it up in cupboard and forgotten about it. When he came home from seeing Fiona, he pulled the bottle out and drank it in front of the fire. I kept asking him why he was so upset — of course I was surprised by the news, too, and they were from different classes and backgrounds — but Fiona was well educated and she'd lived in the Sutcliffe home as a paid companion to Lucretia Sutcliffe, so even though there would be gossip, it should be alright. But nothing I said made any difference. He just sat there, staring into the fire and drinking. Now that I think about it, he wasn't just upset, he was stunned."

Hatchet asked, "What do you mean?"

"It was as if he'd found out something that had shocked him to his very core. I remember now, at one point, he looked up

156

from the fire and there were tears in his eyes."

"He said nothing?" Ruth asked.

"The only thing I recall is him muttering that a marriage based on mutual greed was doomed to failure. At the time, I thought he was referring to Fiona wanting to move up the social scale, but now I'm not so sure what he meant." Mrs. Jeffries gave herself a gentle shake as she glanced at the faces of the others. Everyone was staring at her with expressions of worry and concern on their faces. "It's alright, I'm fine. Thinking about David, even of one of lowest moments in our marriage, makes me happy. But I'm annoyed with myself for having forgotten this particular incident. It might be important." She made up her mind to go and have another word with her sister-in-law. Something had happened between David and Fiona when he'd confronted her about her sudden engagement to Sutcliffe, and even if it had nothing to do with Dearman's murder, Mrs. Jeffries wanted to get to the bottom of it.

"You probably wanted to forget it," Ruth said. "All married women have times in their marriages they don't wish to think about, even those of us who were wed to good men."

"Who was the other woman?" Phyllis asked Luty. "Did your source know her name?"

Luty grinned broadly. "He did. Sutcliffe was supposed to marry Antonia Whitley, who later became Antonia Meadows."

"You mean Lucretia Dearman's friend?" Wiggins asked. "The lady that lives 'ere in London?"

"That's right. Basil said she was the one everyone thought Sutcliffe would marry. He'd been escortin' her to parties and payin' her the kind of attention that usually means a feller is serious about a gal. But when he announced he was gettin' married, it wasn't to her."

"I'll bet she was very humiliated." Ruth shook her head sympathetically.

"She was. That's why she married Thaddeus Meadows," Mrs. Jeffries said quickly. "I've been so stupid. I should have made the connection the moment I heard her name. Meadows had been in the background the entire time Antonia Whitley was being courted by Sutcliffe." She was amazed at how it was all coming back to her. "I remember now — she and Meadows married within a week of Fiona and John."

"When did she come to London?" Hatchet asked curiously.

"I don't know," she replied.

"Maybe we ought to find out," Phyllis suggested. "Seems like half of Yorkshire ended up coming to London. Maybe there's a reason."

Mrs. Jeffries nodded in agreement. Her old memories had shaken her to her core, but she wasn't going to let that stop her from doing what was right. "I think we ought to broaden the scope of our investigation," she announced.

"But we're already stretched thin as it is," Mrs. Goodge protested.

"I know, but Phyllis is right, a number of people from Yorkshire ended up following the Sutcliffes to London."

"You think that might have anything to do with Dearman's murder?" Ruth looked doubtful. "Surely most of them came because they worked for the company."

"That's true of Ronald and Lucretia Dearman and both the Sutcliffes, but what about Antonia Meadows? As I recall, she was nothing more than a close friend of Lucretia's, but she's here in London as well. When I left Yorkshire, I had a number of very dear, devoted friends, and not one of them followed me."

Mrs. Jeffries stepped into the Dirty Duck

Pub and stood by the door. The room was crowded with day laborers, van drivers, dock workers, and shop clerks. The tables and the benches along the walls were filled. A trio of bread sellers holding gin glasses clustered together in front of the fire with their empty baskets stacked on the hearth.

She took a deep breath, inhaling the sharp tang of cigar smoke mingled with the scent of barley and beer. She surveyed the room, studying the faces and hoping her quarry was here. This was Smythe's territory and she wasn't sure of her welcome.

She spotted him sitting at a table on the far side of the spacious room. He wasn't alone. Sitting next to him was a well-dressed man wearing a black greatcoat. Just then Blimpey Groggins glanced her way and their gazes met. She stared him directly in the eye, wondering if the fact that she and the others had once helped him would be of any value now.

He grinned broadly and then turned back to his companion. He said a few words, and the man nodded and then got up and left. Mrs. Jeffries headed toward Blimpey's table.

"This is a pleasant surprise." Blimpey rose to his feet as she approached. He pointed to the stool that had just been vacated. "Sit yerself down, Mrs. Jeffries. Would you like somethin' to drink? How about a sherry? Smythe tells me yer partial to that brew."

It was still early in the day and she started to refuse, but then just as quickly changed her mind. She might end up needing that drink before this was over. "Thank you, Blimpey, that would be very nice." She sat down and took off her gloves as he waved the bar maid over.

"A glass of sherry for the lady and a pint for me," he said to the girl as she drew close. She nodded and went back behind the bar.

"I hope you don't mind my dropping in like this," Mrs. Jeffries said apologetically. Now that she was here, she wasn't certain how to handle the situation. He owed her nothing. Yes, they'd once helped Blimpey, but he'd repaid them handsomely and she knew he didn't work for free.

This was Blimpey's business. He bought and sold information. She was the only one in the household who knew that Smythe used his services every time they had a case; but Smythe was wealthy and he could afford Blimpey's high prices. She wondered if she was supposed to negotiate or if he charged a flat fee. Smythe had told her that Blimpey had started out as a second-story thief, but after a nasty fall and a painful run-in with a mastiff, he'd decided to make

161

his living by using his incredible memory skills instead of risking life, limb, and liberty. Once he heard, saw, or even read something, it stayed in his brain forever. He now had a network of paid informants that covered not only the criminal activities of London's underworld, but also every important institution in England: Parliament, shipping lines, police stations, magistrates courts, insurance companies, hospitals, the Old Bailey, and even the newspapers. But Blimpey had standards — he wouldn't trade in information that harmed women or children. He was old-fashioned that way.

"Yer always welcome 'ere, Mrs. Jeffries," Blimpey said solemnly. "But I'll admit I'm a bit surprised. I've not 'eard of the inspector gettin' a murder. I thought he was workin' on that fraud case." The barmaid came and put their drinks on the table.

To give herself time to think before she answered, Mrs. Jeffries picked up her sherry and took a sip. Surprised, she stared at the amber liquid. "This is Harvey's Bristol Cream," she exclaimed.

He laughed. "Were you expectin' the cheap stuff?"

"I'm sorry, I didn't mean it that way," she explained. "Please, don't be offended."

"I'm not." He regarded her steadily. "But

you've not answered my question."

"You're right, of course. The inspector hasn't a murder at the moment, but I do need some help with another case."

"And what would that be?" He picked up his pint and took a sip.

Mrs. Jeffries took a deep breath. "Oh dear, this is far more difficult than I thought it would be. You see, it's rather complicated."

"Life usually is," he commented.

"There is a murder, but it's one that's being investigated by Inspector Nivens."

"You mean the Dearman murder? But what's that got to do with you?" he asked. "No offense meant, but I can't see your lot lendin' that toff Nivens a 'and. He's about as well liked as a case of cholera."

She laughed again. "We're not helping him. We've been asked by another interested party to look into the case. Oh, what's the use, there's no point in being coy about this — with your resources you're going to find out everything anyway. My sister-in-law is married to John Sutcliffe, and Dearman worked at Sutcliffe Manufacturing. He was murdered in his office."

"I know," he said. "He was shot. But go on."

"Fiona — she's my sister-in-law — is afraid, terrified actually, that she's going to become the prime suspect, so she asked me to help her, and I've agreed," Mrs. Jeffries explained. "That's where you come in."

"You told her that you helped the inspector?" he asked, his expression incredulous.

"No, she found out when Nivens was examining Dearman's body," she said. "He's made no secret of the fact that he thinks Inspector Witherspoon has help on his cases." She told him how Fiona had come to hear of her involvement.

Blimpey listened carefully, making no comment until she'd finished. "What is it you want me to do?"

"The same thing you'd do for Smythe," she blurted. "I'll pay you the normal rates. I wouldn't presume upon our acquaintance."

He waved her off impatiently. "I'll not take money from you," he said. "Yer lot helped me when I needed it, and I want to return the favor."

"But you've already returned the favor," she insisted. "I don't want to take advantage of your relationship with Smythe. Besides, you charge him for your services."

He laughed again. "That's because he's rich, but yer not. He'd be right offended if I didn't make 'im pay. But enough of this silly argument. I take it you want me to find out anythin' I can about the Dearman murder, right?"

"Yes, thank you, Blimpey. I'm very grateful you're going to help me."

"Don't mention it, Mrs. Jeffries. You'll just embarrass me."

"What other information do you need from me?"

"Names, I need names. I want to know who hates 'im, who loves 'im, and who he deals with every day of 'is life."

Wiggins put the pint down on the small table and slid onto his stool. "Thanks for talkin' with me," he said.

The young man sitting across from him shrugged. "I didn't have anything else to do. I've got no job thanks to Dearman." He was a taciturn fellow with brown hair, a long, bony face, and deep-set green eyes. His name was James Tremlett. "You said your newspaper would be willing to pay for information, that's right, isn't it?"

"That's right," Wiggins said. He'd had a quick word with Daniel Jones when the clerk had come out of Sutcliffe's for lunch and found out where James Tremlett lived. He'd gone to Tremlett's lodgings and, using the lie about working for a newspaper, convinced the man to talk to him in ex-

165

change for a few pounds. Wiggins felt a bit funny about bribing someone just to chat, and he'd not have done such a thing except that he knew Tremlett was unemployed and needed the money. Besides, it wasn't like it was his money. Before Smythe left, he'd pulled him aside and shoved a fistful of pound notes into his hand. He'd instructed him to use the cash if they got a case and he needed to "cross a few palms with silver" to loosen a few tongues. Wiggins hadn't mentioned the cash to the others because even though Smythe hadn't said to keep quiet about it, he had sensed it wouldn't do to talk about it openly. Wiggins pushed the thought of Smythe and why on earth the coachman had so much money to the back of his mind. "I said I'd pay you for your time and I meant it," he said. "And I'll buy you as many pints as you like as well. You didn't 'ave to speak with me and I'm grateful."

"I don't know that there's much I can tell you," Tremlett said as he picked up his pint and took a sip. "Dearman sacked me over two weeks ago. I've not seen him since."

"How did you find out he'd been murdered?"

"I read about it in the newspapers," he said. "Not that I've got coin enough to buy a newspaper every day. But Mr. Morland — he's got rooms on the ground floor — he gives me his paper when he's through with it. Even though Mr. Dearman wasn't a nice man, I thought it was terrible that he'd been shot."

"Why did he sack you?" Wiggins took a sip and struggled not to make a face. He didn't really like the taste of beer.

"He accused me of not doing my job, but that's not true. I was doing my work. I was a reconciliation clerk and my ledgers were in perfect condition. There wasn't one receipt from any of our vendors that I couldn't account for," he cried. "I was doing a good job."

"But he sacked you anyway," Wiggins pointed out. "He must 'ave 'ad a reason."

"Don't you think I know that? He was very strict with us, but I'd never known him to sack someone for no reason at all. I still don't understand what I did wrong," Tremlett protested. "There were never any complaints about my work or my deportment. I was never late, I never took too long for my lunch, and I never even thought of putting my ledgers away until it was quitting time. But for some odd reason, Mr. Dearman decided I must go."

"He didn't tell you why he was givin' you

the boot?" Wiggins pressed. Surely there was more to the story than the fellow was letting on. "He must 'ave said somethin'."

Tremlett pursed his lips and shook his head. "All he said was that my services were no longer needed. It stunned me, it did. Just a few days earlier I'd stayed late to finish up reconciling the Jenkins account, but did he care? No sir, he'd didn't, he didn't give a toss."

"When you stayed late, did Dearman receive any visitors?"

Tremlett thought for a moment. "You mean in his office?"

"Yes, did anyone come to see 'im?

"No one came to his office, but I did see him with someone that evening."

"Where were they?" Cor blimey, Wiggins thought, getting information out of this fellow was as hard as herding ducks.

"I thought he had gone, but it turned out he hadn't." Tremlett took another sip. "You see, I'd gone to use the facilities just when everyone else was packing it up for the day. When I returned, the outer office was empty but the lamps were still lighted."

"So you were left to lock up?" Wiggins knew the clerks didn't lock up, but he wanted to see what the man would say. It was so ruddy hard to know if people were telling you the truth or just making it up as they went along.

"Goodness no, Sutcliffe's would never allow a clerk to have a set of office keys. Either Mr. Dearman or Mr. Anson always locked the premises," Tremlett said. "Aside from Mr. Sutcliffe, they're the only two who have keys. Mr. Sutcliffe never locked up, of course. So the two of them took turns."

Wiggins perked up. "And because the lamps were still lighted, you knew that one of them was still there?"

"Yes, but I didn't know which one, so I went down the corridor to Mr. Anson's office and saw that he'd gone."

"How did you know he'd left?" Wiggins pressed.

"His lamp was out, and the door to his office was locked. So I knew that Mr. Dearman must be there. They'd never leave lighted lamps on when the office was closed. Mr. Dearman was always nagging us to keep costs down, so I knew he must be about somewhere. I went back to my ledgers. But it got later and later and I started to get concerned. I was afraid there might have been a misunderstanding between Mr. Anson and Mr. Dearman and I was the only one left. I certainly couldn't have locked the place up."

"But you could 'ave gotten the porter to do it, couldn't you?" Wiggins asked. "Surely he 'ad a set of keys. He coulda locked up for you."

"Yes, but I wouldn't have liked to do such a thing." Tremlett sighed. "The porter would have reported it to Mr. Sutcliffe."

"But it wouldn't 'ave been your fault that one of them forgot to do it. Why should you care?"

"I cared because I like Mr. Anson. He's a decent sort of chap, and he and Mr. Dearman hated each other. They'd had some conflicts ever since Mr. Anson was hired, and frankly, I was afraid if it was Mr. Anson who'd forgotten to lock up, that Mr. Dearman would use the incident against him. But as it was, it wasn't Mr. Anson who was responsible that night, it was Mr. Dearman. I peeked into his office and saw that his lamp was still on, so I knew he must be about somewhere. So I waited another ten minutes, but he still hadn't come back. I decided to go down and ask the porter if he'd seen him."

"What time was this?" Wiggins took another swig of his beer.

"It was almost seven o'clock," Tremlett replied. "That's an hour after we close for the day, and I couldn't imagine where Mr.

Dearman had got to, but when I opened the outer office door, I heard his voice. I was so relieved that I stuck my head out into the hall. I saw him at the far end of the corridor by the back stairs."

"What was he doin' there?" Wiggins asked. "Had he nipped out for a quick drink at the pub?"

"He might have. He was with someone."

"Did you see who it was?"

Tremlett shook his head. "No. Whoever it was stood back on the landing. But I know someone else was there because just then, I saw a hand come out and hand him an envelope. Then I heard the murmur of voices. I couldn't hear what they were saying, but I know they spoke for a moment or two. So I closed the door and went back to my desk. A few minutes later, Mr. Dearman came in and told me to pack it in as he needed to leave. So I did."

Wiggins thought for a moment. "Had Dearman seen you when you peeked out into the hall?"

"I don't think so," he murmured. "But he probably heard the door when I closed it. The wood is warped and you've got to give it a good yank to get it shut properly."

"How long after this incident was it before he sacked you?"

"It was two days later. As I said, he called me into his office. He told me my services were no longer required." Tremlett shook his head, his expression confused. "I kept asking him what I'd done wrong, but all he said was that I wasn't needed and for me to get out. I was so upset, I went to Mr. Anson's office to see if he could help me, but he was gone. I'd forgotten that he'd gone to Southampton on business. So I had no choice. I packed up my desk and left."

Wiggins stared at the young man. He couldn't believe the fellow was so dim he couldn't see the connection between what Tremlett had seen in the hall and his getting the sack two days later. But why would Dearman have waited two days? "You said that Mr. Anson was in Southampton the day you got let? Had Mr. Anson been in the office the previous day?"

"Oh yes, he'd asked me for a list of any outstanding receipts for Drego and Everette — they're a shipyard, and that's who he was going to see in Southampton."

"You said that Mr. Anson and Dearman didn't 'ave much use for one another. So tell me this, could Mr. Anson have helped you? Could he have overruled Dearman's decision?"

Tremlett nodded eagerly. "That's why I

rushed to his office. Like I said, he's a good person, and he wasn't scared of Dearman's temper. He'd already forced Dearman to keep the typewriter girl on staff. So I was hoping he could help me, but I'd forgotten that he was out of the office."

"What kind of envelope was it — the one Mr. Dearman was handed in the hallway, I mean?" Wiggins asked. An idea was beginning to form in his mind. He didn't want to jump to any conclusions about the case, not at this point anyway, but he couldn't shake the feeling that what Tremlett had seen was important.

"What do you mean? It was just an envelope like the ones we have in the office," he said. "The kind you use for documents rather than correspondence. We use them to send contracts and such to our vendors and customers."

Wiggins nodded. "Could you tell if the person talkin' to Dearman was a man or a woman?"

"I told you, I didn't see them."

"But you saw the hand," Wiggins pointed out. "Was it a man's hand or a woman's?"

"The lighting was dim, and it's a long hallway. All I saw was a black gloved hand giving Mr. Dearman the envelope."

"And this was definitely two days before

you were sacked, right?"

Tremlett laughed harshly. "I'm not likely to forget, now, am I?" He drained his glass and then smiled. "Mind you, I'm glad I've had a chance to talk about it. It's given me an idea."

"What kind of idea?"

"Well, seems to me that now that Mr. Dearman is dead, I can ask Mr. Anson if I can have my old job back." He cocked his head to one side. "Do you think I have to wait until after he's been buried before I go see Mr. Anson?"

Mrs. Goodge put the plate of scones on the table and sat down opposite her guest. "Please, help yourself. I'm so glad you were able to come and see me," she said.

Lottie Brimley laughed heartily and put one of the triangle-shaped pastries on her plate. She was a tall, thin woman with salt-and-pepper hair, a broad face, and brown eyes. "I was thrilled to get your note." She reached for the butter pot, picked up her knife, and speared a good tablespoon. "It's been years since we worked together. I didn't think you'd remember me. I was just a scullery maid back then." She slathered the butter onto her scone.

"Of course I remember you," Mrs.

Goodge declared. "I know it's been more than twenty years, but you made a strong impression on me. I always admired your cheerful and observant nature." This was a bold-faced lie; Lottie was good natured, but the cook certainly didn't recall her being particularly observant. However, when one of her other sources had mentioned that Lottie had moved to York to work for a family there but was now back and living in London, Mrs. Goodge had sent her a note inviting her to tea. Thus far, Lottie Brimley was the only acquaintance she had from the old days who had gone anywhere close to where the principals in this ruddy case had come from. She counted herself lucky that Lottie had returned to London.

"What a lovely thing to say," Lottie exclaimed. Her smile grew even wider. "I used to be terrified of you. I'd no idea you thought I was anything more than a green girl who couldn't cut radishes into fancy shapes."

Mrs. Goodge laughed. "Did I really scare you? Oh dear, I'm sorry. I thought I was the only one who lived in fear back in those days. If you'll remember, someone from that household was always gettin' sacked."

Lottie took a bite and nodded in agreement. "You're right about that. That's one of the reasons I left. Mind you, right after you left to go to . . ." Her voice trailed off and she frowned. "Where did you go?"

"I went to work for Lord Rotherhide," the cook said. "I went there right after leavin' the Rampling house. Where did you go?"

"Oh, I went north to York and got a position as a downstairs maid." She laughed. "I knew I'd no talent for cooking, so I set my sights on becoming a housekeeper. I worked for the Donnelly family for several years and then got a position as housekeeper to a nice gentleman named Mr. Keighley. He was a very good employer, single, not fussy, and as long as the house ran properly, he left me alone. He's the reason I was able to retire to a nice flat near my sister and her family. When he passed away, he left decent-sized legacies to all his servants. Well, he would, wouldn't he. He had no family to speak of, and we'd taken good care of him, especially when he was ill there at the end."

"It was good of him to remember those that did for him. So often people forget and even if they've no family, they leave it all to the church or a charity." She took a deep breath. "I was wonderin' if you've —"

"Mr. Keighley didn't go to church," Lottie interrupted. "Once you work for a single gentleman, you'd never want to work taking care of a family again, it's too much bother. Mind you, you work for a single gentleman, so I bet you'd say the same, wouldn't you. Charlotte told me that you work for a policeman." She looked around at the large, well-stocked, bright kitchen. "He must have plenty of money if he can run a household this size."

"He does and he is a policeman," Mrs. Goodge replied. She realized too late that she'd forgotten what a chatterbox Lottie had been. She'd gotten her name and address from Charlotte Temple, another old associate, but she'd need to talk fast if she was to get a word in edgewise. "Now, when you were up north, did you ever hear of a family named Sutcliffe?"

"You mean the family that owns Sutcliffe Manufacturing?"

"Yes, those people, I was wonderin' —"

"Everybody in York knew who they were." Lottie continued as though the cook hadn't spoken. "They employed half the city. Mind you, everyone's nose was out of joint when they moved the head office down here to London, but they did keep most of the plant work in York. They make gears or something like that. I know because Mr. Keighley — he was a solicitor — did some of the legal work for the company."

Mrs. Goodge straightened to attention. "You worked for the Sutcliffe lawyer?"

"He didn't handle all their legal work." She popped another bite into her mouth and chewed. "Just some of their contracts with other companies. Sutcliffe's spread the wealth around a bit. That's one of the reasons they were so well liked by the local community."

"You know that one of their general managers was just murdered, don't you?" Mrs. Goodge decided to get right to the heart of the matter. Lottie talked so much that even if she went all over London telling everyone she'd been here, no one would pay much attention to her. That's what happened when you got a reputation as a talker. People simply didn't pay you much mind.

"Ronald Dearman," she said. "I read about him in the newspapers."

"You'd never heard of him before? You'd never heard your old employer mention his name?"

Lottie gave a negative shake of her head. "No, not that I can recall. Mr. Keighley wasn't a great talker. Once he got home from work, he liked his dinner, and then he'd retire to the drawing room with a glass of whiskey and the newspaper."

"So he never spoke much about Mr. and Mrs. Sutcliffe or the Dearmans? Lucretia Dearman was a Sutcliffe, surely you'd heard of her."

Lottie glanced at her now-empty plate. "May I have another?" She nodded toward the plate of scones.

"Please do, that's why I made them," the cook said quickly. "Now about the Dearmans . . ."

"You're a curious one, aren't you." Lottie helped herself to another scone. "As I recall, you never allowed us to gossip when you ran the kitchen at the Rampling house."

"Yes, well, I was much stupider back then." The cook chuckled. "But I've come to my senses. I love gossip. Especially about people who get their names in the paper, even if it is as a murder victim."

Lottie laughed as she spread more butter on her pastry. "Me, too. You know that Mrs. Dearman's best friend was all set to marry John Sutcliffe when he up and married that paid companion?"

"Yes, I'd heard that much." Mrs. Goodge poured them both more tea and then gently shoved the cream and sugar toward her guest.

"Everyone pretended to be so surprised when it happened, but the maid that worked in the house next to us told me that she'd heard that Sutcliffe had his eye on the companion all along and that he'd only been publicly courting Antonia Whitley so his parents would leave him alone."

Mrs. Goodge wanted to scream in frustration. Lottie jumped from subject to subject in the blink of an eye. But she needed some information from this woman, so she'd do her best to be patient.

"It was sad about her; she became Antonia Meadows," Lottie explained. "Mr. Keighley did the marriage settlement for her and Thaddeus Meadows. She married him right after John Sutcliffe up and married, and everyone claimed that Meadows caught her because her pride was wounded. It wasn't a very good marriage, either. The Meadows men were notorious for being mean and cheap. Everyone thought the family was so wealthy, but it turned out they weren't. When old George Meadows, he was Thaddeus' father, up and died, there wasn't anything left, and the gossip was that he'd gambled everything away. His wife had to sell their home and move in with her daughter. Mind you, Thaddeus was lucky. Some relative of his had died and left him a modest yearly income and a house here in London. Thaddeus was the lucky one in that family. Though I did hear that he died recently."

Mrs. Jeffries stepped off the omnibus and onto the pavement. She had gotten off a half mile from her usual stop because she wanted to walk the rest of the way home; she wanted to think. She started up Holland Road, walking slowly past the six-story brown brick and white town houses toward Upper Edmonton Gardens. One part of her mind paid attention to her surroundings while the rest of her thoughts went over and over what they knew thus far. It wasn't much. Ronald Dearman wasn't a much loved man. His wife hated him, his servants feared him, and he kept his office staff in a constant state of anxiety, so to speak. She frowned as she tried to recall the details of the murder itself. Fact: He'd been killed at the end of a workday when the office was empty but the building itself still had people coming and going. The employment bureau on the third floor was open until seven so the day laborers could collect their pay. But they generally used the back stairs, not the front staircase. She smiled and nodded politely at a well-dressed matron she'd seen in the communal garden.

But what about the porter? He came on

at half past six. So if the murderer came in the front way, he — or *she*, Mrs. Jeffries reminded herself — risked being seen by the porter, but if he used the back staircase, he risked running into a day laborer. Unless the murderer knew that there was a small window of time when it could be done with only a small chance of being seen by anyone. Which meant the killer either knew the comings and goings of the building workers or had watched the place. Or perhaps he simply was incredibly lucky, she thought. That had happened any number of times in their previous cases. She picked up her pace and as she did, snatches of conversation and ideas flicked in and out of her consciousness so quickly they made no sense at all.

A cold gust of wind slammed into her, and she pulled her cloak tighter and lowered her head as her eyes watered. Hansom cabs, delivery vans, and carriages drove briskly up and down the roadway. She moved to one side as a shoeblack lad carrying his box hurried past her, heading for Uxbridge Road Station where he'd no doubt pick up plenty of custom from the afternoon trains as people came home from work.

There was a break in the traffic, so she nipped across the road, dodging past a cooper's van that appeared out of nowhere.

When she stepped onto the pavement, she slowed her steps and decided to try and think logically about this case. To begin with, Dearman was murdered in his place of work *and* after everyone else had gone home. The weapon was a gun, which meant the murder was a planned event. People simply didn't walk about the city on the off chance they'd have an opportunity to shoot an enemy. So if the murder was premeditated, she was going to assume the killer didn't get lucky but knew the layout of the office and the comings and goings of everyone in the building. But that information wouldn't have been hard to gain, she reminded herself.

Second, the body wasn't discovered till the next morning. Was that part of the killer's plan? She was going to assume it was. If so, that meant that he or she must have known that Lucretia Dearman wouldn't raise the alarm for hours. Mrs. Jeffries stopped and stared straight ahead as that idea blossomed into another. Goodness, that would mean that whoever murdered him knew enough about his marriage to know that he and his wife had separate rooms *and* that when he was late, she didn't bother to wait up for him. That was the kind of intimate knowledge that few people outside the household would know and certainly not the kind of detail that Dearman would have shared with his employees. But then again, servants talked and one of them could very easily have mentioned it.

"Are you alright, Mrs. Jeffries?" said a young voice from behind her.

She whirled about to see two street lads staring at her. The taller of the two had curly red hair under his gray flat cap and wore a threadbare brown jacket that was too big for him. He looked vaguely familiar to her. The other boy was brown haired, hatless, and wore a grubby, shapeless blue coat. "I'm fine, thank you." She smiled. "Do I know you?"

" 'Course you do," the redhead replied. "We've taken messages for you a time or two. Usually to the police station on Ladbroke Road. We were hoping you'd stopped because you were waitin' for us, you know, maybe you wanted to hire us."

"I'm sorry, I've nothing for you today. I simply stopped because I was thinking, that's all." London was full of young boys, generally from very poor families, who roamed the streets hoping to earn a bob or two by taking notes, small packages, and messages between one place and another.

"Sorry for botherin' you." The redhead

doffed his cap. "But if you need us for anythin', one of us is generally in front of the station. That's our patch." With that, they took off running, flying past her toward the corner.

Mrs. Jeffries resumed walking, her mind working furiously as she went over and over the details they knew thus far. She reached the corner of Upper Edmonton Garden just as the street lads dashed across the road, and for the briefest moment, an idea flashed through her mind. But it was gone before she could grab it.

CHAPTER 6

Constable Barnes waited till the foyer was empty before he opened the heavy double doors and stepped inside. Eddie Harwood glanced up at the sound of the constable's footsteps on the wooden floor. "You picked a good time to come," he commented. "It's gone quiet. The CI is in a long meeting, and last I looked, none of Nivens' minions are about."

Barnes grinned. "Thanks, Eddie. What time is your shift over?"

"In another thirty minutes. I was thinking we could go have a pint when you've finished looking over the report. I had a quick glance at it and it's not too long."

"That'll be fine, Eddie." Barnes kept his smile firmly in place. He'd sensed there'd be a price to pay for the man's help, and he'd suspected it would be an evening drink. Eddie had no reason to hurry home, but luckily, Barnes had told his good wife he'd be late so she wouldn't worry. "Is there a place I can use that's a bit private? Maybe none of his minions are here, but Nivens has eyes everywhere and I'd not like him to cotton onto the fact I'm reading his reports before they get to the chief inspector."

Harwood jerked his thumb straight up. "I've left an office unlocked. It was Inspector Tarbell's old office. He retired last week, and they've not reassigned the space. Do you know where it is? It's the first one in the corridor by the staircase."

"I know which one it is," Barnes replied.

Harwood pulled a flat, brown envelope out from under the counter and handed it across. "By the way, you may want to have a word with Charlie Wakeham. He's working this case, and he doesn't like Nivens much. He's a sharp lad, and I know he thinks highly of you and the inspector. He might be able to add the bits and pieces that Nivens hasn't put in his report, if you know what I mean."

Barnes nodded. He knew exactly what Eddie meant; there were always small details that were left out of official reports. "That's a good idea. Is Wakeham the sort that can hold his tongue?" He took the proffered envelope.

"He is and he generally has a drink at the

Blakely Arms when he gets off work. Do you know the place? If you want, I can ask him to meet us there tomorrow evening."

"I know where it is," Barnes said. "And I'd appreciate having a word with him. But I don't want you to go to any trouble —"

"It's no trouble at all," Eddie interrupted.

"Good, then, I'll see you in a bit." He turned and hurried up the staircase. When he reached the top, he slowed his steps and stuck his head into the corridor before stepping out into the open. He'd been exaggerating when he'd said that Nivens had eyes everywhere; the truth was most of the rank and file loathed the fellow, but that didn't mean there wasn't some smarmy little sod who'd run tattling to him. It was best if no one saw him going into an empty office.

The corridor was clear, so he stepped into the office and closed the door quietly behind him. The room was dim, but there was enough light from outside so that he could make his way to the desk. Barnes didn't want anyone walking past to wonder why there was light coming from an empty office, so he ignored the lamp on the desk and pulled the chair around so he'd be facing the window. He sat down and took the report out of the envelope. He balanced the pages across his knees and fished his small hand lantern out of his jacket pocket. With his back to the office door, he readied the light and aimed it at the paper. He began to read the witness statements.

Barnes frowned as he scanned the first page. He flicked to the second page, his frown deepening to a scowl as he realized that in every single interview with witnesses, the answers to Nivens' questions were so short as to be meaningless. The stupid sod was still up to his old tricks of intimidating and bullying anyone he considered lower class, namely, the Sutcliffe office clerks and any poor servant who happened to cross his path. Good God, the man had been a copper long enough to know that if you wanted to get any useful information, you needed to get the witness to talk freely, get them relaxed, let them feel respected. Barnes sighed and continued reading; complaining about the man wouldn't do any good. Nivens' political and family connections were too strong, and in all fairness, he did have a decent record for solving house burglaries. But the rumor was that he used a network of paid informants for those cases. Too bad his ruddy informants couldn't help him solve this one properly, because he certainly wasn't going to do it with his shoddy detective work, Barnes told himself. He squinted as he got to the last page and put the hand lamp closer to the paper so he could finish the last few paragraphs. Though he had a good memory, he knew that he'd not recall everything, so as soon as he finished reading, he took out his notebook and began writing.

Phyllis was the last one to arrive back for their afternoon meeting. She rushed into the kitchen, shedding her coat and hat as she moved. "I'm so sorry to be late, but it took a bit longer to get back than I thought," she explained.

"That's fine," Mrs. Jeffries said. "I was late getting back as well."

"We've only just sat down," Mrs. Goodge added.

Everyone helped themselves to seedcake while they waited for the maid to take her place at the table. When she was settled, Mrs. Jeffries asked, "Who would like to go first?"

"I'm not certain I've anything of consequence to report," Ruth said hesitantly. "But I did learn something rather odd about the victim. Ronald Dearman was a snoop."

"A snoop!" the cook exclaimed. "What do you mean by that?"

"Perhaps I'd better explain." Ruth put down her teacup. "I had lunch today with several of my friends, and naturally, the murder came up in conversation. I was quite excited until I realized the only facts anyone had was what they'd read in the newspaper, but then Susanna Sinclair mentioned that her sister knew the Dearmans and that she'd stopped inviting them to her home because Ronald Dearman was a terrible snoop. When I asked her to explain, she said that on the two occasions the Dearmans had come to her sister's home, he was seen picking up private letters left on the mantle to be mailed out and looking at the names and addresses, and what's worse, he was peeking in drawers."

"The sister had seen this with her own eyes?" Mrs. Jeffries clarified as a glimmer of an idea began to take shape in the back of her mind.

Ruth shook her head. "No, both times it was the servants who told her what they'd seen him doing. Susanna says her sister's servants have been with her for years and aren't the kind of people who make up stories about the household's guests."

"What exactly did they see Dearman doing?" Hatchet asked. "If it was just looking at a few letters on a mantelpiece, well, let's admit it, we've all done that."

"No, no, that was the least of it," Ruth said quickly. "Apparently, both of the times he was a guest, he was seen going into the her husband's study. But what he didn't know is that there's one of those tiny doors on the other side of the study that leads to the back staircase the servants use, and the first time he was seen going into the room, the downstairs maid was coming in to clean. She stepped back when she heard there was someone there, thinking it was the master, but then she looked through the crack in door and saw Dearman rifling through the desk."

"Why didn't she go get the housekeeper or the mistress?" Wiggins demanded. "That's what I'd do if I saw someone goin' through the inspector's things."

"I asked that very question, and Susanna told me the girl was more or less trapped in her spot. The door was cracked open, but Dearman hadn't heard her and she was afraid if she moved, he'd realize someone was there," Ruth explained. "The second time the Dearmans came, the housekeeper kept an eye on him, and when he excused himself, she nipped into the study and watched him do the same thing again. I know it's not very useful information, but it does tell us something about his character."

"I think it might tell us more than that," the housekeeper murmured. "People snoop to satisfy their curiosity when it's easy, but from what you've described, he went much further than that."

"What are you thinking, Mrs. Jeffries?" Hatchet asked curiously.

"I'm not sure, and we all know the dangers of jumping to conclusions," she admitted. "But I think it would be a good idea if one of us found out a bit more about the victim's habit of poking his nose where it didn't belong."

"I'll do it," Hatchet said. "It should be easy enough, and I've not had much success finding out anything else."

"Can I go next?" Mrs. Goodge asked. She waited a brief moment and then plunged ahead. She told them about her visit from Lottie Brimley. When she'd finished, she sat back in her chair. "I don't think this means anythin', but at least we now know a bit more about the relationship between the Sutcliffes and Antonia Meadows, or Antonia Whitley as she was known then."

"Mrs. Meadows was at the dinner party at the Sutcliffe house," Phyllis reminded them. "She might have overheard Mrs. Sutcliffe threatening Mr. Dearman and decided to take advantage of the situation . . ." Her voice trailed off. "Sorry, I got carried away. She's about the only person we know of who didn't have a reason to want Dearman dead."

"Don't apologize, Phyllis," Mrs. Jeffries said. "You were right to remind us that she was there that night. For all we know, she hated him, too." She made the comment to bolster the girl's confidence; she didn't want Phyllis clamming up on them just when she'd begun to relax and contribute. But the truth was, Antonia Meadows and her marriage were so far in the past she didn't see how it could have any bearing on the murder. Nonetheless, every scrap of information helped.

"I'll add my bit, then," Wiggins said. He told them about his meeting with James Tremlett. He took his time and made sure he didn't leave out any details. When he'd finished, he reached for the teapot and poured himself another cup.

"Sounds to me like our victim is more than just a snoop," Luty said. "It sounds to me like he was a blackmailer and poor James Tremlett was unluckly enough to witness him gettin' a payment from one of his victims."

Mrs. Jeffries had been thinking the same

194

thing. "It does indeed sound suspicious. But I must caution us against rushing to judgment."

"But why else would he have sacked Tremlett? He told Wiggins his work was excellent and he'd never missed a day's work," Ruth insisted.

"But we've only his word for that," Mrs. Jeffries replied. "I agree with all of you, this does show Dearman in a very different light. But we can't assume he was a blackmailer, and I know that's what you're all thinking."

"What was in the envelope, then?" Wiggins asked forcefully. "If it was a letter, it could 'ave been mailed to the office. But instead, someone brought it to 'im and then took care to stay out of sight."

"But there could be another explanation." Mrs. Jeffries frowned. "I can't think of one off the top of my head, but I do know that we mustn't assume facts without evidence."

"But this incident is evidence," the cook argued. "It's not like you're goin' to find people willin' to come forth and admit Dearman was blackmailin' them."

"But there are other ways to find out," Hatchet said. "And I agree with Mrs. Jeffries; as suspicious as this sounds, we've been fooled before. I think I can find out for certain one way or another. I've some very good sources I can tap for this kind of information."

"I suppose you'll be askin' one of your criminal acquaintances about him." Luty snorted delicately.

"My sources run the entire gamut of our society," he replied pompously. "Which, in this specific incidence, should prove useful."

"I've a source to ask as well," Mrs. Jeffries added. Finding out if Dearman was a blackmailer should be child's play for someone like Blimpey Groggins. "And until we know for sure what Dearman's snooping means, we must keep an open mind. Now, does anyone else have anything to report?"

No one did.

Barnes stuck his head into the corridor, saw that it was empty, and then eased out of the office, taking care to shut the door quietly. He hurried down the stairs. As he reached the foyer, Eddie Harwood glanced up. He walked briskly to Eddie's desk and handed him the envelope. "Thanks, Eddie, that was helpful."

"Good." Eddie's eyes suddenly widened as the front door flew open and two policemen, one in plainclothes and one in uniform, stepped inside.

"Make certain that the constables re-interview all the clerks at the Sutcliffe office and do another search of the premises." Inspector Nivens voice boomed importantly as he barked out instructions to Morehead, who was trailing behind. "We've still not been able to account for how the door was locked."

"Yes, sir," Morehead said.

Barnes had time to turn his back toward Nivens. The inspector gave Eddie only the briefest of nods as he stomped across the floor, continuing to shoot orders at the hapless Morehead. They reached the staircase, and Barnes angled his body so that he still had his back to Nivens. He had every right to be there, of course, but the less Nivens saw him, the less likely the fellow was to start asking questions.

Nivens kept on barking out commands as the two men climbed the stairs. Barnes sagged in relief but it was short-lived; the front door opened again and a constable entered. "Hey, is that you, Barnes?" he called from the door. "Why, you old dog, I've not seen you in donkey's years. Do you have time for a pint?"

Nivens halted with his foot in the air; he spun around, grabbing the banister while simultaneously sticking his neck out to see if it was indeed that damned Constable Barnes at the front counter. But as he moved, he stumbled and lost his footing. Morehead grabbed at him, trying to halt his fall, but he missed the mark and inadvertently knocked the inspector's arm, causing Nivens to lose his tenuous grip on the banister and, consequently, what remained of his balance. "Bloody hell, are you mad?" Nivens screamed as his considerable bulk tumbled down the staircase. He thumped, screamed, and thrashed, making the most awful noises until he finally came to a halt at the bottom.

"Oh my God." Morehead scrambled after him. "Are you alright, sir?"

Eddie, the newly arrived constable, and Barnes moved simultaneously toward the fallen man.

"Of course I'm not alright, you clumsy oaf, you pushed me down the bloody stairs!" he shouted. He grabbed the bottom of the banister rail and tried to get up. "Oh . . ." He yelped as his right foot collapsed beneath him and he crumbled back to the floor. "You bloody fool, you've caused me to sprain my ankle. Yee gods, this hurts like the devil." He rolled to one side and stuck out his injured limb. He directed a steady stream of abuse at Morehead as he tried to maneuver himself into a position that didn't cause him pain.

"I assure you, sir, that wasn't my intention. I was trying to help," Morehead said. He stopped halfway down the stairs and looked over his shoulder at the group of onlookers who'd been attracted by the noise.

"Good gracious, what is all this ruckus?" The crowd parted and Chief Inspector Barrows clattered down the staircase. Morehead stepped back to let him pass. A man dressed in a business suit followed him. "What on earth have you done to yourself, Nivens?" the chief inspector asked.

"I didn't do anything. This fool" — he jerked his head at Constable Morehead — "caused me to lose my footing and fall. I think I've sprained my ankle." He put his right hand down on the floor to lever himself up and then yelped in pain. "Oh no, I think my wrist is sprained as well."

The man following the chief inspector stepped around him and dropped down beside the fallen Nivens. Barnes saw that it was Dr. Bosworth.

"Let me take a look at it," he ordered. He pushed up Nivens' trouser leg and yanked down his sock.

Nivens cried out in pain. "Be careful,

man, that hurts."

The ankle was red and already beginning to swell. Bosworth lifted it gently, causing Nivens to wince and moan. He tried moving the joint, and Nivens cried out, "Oh my God, what are you doing? That bloody hurts."

Bosworth looked at Nivens. "I'm afraid it's not just sprained, it's broken."

"Well that's not good news." Chief Inspector Barrows looked at Nivens. "Gracious, man, you ought to take better care of yourself." He looked at Bosworth. "How's his wrist?"

"Broken, oh no, it can't be broken. Are you sure, are you absolutely sure?" Nivens implored the doctor.

"I'm positive," he replied. "And for a man of your age and weight, it's going to take a number of weeks before you can walk on it."

"No, no, this can't be happening to me." Nivens turned his fury on Morehead. "This is all your fault! You did this on purpose. I should have known not to trust you. You're an ambitious little sod and you want me out of the way."

"I was only trying to break your fall, sir." Morehead regarded him steadily. He wasn't going to admit wrongdoing in front of the chief inspector. "You were the one who turned suddenly and stumbled down the steps."

"Only because I wanted to find out what Constable Barnes was doing here," Nivens snapped. He held up his arm so that Bosworth, who'd finally stopped poking at his ankle, could have a look at the wrist.

"Now, now, Inspector, calm yourself," Barrows ordered. "Shouting at everyone isn't going to help matters." He glanced at Barnes. "Have you brought the report on Witherspoon's fraud case?"

"Yes, sir, the inspector wanted to get it here as quickly as possible."

"Is most of the work finished?" Barrows asked.

"Yes, sir," Barnes lied. He knew what was coming. "Just a bit of clean up to be done on that case."

"Good, we can assign someone else to finish it up."

"Why is someone else going to be assigned to the fraud?" Nivens jerked his hand away from the doctor and grabbed on to the bottom of the banister. He tried to hoist himself to his feet.

Barrows ignored him. "Just as well you're here, Constable Barnes. It'll save us having to telegraph Ladbroke Road Station. Do you still pass by the inspector's house on your way home?" At the constable's affirmative nod, he continued. "Then could you please tell Inspector Witherspoon he's to report to my office tomorrow morning. He'll need to take over the Dearman case. The Home Office is putting a bit of pressure on, and they want this one settled quickly."

"But that's my case," Nivens protested as he sank back down. "You can't take it away. I can still work it, I can still do it. I can get one of those wheeled chairs."

"Don't be ridiculous." Barrows gave him an irritable glance. "You can't investigate a murder in one of those contraptions, and we can't wait weeks and weeks to catch a killer. Sorry, Nivens, but this one is going to Witherspoon."

"Weeks and weeks? This isn't fair, it's not fair at all," Nivens complained. He glared first at Morehead. "This is your fault." And then at Barnes. "And yours. You've both caused me to lose my case. I won't forget this, indeed I won't."

"Oh for God's sake, man," Barrows interrupted impatiently. "You had an accident and that's that. Now, I'll hear no more about it." He turned his attention to the knot of constables that had gathered at the top of the staircase. "Bring a stretcher and take the inspector to hospital."

But despite Barrows' warning, Nivens was still complaining about the unfairness of it as he was carted off to the infirmary.

"The evidence speaks for itself," Witherspoon said as he settled back in his chair. "The shareholders were most definitely defrauded by the company management."

"So the case is concluded?" Mrs. Jeffries asked. "Does that mean you'll be through with it?"

"Oh no, we've uncovered the evidence, but now I've got to ensure that we can prove it was the —" He broke off as they heard knocking on the front door. Mrs. Jeffries started to get up but sank back down as footsteps pounded in the hallway. "Are we expecting anyone?" Witherspoon asked.

"No," she replied. A moment later, Phyllis stuck her head into the room. "Constable Barnes is here to see you, sir. Shall I show him in?"

"Of course." Witherspoon put his drink on the side table as Barnes stepped into the drawing room. "Gracious, Constable, what on earth are you doing here? Is there a problem? I thought you were going straight home from the Yard."

"I was, sir, but something's happened." Barnes nodded politely to Mrs. Jeffries. "While I was there, Inspector Nivens tripped and broke his ankle."

"Broke his ankle." Witherspoon clucked his tongue sympathetically. "Oh my goodness, that must have hurt dreadfully."

"Chief Inspector Barrows happened to be coming down the stairs when it happened, sir, and well, the situation is he wants you to report to his office tomorrow morning. You're going to be getting the Dearman case."

Witherspoon sighed heavily. "Oh dear, I imagine the inspector wasn't happy about that."

"He was somewhat upset, and the chief inspector said they're getting pressure from the Home Office to get it solved, so there's nary he can do about it. Besides, he'll not be able to walk for a number of weeks."

"And you're sure his ankle was actually broken, not just sprained?" Witherspoon queried.

"Yes, sir, Dr. Bosworth happened to be there as well, he had a look at it and he was certain."

"Would you care for a sherry, Constable?" Mrs. Jeffries offered.

"Thank you, but no, I've got to get home.

My wife is waiting supper on me. I just came by to give the inspector the message."

"Thank you, Constable," Witherspoon said. "It was good of you to stop in. I'll see you in the morning."

"I'll walk you to the door, Constable." Mrs. Jeffries put her sherry down and got up. As soon as they were out of the drawing room and out of earshot, she looked at Barnes. "This is an unexpected turn of events."

"It is, indeed." Barnes chuckled. "I ought to feel guilty, but I don't." They'd reached the front door.

"Why should you feel guilty? You didn't push him down the stairs, did you?"

He laughed outright. "No, but in all honestly, there's been a time or two in my dealings with the man when I was sorely tempted to give him a hardy shove. But it was still due to me that he fell. I was at the Yard, and I happened to be standing at the front counter in the foyer when Nivens came in. I'd managed to turn my back so he wouldn't see me, but just as he was halfway up the stairs, an old friend of mine came in and greeted me by name. Nivens whirled around, lost his footing, and fell. Mind you, it'll probably work out for the best. Solving this one without our inspector wasn't going to be easy. Are you going to tell him that one of the suspects is your sister-in-law?"

"I suppose I'll have to," she murmured. "If he finds out and I haven't told him, he might be upset. On the other hand, there's a good chance he might not find out we're related. I've had nothing to do with Fiona for years."

"True." Barnes reached for the handle and turned the doorknob. "But her full name is listed in the reports. If he spots 'Jeffries' and realizes she's from Yorkshire as well, he'll ask."

"I know," she replied.

Barnes pulled the door open. "You don't have to tell him she came to you for help. You can just say she's your sister-in-law and that when you heard about the murder, you went to see her for moral support. Think about it."

Mrs. Jeffries tossed and turned most of the night but by the morning, she had made up her mind. "Sir, there's something about this case you ought to know," she said as she put a plate of bacon and eggs in front of him.

Witherspoon, who'd just reached for his serviette, dropped it onto his lap. "Something I ought to know?" he repeated. "That sounds ominous. What is it?"

"Well, sir, one of the suspects in the Dearman case is a relative," she explained. "Mrs. Sutcliffe is my late husband's sister."

He stared at her with an expression of disbelief on his face. "I didn't know you had any family here in London."

"I don't really consider her family," she replied. "Once she was married, she wanted very little to do with David and me. When David died and I came to London, I practically forgot about her."

"You didn't know she was here?"

"I'd heard they moved the company to London, and I did go to Christmas tea there a time or two, but we had nothing in common, so I stopped attending. When I read about the murder, I went to see her, you know, to offer moral support. She's very frightened, and she was my husband's sister."

"And she's a suspect?" he pressed.

"I'm afraid so." She knew she had to tread carefully here. She didn't want to lie, but it would be best if she was vague about the real circumstances of how she acquired her knowledge about the case. "I saw the company name in the newspaper account of the murder. So I went to see her. She mentioned that she'd had an argument with the deceased several days before he was killed and she knew that once the police found out, it would look very bad for her. I tried to reassure her, sir, and frankly, I was alarmed when I realized that Inspector Nivens was in charge. He's not experienced in murder investigations. To tell the truth, I'm rather relieved that you've got the case now. You'll find the true culprit."

"I'm gratified and humbled by your faith in my abilities." He smiled uncertainly. "But I'll have to mention your connection to the chief inspector."

"Of course you will, sir." She poured his tea.

"But as she isn't a blood relative and you haven't seen her in years, I don't expect it'll make any difference to our investigation." He spread the serviette over his lap and picked up his fork. "But I appreciate your telling me about this. Are you going to go to her house again?"

"Not if you'd prefer I didn't, sir," she said. She was planning on seeing her today if possible. She had a number of things she needed to ask her.

"I'm not sure that's a very good idea." He scooped a forkful of egg into his mouth.

"Then I won't go, sir," Mrs. Jeffries said

quickly. She'd send Phyllis with a note, and Fiona could meet her at the Lyons tea shop in Oxford Street. "I don't want to do anything that might disturb or impede your investigation, especially as you'll be getting a bit of a late start on the case."

Phyllis got off the omnibus at the Kensington High Street. Holding her bonnet ribbons tight against the wind, she stepped onto the pavement and surveyed the row of shops lining this side of the busy thoroughfare. She was in front of a fishmonger's, but the small shop was already filled with customers, so she knew they wouldn't be in a chatting mood. She walked on, coming abreast of a baker's where she stopped and peered through the window. "Blast," she muttered, "they're full, too." Well, of course they are, she thought. It's ten o'clock in the morning and every household in Kensington is doing their shopping. "Excuse me." A dark-haired young woman smiled apologetically as she pushed past her and into the shop.

"Sorry," Phyllis murmured as she hastily stepped back. Hanging about here was pointless, but she'd come to this neighborhood because both the Dearman household and Antonia Meadows lived nearby and she'd hoped to pick up something from the clerks and shopkeepers. Clearly, that wasn't going to work this morning. But Phyllis was determined to learn something. She'd do what Wiggins did; she'd go right to their houses and hope she could find someone who was in the mood for a chat.

But an hour later, she was chilled to the bone and her feet hurt. She'd found the Dearman house first, but just as she'd arrived, Inspector Witherspoon and Constable Barnes had stepped out of a hansom cab. She'd made a run for it, keeping her head down and praying that her employer wouldn't look in her direction. She'd gone a good half a mile before she'd felt safe, and then found that she'd gotten so twisted and turned around that she was lost. It took another half hour for her to find her way to Church Street, a place she recognized. From there it was only a short walk to the high street and the police station, where she wisely went in and asked for directions.

"Let's hope I have better luck here," she muttered as she rounded the corner onto Garrick Road. Antonia Meadows lived at number 14. She slowed her pace as she came abreast of the three-story brown brick detached house set back from the street behind a black wrought iron fence. She saw that though the gate was closed, the latch was held by a piece of wire, and there were chunks missing from the concrete walkway. The stone on the stairs was crumbling, and the white window frames were badly in need of paint. She increased her pace, intending to go to the corner, turn around, and come back, but she'd not taken more than a few steps before she heard a door slam shut. Stopping, she saw a young girl carrying a shopping basket come up the muddy pathway on the side of the house.

Phyllis dashed across the street and ducked behind a tree. She watched the girl come out, turn left, and walk toward Notting Hill Gate. Phyllis let her get a bit farther away before she moved from the safety of her hiding place and followed her. But the girl walked so slowly that she had a tough time hanging back far enough not to get noticed. Finally, the lass turned onto the busy high street.

But again, the girl dawdled, stopping to look in windows, gawking at the traffic on the street, and staring at the well-dressed women going in and out of the shops. Phyllis couldn't stand it anymore; she sidled up to the girl as she stood in front of a confectioner's, her gaze fixed on a plate of cream buns.

"Those look lovely, don't they?" Phyllis murmured.

The girl turned and stared at her. She had dark blonde hair, blue eyes, and a narrow face with thin lips. "Good enough to eat," she finally replied. She cocked her head to one side and eyed her suspiciously. "I've never seen you before. Do you live round here?"

Phyllis hesitated for a brief moment. She had the strangest feeling that being honest would work with this one. She had no idea why she was so certain, but she was, and Betsy had told her to trust her instincts. But what if she was wrong? What if the girl balked at being questioned and told Inspector Witherspoon about being accosted in the street by someone digging for information. "No, I was following you hoping you'd speak to me."

"Why should I want to talk to you? I don't know you from Adam." The girl turned her attention back to the window.

"Of course you don't," Phyllis tried again. "But I'm hoping you'll be able to help me. My name is Mollie Brent, and my master works for a newspaper." Even though she thought being honest with the girl might be best, she wouldn't risk using her real name.

"What's that got to do with me?"

"I saw you come out of the Meadows' house, right, and Mrs. Meadows is good friends with Ronald Dearman's widow." She was making it up as she went along. "And my master will pay me for any information I can give him about the murder case."

The girl dragged her gaze away from the display of treats and looked Phyllis directly in the eye. "What'll you pay me?" she asked bluntly.

"I'll buy us a couple of those buns, and I'll give you a tanner."

"A tanner, that's just a sixpence!" She laughed. "That's not very much." Her eyes narrowed. "Make it a shilling and I'll do it."

"I can't do that. All I'm going to get is a shilling, and that's only if I give him something useful he can put in his newspaper," Phyllis retorted. She was beginning to enjoy herself. "And maybe this Mrs. Meadows doesn't know anything. . . ." She gave a shrug and started to walk away.

"Wait. Alright, then." The girl grabbed her arm. "I'll do it. But you've got to buy me two of them buns. There's a church just around the corner." She pointed down the street. "St. George's, there's a bench outside the gate. I'll wait for you there."

Five minutes later, Phyllis settled down

next to her informant. "What's your name, then?"

"Blanche Keating." The girl took a bite out of the bun and then hastily licked her lips to capture the escaping cream. "Mmm . . . this is so good."

"Don't you get enough food where you work?" Phyllis took her bun out of her shopping basket.

"We do now," Blanche replied. "Mr. Meadows died six months ago, and he was a right cheap old bastard. There was never enough to eat. He was always yellin' at the mistress about how much it cost to keep us. But he's gone now, and Mrs. Meadows isn't near as mean with food. Mind you, we don't get food like this, but we do get enough to eat now."

"How many are you?" Phyllis took a bite.

"Just me and the cook." Blanche grinned. "There's another girl that comes in twice a week to help with the heavy cleanin'."

Phyllis didn't care about the late, unmourned Mr. Meadows; she wanted to find out about the victim's household. "Does Mrs. Dearman come to your home often?"

"She does now." Blanche stuffed the last of her bun into her mouth, chewed, and swallowed. "She and Mrs. Meadows are as thick as thieves. They always were, but when

Mr. Meadows was alive, Mrs. Meadows went to the Dearman house most of the time. Like I said, he'd have a real nasty go at the mistress if he saw too much tea had been used in the week, and he'd never have allowed nice buns or treats to be bought."

"Wouldn't the cook have made tea cakes and that sort of thing?" Phyllis asked curiously.

Blanche shook her head. "Nah, she's not a real cook; she does mainly fry-ups and roasts. She can't bake worth a tinker's damn. The only reason Mrs. Meadows doesn't sack her is because she works cheap. But then again, so do I."

"Why don't you try and find another position?" Phyllis asked reasonably.

"I was goin' to." Blanche shrugged. "But then he up and died. That's when Mrs. Meadows let us have more food and stopped makin' us pay for our tea and sugar every quarter. So I thought I'd stay on. The work's not hard and she's easy enough to do for, but now I'm not too sure. Are there any jobs goin' where you work?"

"No, sorry." Phyllis smiled sympathetically. She wanted to get the conversation back to Ronald Dearman, but just as she opened her mouth, another thought nudged at the back of her mind. "But what made you change your mind about staying on with Mrs. Meadows? You just said she's easy to do for."

"She is, but a couple of months ago, she started actin' strange, sellin' off all the master's things, you know, his watch, his desk, cuff links, and even his clothes. It got me to thinkin' that she's runnin' low on money even though I know she's gettin' the master's income. He'd no one else to leave it to but her. If she's having trouble makin' ends meet, she'll be chuckin' one of us out the door, and it's always easier to find a position when you've already got a job, if you know what I mean. Besides, I think she and Mrs. Dearman are plannin' on doin' some travelin' to the Continent, and if that happens, she'll not keep either of us on."

"How do you know that?"

"Because I overhead them makin' plans yesterday." Blanche picked up her second bun. "Mrs. Dearman stopped in to borrow a black veil for her widow's bonnet from Mrs. Meadows. As I was bringin' in the tea tray, I overheard Mrs. Meadows tellin' Mrs. Dearman that she'd been to Thomas Cook's and they had a tour to Italy next month and that it was reasonably priced. Then she started tellin' her about a round-the-world tour they offered for a hundred and five pounds! Mrs. Dearman got ever so excited and started askin' questions, but then they noticed me standin' there in the doorway with the tray and they shut up."

"They're both widow ladies; maybe having something to look forward to helps with their grieving," Phyllis murmured. She tried to think of what to ask next.

"Grief." Blanch laughed. "Don't be daft. From what I could see, neither woman was all that upset to be widowed. Mr. Dearman was as nasty a man as Mr. Meadows, he just couldn't be so cheap because he worked for his wife's brother, so she didn't have it as hard." She began eating her second pastry.

"My master mentioned that they'd already found out it wasn't a happy marriage," she said.

"Mrs. Dearman was always complainin' to Mrs. Meadows about how marryin' him was the worst mistake of her life. I know what she meant, too. There was somethin' sly and horrid about the fellow. The day before Mr. Meadows succumbed to the pneumonia, Mr. Dearman was creepin' about outside the house. I saw him — he was skulkin' about, peekin' in the windows, even Mr. Meadows' sickroom window. That weren't the first time, either. Cook claims she saw him outside the windows, too. Mind you, he always pretended he was just droppin' somethin' by the house and that he'd knocked and no one had come to the door. But he was lyin'. He was just one of those people like my Aunt Agnes. She was always stickin' her nose where it didn't belong and then droppin' hints that you'd better be nice to her or she'd tell the world your secrets."

"Nivens' reports are all being sent to the station," Constable Barnes said as he and Witherspoon got out of the hansom in front of the Dearman residence, a five-story gray brick house with a white facade. "And I made certain that Dr. Bosworth's postmortem report was to be included."

"That should help us catch up." Witherspoon started up the walkway. "However, I think it's important that we do our own interviews. Perhaps I ought to have gone to the Sutcliffe offices first; after all, that's where he was murdered. But I prefer to interview the people closest to the victim as soon as possible."

"I agree, sir. Murder is usually done by the 'nearest and dearest,' as we say in the trade." They climbed the short staircase, and Barnes banged the knocker.

A few minutes later, the housekeeper escorted them into the drawing room. Lucretia Dearman and another woman, both of them dressed in black, were sitting on the settee.

"I'm Lucretia Dearman," one of the women said. "And this is Mrs. Meadows. I don't know why you've shown up here. I've already told that other policeman everything I know."

"I'm Inspector Witherspoon and this is Constable Barnes." Witherspoon gestured politely toward the constable. "I do hate to intrude, but I'm afraid the other inspector met with an accident and I'm taking over the investigation."

"Surely he wrote down what we told him," Mrs. Meadows said dryly. "Can't you just read his report and leave poor Mrs. Dearman alone? She's planning the funeral."

Witherspoon sighed. He and Barnes weren't going to be asked to sit down, and this wasn't going to be a fast interview. "I understand that, ma'am, but this is a murder case and we've a number of questions to ask."

"Go ahead," Lucretia Dearman said ungraciously. "But be quick about it. I've the vicar coming in half an hour."

Witherspoon glanced around the drawing room, noting there were no formal signs of mourning. The mirror over the mantelpiece wasn't covered, nor was there black crepe draped around the windows. But that didn't necessarily mean anything. "Why did you wait until the morning to go to your husband's office?" he asked. "Weren't you concerned when your husband didn't come home that night from work?"

"I didn't know he hadn't come home," she snapped. "He knows what time dinner is served, and when he didn't come home, I assumed he was working late. I had my dinner and then retired. It wasn't until the next morning that I realized he'd not come home at all."

"What about your servants? Did they bolt the door knowing the master was still out?"

"My husband has keys, and he'd have bolted the door himself when he came home."

"Was it unusual for him to stay out all night?" Barnes asked.

"Of course it was unusual," Lucretia replied acidly. "He might work late, but he didn't stay out all night."

"When you realized your husband was missing, why did you go to Mrs. Sutcliffe's home?" the inspector asked. "Why didn't you go directly to the Sutcliffe office?"

"I didn't have keys, and I knew that my brother did," she replied.

"But wouldn't the porter have let you in?" Barnes queried.

"Why should I bother with the porter when I knew John could handle the matter?" she sniffed. "Really, I don't understand why you're going on and on about this. I explained it to that other policeman. Unfortunately, I'd forgotten that John was out of town on business, so it ended up that the porter had to let us in after all. It was most inconvenient."

"Did your husband have any enemies? Had he had any recent trouble with anyone?" Witherspoon asked.

Lucretia looked down at her hands and then back up at the two policemen. "He wasn't a well-liked person," she said, "but I wouldn't say he had enemies."

Antonia Meadows patted her arm. "Lucretia, dear, I know this is difficult for you. But you must tell these gentlemen the truth."

Lucretia gaped at her. "What on earth are you talking about? I am telling the truth."

"Now, now, dear, I understand it's painful, but it's necessary." She looked up at the two men. "Ronald did have trouble with someone recently."

"Antonia, what are you saying?" Lucretia demanded.

"We were at a dinner party at the Sutcliffe house last Saturday," she continued. "And I overheard Fiona Sutcliffe threatening to kill him."

CHAPTER 7

"Antonia, what on earth are you talking about?" Lucretia demanded again.

Antonia smiled sadly. "Forgive me, dear," she said to her friend, "but I must tell them what I heard. I didn't say anything about it before because she's part of your family. But I can no longer keep silent." She turned to Witherspoon. "After dinner, John said he wanted to show us all a new map he'd acquired. He collects them. We got up and as we were leaving the dining room, Ronald and Fiona both commented that they'd already seen it so they'd go on into the drawing room. We went upstairs to John's sitting room."

"Who is 'we'?" Witherspoon asked.

"Myself, Henry Anson, and his fiancée, Miss Amy Throckmorton," she replied. "John got the map out and spread it so we could all see it. It was a map of the Alaskan Wilderness and not that interesting. But

Henry Anson seemed to find it fascinating, and he began asking questions. I got bored and a bit chilled, so I came back downstairs to find my shawl. To get to the cloakroom you must walk past John's study, and as I came past, I overheard Fiona yelling, so naturally, I stopped to see what was wrong. I started to go in, but then I heard Ronald's voice."

"What did he say?" the inspector pressed.

"He said she'd better listen to him" — she cast a worried glance at Lucretia — "and then I heard Fiona say that she didn't care if he did have the box, it proved nothing, and that if he tried to make trouble, she'd kill him."

Lucretia closed her eyes briefly. "Why didn't you tell me this before?"

"Dearest, I'm sorry, but I simply thought it was an argument, I didn't take it seriously. Then when Ronald was murdered, I was so confused. I didn't know what to do."

"You could have told the police," Barnes said dryly.

The tea shop was crowded, and it took her a few moments to spot Fiona. She was sitting in the rear with her back turned away from the window. Tucking her umbrella under her arm, Mrs. Jeffries made her way between the closely packed tables and chairs. As she approached, Fiona turned and gave her a hesitant smile.

"Thank you for meeting me here." Mrs. Jeffries sat down opposite her sister-in-law. "It was good of you to order tea." A silver teapot, two cups, and a tray of fancy biscuits were already on the table. "There's been a serious change in the investigation, and I couldn't risk meeting at your home."

"So I gathered when I received your note." Fiona poured a cup of tea and passed it to Mrs. Jeffries. "What has happened?"

"Inspector Nivens has had an accident, and Inspector Witherspoon will be taking over the investigation. Which ought to work to your benefit. He never arrests innocent people."

"Never?" Fiona looked skeptical. "You mean he's never made a mistake?"

"Of course he's made mistakes." She took a quick sip of the warming brew and helped herself to a biscuit. "But we make sure they are rectified before an arrest is made. Take my word for it, you're in much better hands now than when Nivens was in charge. The only thing *he* cares about is making an arrest and getting his name in the paper."

"That was the impression I got as well," she admitted. "Does Inspector Witherspoon know that we're related?"

"He does now. I told him this morning. Too many people already know of our connection, so I thought it best to speak up." She nibbled a bit of the chocolate off the edge of the biscuit and laid it down on the saucer. "But I made it very clear we're not close and that I've had no relationship with you for years."

Fiona smiled wistfully. "I suppose I had that coming."

"I didn't say it to hurt you, Fiona, but only to make you aware of the situation. You forget, I not only work for a policeman but I was married to one for many years and I know how they think. They are far less suspicious of information that is freely given than facts they have to dig out for themselves. Inspector Witherspoon would have found out about our relationship, and when he did, he'd wonder why we'd kept it hidden."

"Forgive me, I didn't mean to sound so maudlin. Nor did I mean to doubt his or your ability to help me. I'm just so very upset about this wretched mess. This has been very difficult for both of us."

"Of course it's been difficult," Mrs. Jeffries said briskly. "But all that aside, there are a number of questions I must ask you. First of all, when did Mr. and Mrs. Meadows come to London?"

Fiona frowned. "I'm not sure of the exact date, but it was seven or eight years ago. Lucretia could give a more precise accounting. But Thaddeus Meadows is dead. He passed away about six months ago. He died of pneumonia."

"I know."

She nodded and continued. "Lucretia was delighted. She and Antonia have been friends since they were children. Why do you ask?"

"Everyone in Ronald Dearman's circle of family, friends, and work colleagues must be considered a possible suspect in his murder."

"But Antonia and Ronald had very little to do with one another. He considered her a fool, and she wasn't shy about telling people she thought him a brute."

"They may have not had much to do with one another, but apparently, there was no love lost between them," Mrs. Jeffries said. "Do you know why they came to London?"

"I can't say for certain, and Lucretia would die before she'd ever confide in me, but the gossip I heard is that Thaddeus Meadows inherited a house and a small yearly income from his godfather. He wasn't doing well in York; apparently, the family fortunes had turned sour, so he sold off their home there and moved to London. Antonia was happy with the change. She hated being separated from Lucretia. Those two are closer than most sisters, which is perhaps one of the reasons Ronald disliked her so much."

"So their coming here had nothing to do with Sutcliffe Manufacturing?"

"Not at all. Thaddeus was a small shareholder in the company, but he had no more than hundreds of other shareholders. He had nothing to do with the management or the running of the firm."

"What happened to those shares when he died?"

"I've not heard that he had any other heirs, so I imagine they went to Antonia. As far as I know, she inherited everything. The shares are worth a great deal more than they were when he first acquired them."

"They had no children?" Mrs. Jeffries pressed.

A shadow flitted across Fiona's face for a brief moment. "No, there were rumors that Antonia lost a baby early in her marriage, but again, I've no idea if it's true."

"I've heard that Ronald Dearman was a snoop," Mrs. Jeffries said. "Is it true?"

"Absolutely." Fiona looked disgusted. "When they came to dine, I hid all our correspondence. You know what I mean, invitations and calling cards, that sort of thing one leaves on the mantelpiece as a reminder of a social obligation. Ronald had no compunction whatsoever about reading them. He wasn't even embarrassed when he was caught. He'd just make up a lie that the paper fell and he'd picked it up and was putting it back. One time John caught him in the study, going through his desk drawers. He claimed he was looking for a piece of notepaper, but I didn't believe him."

"Did John?"

"He pretended he did." She shrugged. "But I think he had his doubts. I know that after that incident, he took to locking the desk."

Mrs. Jeffries regarded her steadily. "Why didn't you tell me this before? It is rather pertinent information."

Fiona raised her eyebrows. "It never occurred to me to mention it. The man had a substantial number of character flaws. I saw no reason to single that one out for special attention."

"Didn't you?" She smiled. She knew Fiona was lying, that she'd deliberately kept this information secret. But why? "Come now, Fiona, you're a smart woman. Surely you must have realized that people who nose about in other people's business with the kind of single-minded fervor that Dearman possessed must have a reason for doing so."

"He just liked knowing things about people, that's all," she insisted.

Mrs. Jeffries was losing patience. "That's absurd. No one in his class risks becoming a social pariah just because they like 'knowing things.' We found out about his little habit of snooping in drawers and peeking in windows in just a few days. How long do you think it's going to be before the police know what he was up to?"

"I don't know what kind of gossip you've heard, but he was just a common garden variety snoop —"

Mrs. Jeffries interrupted. "He was a blackmailer. He discovered people's secrets and blackmailed them." She was shooting in the dark here, the very thing she'd warned the others about just this morning, but she needed to shake Fiona enough to get the truth out of the woman.

"How do you know that?" Fiona cried. Conversation at the nearest tables stopped as well-dressed matrons turned to stare at them with expressions of disapproval. She smiled apologetically and lowered her voice. "Do you have evidence that he was black-mailing anyone? Do you know that for a fact, or are you just guessing?"

And with that, Mrs. Jeffries knew her suspicions had been confirmed. Dearman had threatened to blackmail Fiona; she could see it in the sudden fear that flashed across Fiona's face and in the way her hands clenched into fists. Mrs. Jeffries leaned forward and looked her straight in the eye. "I do know it for a fact. He tried to black-mail you. What's more, if I can find out so easily, so can the police, and they won't be nearly as tolerant of your privacy as I was."

Fiona's face drained of color. "Alright, he was trying to blackmail me, but I didn't kill him."

"What did he have on you?" Mrs. Jeffries asked bluntly.

"Oh dear God, don't ask me that, I can't tell you, I simply can't. It doesn't just involve me. It's not my secret to tell."

"Then whose is it? Fiona, you don't seem to understand —"

"But I do," she interrupted. "I know what I'm doing. Even though I didn't kill him, I know that I'm a suspect and there's a chance I'll face the hangman. But that's a risk I'll have to take."

Mrs. Jeffries said nothing. She had her answer now; there was only one person that Fiona would sacrifice herself for, her husband. "Does John own a gun?"

Fiona drew back. "Why do you ask?"

"Because the police are going to ask, and I suggest you don't lie to them. They'll have asked your servants as well."

Her eyes suddenly filled with tears, and she looked down at her hands. She took a long, ragged breath and lifted her chin. "He owns a gun. He keeps it in the drawer in his sitting room."

The room went silent as the two policemen stepped into the outer office of Sutcliffe Manufacturing. Two rows of clerks paused over their ledgers, and the typewriter girl, alone in a spot by the window, stopped her work and stared at them with open curiosity. The chief clerk, an older man with a prominent overbite, scurried out from behind his high desk in the corner of the room. He didn't look pleased to see them. "Back again, are you? How many more times are you going to disrupt our office? We're already behind in our accounts."

"As many times as it takes to find Mr. Dearman's murderer," Barnes said softly. "We'd like to have a word with Mr. Anson.

Please tell him we're here."

"Wait here, and I'll see if he is available." The clerk gave them one last disapproving frown and hurried down the hallway.

Witherspoon pointed to a closed door on the far side of the room. "I wonder if that is the victim's office."

"Indeed it is, sir," the clerk closest to them said. "I'm Daniel Jones. That's where he was murdered."

"The other private offices are down that hall?" Witherspoon pointed in the opposite direction. "Is that correct?"

Jones nodded. "Yes, Mr. Dearman's office is separated from the others. You can see all of us from his room, and he liked that. He was in charge of us, sir."

"Who is in charge now?" Barnes asked.

Just then, they heard the voices, then footsteps, and a tall man wearing a dark blue suit emerged. He was followed by the clerk.

"Mr. Anson?" Witherspoon asked.

"I'm Anson." His face creased in a puzzled frown as he came toward the two policemen. "I'm afraid I don't understand. I thought you'd already taken statements and questioned the staff. Do you need to speak to us again?"

Witherspoon smiled apologetically and

233

extended his hand. "We haven't met, sir. I'm Inspector Witherspoon, and this is Constable Barnes." Anson took the proffered hand. "I know it's confusing," he continued, "but Inspector Nivens met with an accident and I'm taking over. I know it's inconvenient, but we will need to look at Mr. Dearman's office and speak to your staff again."

"I've already told them these disruptions have put us very behind in our accounts," the clerk said quickly.

"I'm sure you have, Mr. Dennis. Go on with your duties. I'll take care of this matter." He waved the clerk back to his corner and turned to Witherspoon. "We'll cooperate in any way we can. But as Mr. Dennis has just said, we'd like to get back to doing business. We're falling behind in our accounts department."

"Thank you, we appreciate your position. We'll do our best to get this over with as quickly and efficiently as possible. But I must remind you that this is a murder investigation and it's essential we interview everyone."

"But you've already done that," Anson protested. "The police were here for two days taking statements from the staff. You're not starting over, are you? Surely the original reports are available to you."

"They are, sir," Barnes said. "But we'd prefer to conduct our own interviews. It won't take long."

"I suppose I've no choice in the matter. Who would you like to speak with first?"

Barnes said, "If it's all the same to you, sir, we'd like to have a word with you."

"I've already given a very lengthy statement. I spoke to a Constable Morehead, and I know he took note of everything I said, but if you think this is really necessary, then let's go into my office."

He motioned for them to follow. Once inside, he pointed to two straight-backed chairs in front of the desk. "Please sit down," he said, taking this seat.

The two policemen sat, and Barnes whipped out his little brown notebook. "Do you know of anyone who would have wanted to harm Mr. Dearman?" he asked.

Anson's eyebrows rose. "As I told the other constable, Dearman wasn't a nice person. Everyone here either disliked him or feared him. But if you're asking if I know of anyone who hated him enough to kill him, then I'm afraid the answer is no."

"How about you, sir?" Witherspoon asked. "You told Constable Morehead that the two of you didn't get along." This was a guess

235

on his part; he'd not read any of the statements yet.

"We didn't get along at all. Dearman resented my presence here and tried his best to get Mr. Sutcliffe to either move my office to the Battersea plant or terminate me completely."

"Why did he resent you?" Barnes looked up from his notebook.

"He thought I was trying to take his place." Anson leaned back in his chair and steepled his fingers together. "I run the day-to-day operations of both our manufacturing plants. One is in York and the smaller one is here in London, so I'm gone much of the time. Ronald Dearman used to have my position, but when I came on board this past September, he was put solely in charge of the office management. He's resented me ever since. But the truth of the matter is I was hired because he simply wasn't up to the task. As a matter of fact, when Mr. Sutcliffe recruited me, I got the distinct impression he was going to sack Dearman outright."

"What time did you leave the office on the day of the murder?" Witherspoon unbuttoned his coat. It was very warm in the room.

Anson sighed. "If you've read my state-

236

ment, you'll know I left at five."

"Did you go straight home from here?"

"No, I went to the post office, and then I went to my lodgings to rest before going to my fiancée's home. We had a dinner engagement."

"What is the lady's name, and where does she live?"

"I don't want anyone bothering her with something this distasteful," he retorted.

"Sorry, sir, but we must insist," Witherspoon said. "We'll be as discreet as possible, I assure you."

Anson looked doubtful. "Her name is Miss Amy Throckmorton. Her family lives near Hyde Park, number four, Haddington Place."

"What time did you arrive at the Throckmorton home?" the constable asked.

"I didn't note the time, but I wasn't late, which was amazing as the traffic that evening was dreadful. So I must have arrived close to seven o'clock."

"How did you get there?" Witherspoon asked.

"I took a hansom cab," Anson replied.

"Where did the hansom pick you up? Was it at a stand or in the street?" Barnes asked.

"It was out on the road near my lodging house." He looked confused. "But why do you need to know that?"

"Because we'll need to check with the driver and have him verify your account," the inspector explained politely.

Wiggins grinned to himself as he saw the housemaid stop in front of the pub. She cast a furtive glance over her shoulder, opened the door, and stepped inside. He was after her like a shot. He hoped his luck was changing; he'd spent the day hanging about one place after another and hadn't found anyone willing to give him the time of day.

He went in and stood just inside the door, giving his eyes time to adjust to the dim light. It was a good working-class pub: nothing fancy, sawdust on the floors, wooden benches along the walls, and three small wooden tables. He spotted his quarry standing at the bar. The barman was pouring her drink, and the fellow next to her was chatting with her as if they were old friends. Cor blimey, he thought, looks like she's a regular. He frowned; he'd hoped to catch her on her own. But he moved to the bar and eased into the spot next to her.

"What'll you 'ave, mate?" the barman asked.

"A pint of bitter, please," he replied. He glanced at her and gave her a friendly smile.

But she was knocking back her glass and didn't notice him. She wore a shabby gray jacket over a maid's lavender broadcloth skirt, and now that he was close to her, he could see she was older than he'd first thought. There were streaks of gray in her brown hair and lines etched around her eyes and mouth.

She put the glass down and turned her head, catching him watching her. "What are you starin' at?" she demanded.

"I'm sorry, miss." He gave her another smile. "I meant no disrespect. I was lookin' at you because I thought you were someone else. You look enough like my cousin to be her twin, and as she works round these parts, I thought you was her."

"Oh, that's alright, then," she muttered.

The man standing next to her, a burly fellow with a red complexion and stringy gray hair, poked her in the ribs. "Did you ask her?"

"I tried, but yesterday she was shut up with that friend of hers, and then the vicar and the undertaker come round, and this mornin' she up and disappeared. The housekeeper said she was goin' out to Mr. Dearman's old cottage in Essex and wouldn't be back until late. Tomorrow's the funeral, and I don't feel right sayin' anythin' on the day she's buryin' her husband. Sorry, Sam, I know how badly you need work. I'll try to have a word with her next week. But I do know that she's not hired anyone else for the job."

"That's good, then. What about her friend?" the man said. "Maybe she needs some paintin' done."

"You mean Mrs. Meadows?" She laughed. "You'd need Mrs. Dearman to vouch for you, and she'd not do that unless you'd worked for her first."

He shrugged and tossed back the rest of his drink. "It was just an idea. Anyway, I've got to get back and load the rest of them pallets. It don't pay as well as paintin', but it's better than nothing. Will I see ya tomorrow?"

"I don't think I can get away. She's makin' all of us go to the funeral, and then we've all got to serve at the reception afterward. But at least she's out of the way today, and I can come back this evening for a quick one because the housekeeper will be gone, too."

"Let's meet at half six. I'll be finished workin' by then." He slapped his cap on his head and left.

Wiggins waited until the door closed behind the man before turning to the woman. "Excuse me, miss, but I feel bad about my earlier behavior. It was rude to stare at you, even if I did think you were my cousin. Would you allow me to buy you a drink by way of apology?"

"Oh, you do talk posh," she cried. "But then again, you probably work in a posh house, don't you, and yes, you can buy me another drink." She waved at the barman. "Give us another one 'ere, Johnny, this bloke is payin'."

Johnny duly poured another shot of gin in her glass, and Wiggins handed him the coins.

"I don't want you to get in trouble with your mistress," he began.

But she cut him off with an impatient wave of her hand. "Don't you worry about that. The merry widow has gone to some village in Essex and won't be home until eight o'clock."

He grinned. "I wasn't eavesdroppin', but it did sound like there's a lot of work for your household."

"You mean the funeral and reception." She waved her hand again. "That's no trouble for any of us; all we've got to do is serve. It's to be a cold dish reception, and Cook has already done the beef joint and the ham." She knocked back the rest of her gin. "My mistress isn't goin' to waste any more time on gettin' him planted than she has to. I don't think she even cares if we get the house cleaned properly. She's got the housekeeper off running errands that don't have anythin' to do with the funeral, she's gone off to his cottage in Essex, a place she's never gone to as long as I've worked for her, and she sent me next door this morning to ask the neighbors to send their footman to Liverpool Street Station to meet the seven thirty-five train."

"Why does she need a footman to meet her?" he asked. He nodded at the barman to pour her another one.

"To help with the boxes." She smiled her thanks at the barman. "She's bringin' some of his old stuff back from the cottage. Maybe she's lookin' for an old suit to bury him in — I wouldn't put it past her. God knows there was no love lost between the two of 'em, and now that he's dead, I expect she'll be scarperin' off to someplace warm."

"She's leavin' the country?" He wanted to make sure he got this part correct.

"I don't know for certain that's what she's plannin', and if you'd asked me last week, I'd said she didn't have enough money to go to Brighton and back, but now that he's gone, she's spendin' fast enough."

"Maybe she's goin' to inherit from him," Wiggins suggested.

"Could be. He had plenty he didn't tell her about, that's for certain." She took a sip of her gin. "He was never short of cash, I can tell you that." She winked and poked him in the arm.

"Why, you clever woman, how did ya find that out?"

"I do the cleanin' upstairs, and twice now, when he didn't know I was up there, I've seen him pullin' big wads of cash out of his pocket and stuffin' it into his travelin' bag. Now, I ask you, why would he be doin' that if he wasn't tryin' to hide money from his missus?"

"Don't be alarmed, sir." Witherspoon rose to his feet. "We check everyone's movements, not just yours." Barnes put his notebook in his pocket and got up, too.

"I'm relieved it's not just me you're —" Anson broke off as his office door opened. "John, what are you doing here? I thought you were at your sister's helping with the funeral arrangements?"

"She wasn't there. She's probably gone to Mrs. Meadows'. Women are so much more understanding of one another at time like this." He moved farther into the office, his gaze locked on the two policemen. "Back again, are you?" Then he frowned. "Wait a moment, you're not the chap that was here earlier."

."There's been a change in the investigation," Anson said quickly. He introduced them and explained the situation. "They'd finished with me and were going out to interview the staff," he concluded.

"I hope you're better mannered than that other chap." Sutcliffe eyed Witherspoon cautiously. "He was most abrasive and rather rude."

Barnes chuckled, and the inspector tried to keep a straight face but couldn't. "We've heard that complaint before," Witherspoon replied. "I assure you, sir, we do our best to be respectful of witnesses."

"In that case, come along to my office first. You were going to interview me again, weren't you?" He was already at the door and heading for the hallway.

"We were indeed, sir," Witherspoon said as they hurried after him.

Sutcliffe stopped at a door at the end of the corridor and waved them inside. "Please have a seat, gentlemen. Would you like tea?"

"Thank you but no." Witherspoon sank down into one of the two upholstered leather chairs in front of the man's massive

244

desk. Barnes took the other one.

Sutcliffe took his seat. "Right then, let's get on with this. What do you need to know?"

"To begin with, do you know of anyone who might have wished to harm Mr. Dearman?" Witherspoon asked.

Sutcliffe gave a negative shake of his head. "Ronald wasn't a popular person, but I don't know of anyone who would have wanted to kill him. Yet, obviously, someone did."

"Had he sacked anyone recently?" Barnes asked.

"He let James Tremlett, one of the accounting staff, go. That was about ten days ago, I think," Sutcliffe said. "To tell you the truth, I was surprised he'd done it. Tremlett's always been a good worker and completely reliable. But when I asked Ronald about it, he claimed he'd found irregularities in the fellow's work."

"We'll need Tremlett's address," Witherspoon said.

"Of course, I'll have our head clerk get it for you before you leave. Henry didn't look pleased when he said you'd be speaking to the entire staff again. He's a good man, but like so many of the young, he thinks efficiency is a virtue on the par with justice."

"I take it you don't agree?" Barnes asked.

"I did when I was his age." Sutcliffe suddenly smiled and it transformed his face; gone was the stern visage, replaced by the expression of a wise and kind grandfatherly type. "But now that I'm older, I've come to believe that kindness is more important than intelligence and people should be judged on their character and not their class or background." He sighed. "But you didn't come here for a philosophy debate. Go on, ask your questions."

Barnes leaned forward. "Mr. Anson said that Mr. Dearman resented him. Can you comment on that?"

"Henry is being overly sensitive. Ronald most certainly did not resent him. I'll admit there was a bit of conflict between the two of them, but that's to be expected considering that Henry took over much of Ronald's responsibilities. Surely you don't suspect Henry? That's absurd."

"We don't suspect anyone as yet," Witherspoon said quickly. "We're trying to find the truth. But you do admit the men had conflicts?"

"Yes, and that was my fault. I didn't adeptly handle the transition between hiring Henry and easing Ronald out of his responsibilities."

"Why did you decide to decrease Mr. Dearman's role in the company?" Witherspoon shifted in his chair.

"Because he was getting older, Inspector, and I was trying to gently push him toward retiring."

"Mr. Sutcliffe, in your previous statement, you claimed that the victim and Mr. Anson didn't get along, yet now you seem to be implying that there was only the occasional mild disagreement between them," Barnes said. Unlike the inspector, he had read the reports and witness statements. "Which is it?"

Sutcliffe tilted his head to one side. "Uhm, looks like you did read your predecessor's reports."

Barnes nodded. He didn't dare look at Witherspoon; now he was going to have to explain when and where he'd seen the witness statements. Drat.

"Alright, I have tried to tone it down. The truth is they couldn't stand one another. It was getting awkward and I was sorry for it. Ronald wasn't incompetent, but the company had grown so much that I felt we needed someone younger and frankly, better educated. I hired Henry, and within a very short time, he proved so valuable, I put him in charge of the operations of both plants. Of course, Ronald was upset."

"Weren't you going to sack him?" Barnes pressed. "Shouldn't he have been grateful you kept him on at all?"

"Who told you I was going to sack him?" Sutcliffe demanded.

"Henry Anson," the constable said. "He said that when you hired him, you gave him the impression you meant to get rid of Mr. Dearman."

"Henry was mistaken." Sutcliffe got to his feet. "I never had any intention of sacking Ronald. He is my brother-in-law, and such an act would have hurt my sister deeply. Now, if you've no more questions, I really must get to work."

They got up. "I do have one more question, sir." Barnes put his notebook in his jacket pocket. "You went to Birmingham on business the day that Mr. Dearman was killed, is that correct?"

"That's right."

"What train did you take?"

"The five forty-five," he replied. "And I came back the next morning as soon as I heard about Ronald's death."

"How did you hear, sir?" Witherspoon asked.

"Henry sent me a telegram, and I came back immediately."

"Do you have your ticket stub, sir?" Barnes pressed.

"Certainly not, why would I keep such a thing? I threw it away."

"Did you see anyone on the train who you know, anyone who can verify you were there?" the inspector added. He'd no idea what Barnes was doing, but he was going to play along. He trusted the constable completely.

Sutcliffe's eyes widened in surprise. "I saw no one, Inspector. I didn't realize I'd be needing to account for my whereabouts. Surely you don't suspect that I had anything to do with Ronald's murder? Why? I've no reason to want the fellow dead."

"Our questions are just routine, sir," Barnes said quickly. "We're asking everyone to account for themselves."

Hatchet smiled at his companion and signaled the barman for another drink. He, of course, was drinking mineral water, but Alexander Dreyfus loved his gin. They were seated at a small, elegant table in the Kings Spaniel, one of the fanciest pubs in Mayfair. The walls were covered with flocked red silk wallpaper; French embossed glass adorned the wooden panels separating the sections; and from overhead, three red and gold chandeliers cast the room in cheerful light.

"I was surprised to hear from you." Dreyfus nodded his thanks as the waiter put his drink in front of him and then hurried off. "It's been a long time."

"True, but that doesn't mean I neglect my old friend forever," Hatchet replied. He and Dreyfus had once been fast friends, but over the years as their lives had gone in different directions, they had drifted apart. Like Hatchet, Dreyfus had started out in service, but had made a fortune by opening a temporary employment agency supplying "Gentlemen's Gentlemen" to those that could afford his exorbitant fees. "Every time I've sent you a message, you've been either in Paris or Edinburgh. Good Lord, man, don't you ever stay in London?"

Dreyfus laughed. He was a tall man with hazel eyes, a huge forehead, and a fringe of gray hair. "Business, I'm afraid. Even in France and Scotland there's a call for my services. Amazing how many households hire temporary butlers and footman for either special occasions or to impress a dinner guest. But I can't complain; it's made me a rich man. How about you? Are you still working for that American woman? You do know that if you'd come to work for me,

I'd make sure you got only plum jobs right here in London."

This time, Hatchet laughed. "Thank you, Alex, but there's no need for that. I'm well fixed. As a matter of fact, I've plenty of money thanks to some wise investments. The only reason I don't retire is that I enjoy working for my American lady. She's quite the character, and life with her is always interesting."

"I'm glad life has worked out well for you." Alex grinned broadly. "There was a time when it looked as if it wouldn't."

Hatchet knew he was referring to those dark days when he was held firmly in the grip of an addiction often referred to as "demon rum," though at the height of his cravings, anything with alcohol in it would do. "It was my eccentric American lady who found me in an alley in Baltimore and offered me a chance. That's one of the reasons I'll never leave her. But to be perfectly frank, I do have another reason for wanting to see you. I need your help."

"You know I'll help you in any way that I can," Alex replied. "I owe you a great deal."

Hatchet waved him off impatiently. "You don't owe me anything. You'd have done the same for me."

Years earlier, Dreyfus, who was Jewish,

251

had been accosted by a gang of anti-Semitic thugs as he left a pub. Hatchet happened to follow him out, saw him getting attacked, and leapt into the fray himself. The thugs ran off into the night, and Dreyfus and Hatchet had become fast friends. "I know that you'd die before you'd admit this to most people, but you do hear a substantial amount of gossip from your staff, right?"

Alex chuckled. "That's true, but don't tell anyone. All of our advertisements claim we're the very soul of discretion. But I admit that when the men come in to pick up their pay packets, we sit around the fire and have a right good natter. But we make sure we keep it in the family, so to speak. I do draw the line at the staff spreading gossip to outsiders. It would kill my business."

"My lips are sealed, but it would be very helpful to me if you happened to have heard anything about a family named Dearman or Sutcliffe."

"You mean Ronald Dearman, that man who was murdered a few days ago?" Alex took a sip of his gin. "Good Lord, why are you asking questions about that fellow?"

"Let's just say that in recent years, I've frequently found myself in a position to pass along information that helps the police." He was hedging, not wanting to out and out lie

252

to his friend. "Have you heard anything about him? It's important."

"We've never sent anyone to work at the Dearman house. But the Sutcliffes have hired us on several occasions." He frowned. "As a matter of fact, one of the lads mentioned that he'd been on the late train to Birmingham and seen Mr. Sutcliffe."

"He knew Sutcliffe by sight?" Hatchet pressed.

"Oh yes, Leonard's worked for them several times recently. He's a fully trained footman, and they've used him when they've had large parties and such. He's very good at putting gentlemen in their cups and single ladies into hansom cabs. He's a nice boy, too, big as a house and broad shouldered enough so that older ladies frequently request his services when they have to take a late train. That's what he was doing when he saw Sutcliffe. Mrs. Adamson hired him to carry her packages and escort her to Birmingham."

"Do you know exactly when this happened?"

"Monday night." Alex laughed. "I remember because we got the request from Mrs. Adamson as I was leaving and I always leave early on Mondays because it's my whist night. I was annoyed because the messenger from the hotel came late in the afternoon and I was worried that I wouldn't get confirmation from Leonard that he could do it. But he's a reliable lad and got to the office before I had to leave. There was plenty of time for him to get to Mrs. Adamson's hotel and get the two of them on the nine o'clock train to Birmingham."

"Nine o'clock," Hatchet murmured. He wasn't certain, but he thought that Sutcliffe was supposed to have left town much earlier in the day. "Would Leonard be willing to tell this to the police?"

Alex drew back. "Uh, I don't know, Hatchet. I don't want our customers to think we go tattling about their business."

"But this is a murder inquiry," Hatchet said earnestly.

"Can you keep my company name out of it?"

"Should we start interviewing the staff?" Barnes asked as he and Witherspoon left Sutcliffe's office. "Mr. Sutcliffe said we could use Dearman's office. It's empty now, and before I begin calling them in, you can examine it."

"Yes, I'd like to have a good look at it before we begin." He started down the hall and then stopped abruptly. "Constable, there's something I don't understand. You told me earlier that Inspector Nivens' reports are being sent to the station. Well, if they're on the way to the station and you've not been back there since before you went to the Yard yesterday, how did you know what was in Constable Morehead's report?"

"I read it, sir," he admitted. "I'd taken the fraud report over and stopped to have a word with my friend, Eddie Harwood. You remember him, sir, you recommended him for the position."

He nodded. "Yes, of course, go on."

"I happened to see that Nivens' report was sitting under the counter, and I was curious. When Eddie nipped to the back to use the water closet, I had quick glance at the statements."

Witherspoon stared at him for a moment and then shrugged. "Oh well, no harm done, I suppose, and if the truth be told, I suspect we've all had a peek at one another's reports."

"Thank you, sir."

They reached the outer office, and Barnes motioned for the chief clerk. "Mr. Dennis," he said as he approached. "Mr. Sutcliffe said you're to open Mr. Dearman's office. We'll use that to speak to the staff."

"It's not locked," the clerk said. He

opened the door and stepped back. "Who should I send in first?"

"No one as yet." Barnes walked to the window and opened the blinds, flooding the room with pale, gray light. "We want to have a good look around first. I'll let you know when we're ready. Close the door on your way out, please."

When they were alone, Witherspoon looked at the empty chair behind the desk. "He was sitting there when he was killed?"

Barnes nodded. "That's right. The killer probably stood where you're standing. According the report I read, he was found slumped over, facedown on the desk. The murder weapon wasn't here nor anywhere else on the premises."

"So the murderer took it with him." He moved closer and grimaced as he saw the bloodstained desk blotter. "We know the approximate time of death?"

"The last employee left the office at six ten."

"And the office was unlocked at that time?"

"I'm not sure, sir. I didn't get to read all the witness accounts," Barnes said. He had read most of them but didn't think it wise to know too many details.

Witherspoon sighed glumly. "We might as

well get started, then. When we get finished, we may have time to go to the station. I'd like to have a look at Nivens' reports before I do any additional interviewing. Your jumping in when you did with Mr. Sutcliffe was most helpful, and frankly, I'd like to see what Mrs. Sutcliffe said in her statement before we speak to her tomorrow. It's going to be awkward enough as it is."

"Because she's Mrs. Jeffries' sister-in-law?" Barnes walked to the office door and took hold of the knob.

The inspector nodded, lifted the blood-stained blotter off the desk, and peeked underneath.

"I understand Mrs. Jeffries hasn't had much to do with her in the last ten years," Barnes said.

"I know, but even so, family is family."

CHAPTER 8

"Luty, this is a wonderful surprise. I didn't expect to see you here," a woman's voice rose above the din of the crowded room. Luty grinned with delight as a tall, red-haired woman wearing an elaborate blue dress charged toward her. Her long rope of pearls swung wildly as she held her loaded plate high and elbowed her way through the throng clustered at the end of the buffet table. "Thank goodness I ran into you," Alice Wittington exclaimed. "At least now I'll have someone interesting to talk to."

"I was just thinkin' the same thing. Now that you're here, I'm glad I came."

Alice chuckled. "Lady Barraclough is an old snob, but she does do a delightful lunch buffet."

Luty held up her own plate. It was loaded with roast beef, shrimp, a chicken leg, and a huge dollop of duchess potatoes. "Why do you think I'm here? Seein' as we've both got our grub, let's go find us a quiet table. I've got somethin' I want to ask you."

"There's a couple of vacant ones by the terrace door." Alice jerked her head. "Follow me." She turned and used her considerable bulk to clear them a path through the well-dressed women chatting in the aisles and between the closely packed tables. She guided Luty to an empty bistro table for two. They put their plates down and took their seats. Alice waved at a black-coated waiter carrying a tray of champagne, and he hurried over.

"Now don't say you oughtn't to drink this." She handed the flute to Luty. "We're here to eat, drink, be merry, and gossip."

"Amen to that." Luty took a quick sip. "Hmm, this is good."

Alice took a drink. "Ah, Lady Barraclough's cellar never disappoints. What was it you wanted to ask me about?" She put the glass down, picked up her fork, and speared a shrimp.

"You know that fellow that was shot a few days back, Ronald Dearman?" she began. At Alice's nod, she continued. "I was wonderin' if you knew anythin' about him or his family."

Alice chewed her food, her expression thoughtful. "No, I can't say that I do."

Luty's spirits plummeted. "Oh, that's disa—"

"Wait a minute," Alice interrupted. "Ronald Dearman married a Sutcliffe."

"That's right, Lucretia Sutcliffe."

"I don't know much about her, but I was at the announcement of her brother's engagement." Alice laughed heartily. "Oh my God, what a scandal that was. I'll never forget that day. We were all at the village fete where the Sutcliffes have a country home. I'd gone because my brother Baxter — you remember Baxter don't you? Tall fellow, looks a lot like me? — well, anyway, he'd insisted I accompany him to a house party in the area."

"You didn't stay with the Sutcliffes?" Luty interrupted.

"We were staying with Edmund's cousin. This was right after Edmund and I had gotten engaged, and Baxter was feeling left out because his friendship with one of the Ordway twins hadn't worked out as he'd hoped."

Luty nodded. She'd forgotten that though Alice was a really decent woman, she could talk the paint off a wall. "I've met Baxter, he's a right nice man . . . Go on, you were at the village fete."

Alice laughed again. "Oh gracious, it was

wonderful. We were standing about listening to some self-important twit go on and on about something or other when all of a sudden, John Sutcliffe appeared and said he had an announcement." She took another drink.

"Go on." Luty chugged her own drink. "What happened then?"

Alice frowned. "It gets a bit murky here."

"Murky, what do you mean, murky?" Luty waved her now-empty glass at the waiter. Hatchet would be righteously annoyed with her for coming home in her cups; perhaps it would have been better if she'd eaten more before downing so much champagne. But Alice was so slow in getting to the point, it would drive a saint to drink.

"Because Baxter suddenly appeared and began nattering on in my ear about some poor Australian fellow. I finally shushed him so I could hear what Sutcliffe was saying." She took a swig of champagne and giggled. "He was announcing his engagement, and it was to a woman that worked for them. She was a paid companion to his sister or something like that, but the point is, everyone, including the self-important twit, had been expecting him to announce he was marrying someone else. Someone from his own class."

261

Luty smiled her thanks as a waiter appeared and refilled her glass. This was old news. Dang it all, she'd been hoping Alice could give her something new. She tossed the drink back, not caring how perturbed her butler would be when she arrived at their afternoon meeting half drunk.

"But of course," Alice continued, "people stopped talking about the engagement when they heard about the dead man in the pony cart."

"Come in," Inspector Witherspoon called in response to the soft knock on the door. The typewriter girl smiled as she stepped into the office. She was a rather lovely young woman with dark brown hair, brown eyes, high cheekbones, and ivory skin. She was dressed in a gray skirt with a thick black cumberbund around her slender waist, a gray waistcoat, and a pristine white blouse with a cameo broach at the throat. "Please make yourself comfortable. I assure you, this won't take long." He motioned toward the chair. "I'm sorry to have to question you again, Miss . . ."

"Blackburn, Anna Blackburn, and please don't apologize, Inspector. You're the first policeman who I've spoken with," she said as she took her seat.

Witherspoon frowned. "Have you only just started working here?"

"No, I've been here for three months."

The inspector didn't understand. He'd been under the impression that everyone on the staff had been interviewed. Had he misunderstood? He wished Constable Barnes were here to set him straight. But in the interests of efficiency, they'd split the staff list in half and the constable was taking statements in another office.

"You operate one of those typewriting machines, is that correct?"

"That's right, sir. I type invoices, contracts, letters of credit, and correspondence."

"Did you type for Mr. Dearman?"

She nodded. "Yes, but not often, sir. Generally I just did correspondence for Mr. Sutcliffe and Mr. Anson. The late Mr. Dearman rarely used my services."

"Were you in the office this past Monday, the day that Mr. Dearman was murdered?"

"I was, sir," she said. "I was here until closing time."

"Did you see anything unusual or hear anything unusual?"

"No sir, I didn't. Except for Mr. Jones being called into Mr. Dearman's office just before we packed up to leave, it was a day

263

like any other."

"Did you like Mr. Dearman?" Witherspoon asked.

"No sir, I didn't," she declared. "He tried
to replace me, sir, and I thought it most
unfair. If Mr. Anson hadn't intervened on
my behalf, I'd have been let go, and there
was nothing wrong with my work." Her
hands clenched into fists and a red flush
crept up her face. "He told Mr. Anson that
he could find someone cheaper, but that
isn't true. He just wanted to get rid of me."

"Do you have any idea why he'd want to
do such a thing?" Witherspoon asked gently.

"None. I don't know what I could have
done wrong. I work hard. I type invoices
and contracts, and once, I even stayed late
to do a private letter for him. I'm not supposed to do that, but he asked me so I did,
and two days later, he tries to give me the
sack. That's gratitude for you."

"You're not supposed to do private correspondence? Not even for the deputy direc-
tors?"

"No, Mr. Sutcliffe made it very clear when
I was hired that I work for the firm. I'm a
typewriter girl, not a private secretary." She
smiled hesitantly. "But we were alone here
in the office when Mr. Dearman asked me
to do it, and I was afraid to tell him I

couldn't. He claimed the letter was important and that it had to be typed and not written by hand."

He stared at her thoughtfully. "Who was it addressed to?"

"A law firm in Sydney. It was in reply to their letter to Mr. Dearman."

"Do you recall what it was about?"

"Of course I do," she said proudly. "He thanked them for their quick response to his inquiry and asked if it were possible to obtain the papers from the late Mr. Grimshaw's estate. He said he'd be willing to incur all expenses related to granting his request. If it was possible, could they please assess a monetary value to the remainder of the estate, the papers left in their possession, and he'd obtain a letter of credit for any bank they nominated in Sydney."

Witherspoon had no idea what this might mean for the investigation, but he sensed it might be important. "Do you have any idea who the late Mr. Grimshaw might be?"

She shook her head. "No, sir, I'd never heard the name before."

"Could it be one of the firm's customers or a supplier?" he pressed.

"It's possible, I suppose." She shrugged. "But I don't think so. When I mentioned the name to Mr. Anson, he'd never heard of them, either."

"You told Mr. Anson what happened?"

"I most certainly did," she replied. "I'd stayed late and done the man a favor, and two days later, he tried to let me go. The moment I walked out of Mr. Dearman's office, I went straight to Mr. Anson. He wasn't in his office. He'd gone to the plant." She smiled triumphantly. "Mr. Dearman wasn't expecting me to go there, but I did. I told Mr. Anson everything, that Mr. Dearman had bullied me into doing a letter for him and now he was trying to sack me."

"So Mr. Anson saw to it you kept your position," Witherspoon said. "When did this incident occur?"

"Three weeks ago," she replied.

"Do you remember anything else about this incident?" he asked.

She thought for a moment. "I don't think so . . . wait a moment, I tell a lie. There was something else. It was the address on the envelope. It was to Mr. Dearman, but it wasn't a London address, it was a village in Essex."

After leaving the tearoom, Mrs. Jeffries walked in a roundabout fashion toward the river, trying to sort out her feelings. The London streets were crowded with women shopping, street vendors hawking wares, delivery men pushing hand carts stacked high with boxes, and street lads transporting messages. But she was oblivious to it all as she meandered along the roads, deep in thought and paying only enough attention to her surroundings to avoid doing herself or anyone else harm.

Fiona's revelations had disturbed her greatly, and to make matters worse, now her conscience was starting to bother her. Did she have a duty to tell the inspector about Fiona's admission that she had access to a gun? Or was it best to let the police find out for themselves? What did she really believe? Was her sister-in-law really innocent? Was she, by withholding information, helping a murderer walk free? Was Fiona or John capable of murder? That was the real question that was gnawing at her.

Don't be absurd, she chided herself silently. You've no idea who committed this murder, and nothing you've learned points the finger of guilt at any one particular person; none of the clues have formed a pattern as yet. There is no coherent, logical progression that ties any of the facts together in any way that can identify the killer.

She stopped in front of a church and dragged a long, deep breath into her lungs.

This wouldn't do, it wouldn't do at all. She wasn't going to give in to maudlin fits of guilt just because nothing made sense. There's still plenty of time, she told herself. You'll sort it out. You always do.

Overhead, the church bells chimed the hour as a hansom pulled up and a vicar, staring at his pocket watch and muttering to himself, leapt out, paid the driver, and raced into the church. She realized if she was going to have time to take care of her next task before their afternoon meeting, she'd better grab this cab. "Take me to Bridge Road, please. It's near the West India dock."

"Yes, ma'am."

Twenty minutes later, she stepped into the Dirty Duck Pub. Blimpey spotted her and waved her over. "Come take a seat," he invited as she drew close.

"Thank you." She slipped onto the stool. "Sorry to come so unexpectedly, but I was hoping you'd have some information for me."

"You mean because yer guv 'as the case now." Blimpey laughed. "As it 'appens, I do 'ave somethin' you might find interestin'. I was goin' to send a lad over with a note askin' you to drop in, but you've saved me the trouble. But first, would you like somethin' to drink? How about a nice glass of Harvey's? We also do a very superior gin 'ere, none of that rotgut stuff you find in most waterside pubs, or perhaps you'd rather 'ave a pint. We can even do you a cup of tea if you like. Gemma keeps a kettle on the boil in the back."

"Nothing for me, thank you. But how did you know that Inspector Witherspoon had the case now? It wasn't . . ." She trailed off as she realized how foolish she sounded. "Oh dear, how silly of me. Of course, it's your business to know such things."

"It is indeed. I know that Inspector Nivens 'as a broken ankle and a sprained wrist." His smile vanished and he leaned closer to her. "And a word of warnin' 'ere. My sources tell me your guv's goin' to have the 'Ome Office on his back if he don't make an arrest soon."

"That is generally what happens with the inspector's cases," she said. "They are always after him to hurry the investigation."

"This time it's different," he warned. "What they're really scared about is that Nivens might 'ave already mucked things up so badly, your inspector won't be able to sort it out. At that point, they'll pressure him to arrest any Tom, Dick, or Harry that looks half guilty."

"Inspector Witherspoon would never do such a thing," she protested. She clenched her hands into fists as a sudden shaft of fear climbed her spine.

Blimpey nodded sympathetically. "Yer worried about your sister-in-law?"

She forced herself to relax. "Of course. We're not close, we never have been, but she is still in some way family. For my late husband's sake, I have to try and help her."

"The evidence against her is startin' to mount up," he said softly. "And when you 'ear what I've found out, it's goin' to look even worse. Are you sure you don't want that drink?"

"I'll have a sherry."

Blimpey got the barmaid's attention and held up his index finger, then turned and gave Mrs. Jeffries an encouraging smile. "Don't look so worried. You and yer lot will figure it out."

"I'm flattered by your faith in us," she replied. "But I'm still concerned. If what you say is true, they may not give the inspector enough time to find the culprit."

"Look, yer guv's rich, so you know he won't be knucklin' under to the toffs at the HO." He leaned back as their drinks arrived. "Thanks, Gemma." He waited till they were alone again. "Alright, we might as

270

well get on with it. There's two items for you, and they may help sort this out. The first, and to my mind the most important, is that yer victim wasn't pure as driven snow. Ronald Dearman was a blackmailer."

"Are you certain?"

"Don't insult me, Mrs. Jeffries." Blimpey pursed his lips. "Or course I'm sure. My sources know what they're about. Now, I'm not sayin' that the reason Dearman was murdered was because he was blackmailin' someone, but I am sayin' there's a bloomin' good chance yer killer was one of his victims and he or she got fed up with payin' the bloke."

"I meant no offense." She tapped her finger against the stem of her glass. "We'd already suspected he was blackmailing people. It's good to have it confirmed."

"Did you suspect he dealt in volume?"

She frowned. "Does that mean what I think it does?"

"It does." He nodded vigorously. "He 'ad lots of victims goin'. From what my sources found out, Dearman sort of stumbled into bein' a blackmailer because he was always stickin' 'is nose into other people's business and he was smart enough not to bleed 'em to death. He never asked for a fortune; he made 'em pay every month. Dearman called it a fee."

"How many victims does he have?" Mrs. Jeffries asked. She wondered how much he'd demanded from Fiona.

"My sources weren't sure of the exact number he 'ad when he was murdered, but they did find out that he's been doin' it for over fifteen years."

"So he was doing it even before he came to London."

"That's what it looks like." Blimpey took a sip of his beer.

"Do you know who else he might have been blackmailing? Did your sources have any names?"

"No, my source only found out because one of Dearman's victims was in his cups and talkin' a blue streak, but all the fellow would say was what I've already told ya: He'd been doin' it for years and he was smart enough to do the collectin' himself and not to bleed his victims too much." Blimpey nodded appreciatively. "He weren't stupid, that's for certain. He ran it like a business. Keep your fees low enough so that you can keep on collectin'."

"Nonetheless," Mrs. Jeffries pointed out, "he may have been good at running a blackmail business, but at some point, he must have picked the wrong victim. He did end up murdered."

"That's true," Blimpey agreed. "Right then, I'd best tell you the rest." He cleared his throat. "This bit may be shockin' for you, considerin' there's family involved 'ere."

"What is it?" She stared at him curiously, noting that a rosy hue was creeping up his cheeks. "Are you blushing?"

" 'Course not," he said quickly. "It's just — alright, I might as well spit it out. It's about Henry Anson. He's John Sutcliffe's illegitimate son. Apparently, he was carryin' on with Anson's mother before he married your sister-in-law. Anson's thirty-two."

She said nothing; then she lifted her sherry and drained the glass. "John has a son," she murmured. "I had no idea."

"Do you think your sister-in-law does?"

"It's impossible to tell," she replied. She had no love for Fiona, but she didn't rejoice in this news. "But she's the kind of woman who would rather die than have a scandal in the family. Oh dear, I see what you meant earlier. This doesn't look good for her."

"If Dearman found out the truth and threatened her with it, she'd 'ave a good motive for shuttin' 'im up permanently."

"But why target Fiona and not John?" she muttered.

"Because of what you just said," Blimpey shrugged. "She'd rather die than face a scandal. Women like that, women who've married up, will do whatever it takes to 'ang on to their position in society."

Mrs. Jeffries couldn't argue with that; she'd already come to the same conclusion. "Did your source know if Anson knew Sutcliffe was his father?" she asked.

Blimpey shook his head. "He didn't know if Anson knew the situation, but John Sutcliffe knew the truth. That's the real reason that he gave Anson the job."

"We can't wait for him any longer," Mrs. Jeffries looked at the clock. The meeting was supposed to start at half past four and it was already a quarter to five. "We must get on with it. But it's not like Wiggins to be so late."

"I'm sure he's got a reason," the cook muttered. "The lad knows we worry when people don't show up at the proper time."

"Maybe he's following someone," Phyllis suggested.

"I'm sure he's fine," Mrs. Jeffries said with a quick smile to the cook. "He'll probably be here any moment now. Why don't you start." She wanted to distract Mrs. Goodge from worrying about their errant footman.

"I'd like to, but I've not got anythin' to report," Mrs. Goodge said glumly. "I've had half a dozen people through this kitchen today, and not one of them had even heard of the murder. Honestly, you'd think people would take more of an interest in the world, wouldn't you."

"Don't feel bad, Mrs. Goodge. It happens to all of us." Ruth smiled sympathetically.

"I heard a little bit." Luty helped herself to a slice of buttered brown bread. "I ran into a friend at Lady Barraclough's luncheon, and she told me that she was there at the village fete on the day that John Sutcliffe announced his engagement to your sister-in-law." She looked at Mrs. Jeffries. "She said how everyone there was shocked and surprised because they was expectin' him to marry Antonia Meadows, or Antonia Whitley as she was known then."

"Madam, we've already heard this information," Hatchet reminded her.

Luty waved her hand impatiently. "I know that, but what we didn't know is the other interestin' bits that Alice told me. Seems like that very afternoon, the local people found a dead man in a pony trap by the side of the road. He was well dressed and had come all the way from Sydney, Australia. He'd only arrived in England the day before

275

and had just come from the train station. He was on his way to the Sutcliffe house, but he never got there. When they questioned John Sutcliffe, he claimed he'd never heard of the man and had no idea why his name and address would be in the fellow's pocket. His name was Eldon Grimshaw. He was an engineer."

"How did he die?" Hatchet asked.

"The doctor said it was a heart attack." Turning back to Mrs. Jeffries, Luty asked, "Has your sister-in-law ever mentioned this?"

"No, not at all, but I'll ask her about it." Mrs. Jeffries frowned. "But I don't see how this incident could have anything to do with Dearman's murder. Eldon Grimshaw was on his way to visit John, not the murder victim." Something nudged the back of her mind, but it was gone as quickly as it had come.

"Maybe." Luty shrugged. "But all the same, seems to me a dead man in a pony cart is worth mentionin'."

"Of course it is, madam," Hatchet said cheerfully.

Luty shot him a disgruntled frown. "I suppose you found out all sorts of interestin' bits."

He grinned. "One does hate to boast, but

I did find out a tasty morsel or two. Constable Barnes told us that when John Sutcliffe was interviewed, he claimed he was on the late afternoon train to Birmingham. But he wasn't. I've an impeccable source that saw him on the nine o'clock train that night. Which means he was in London when Dearman was murdered."

"But he doesn't have a motive for murdering Dearman," Ruth pointed out. "And there could be other reasons he lied about taking a later train."

"He does have a motive for wanting Dearman dead," Mrs. Jeffries said softly. She smiled self-consciously as everyone looked at her. "I'm sorry, I'll wait and take my turn when Hatchet is finished."

"But I am, Mrs. Jeffries," he said quickly. "Sutcliffe being on the later train was the only information of consequence that I heard. Do go ahead."

"Well, my source had several things to tell me." She took a deep breath. "To begin with, I got confirmation of what we suspected: Ronald Dearman was a blackmailer." She told them the details of her discussion with Blimpey, taking care, of course, not to mention Blimpey's name. "So you see, there are any number of people who had a motive for wanting him dead."

"This is goin' to make it bit harder to find the killer," Mrs. Goodge complained. "We're already spread thin on the ground as it is. What's more, we don't have any way of figurin' out how many people he might have had in his clutches." She crossed her arms over her chest and glanced at the clock again.

"Not necessarily," Mrs. Jeffries replied. "Not when you look at it logically. My source said that Dearman literally found his victims by invading their privacy, or as we've already discussed, by snooping. Which implies that he would only have access to people he saw socially or who worked at Sutcliffe's."

"I don't think he'd bother with the accounts clerks and the typewriter girl." Phyllis reached for a currant scone. "They'd not make enough money to be worthwhile victims. But Mr. Anson and Mr. Sutcliffe and the managers at the Sutcliffe plants might be good pickings."

"And those would also be the sort of people he saw socially," the housekeeper murmured.

Ruth nodded in agreement. "That makes sense. People can always find a reason to have a nice hunt around someone else's home at social functions. I've caught several ladies going through the medicine chest in my dressing room and then claiming they didn't want to bother me by asking for a headache powder. So perhaps identifying Dearman's victims won't be that difficult after all."

"Let's hope so," Mrs. Jeffries said fervently. "The other useful information I received is about Henry Anson. He's John Sutcliffe's illegitimate son."

No one said anything for a moment. "Now that's what I call a surprise," Luty finally announced. "Does your sister-in-law know?"

"I don't know." Mrs. Jeffries reached for her teacup. "But if she did and Dearman found out about it, he could use it to blackmail her. She'd do anything to avoid a scandal. What's more, it's put me in a very awkward position. I don't know what to do. If I say something and she doesn't know, it's going to hurt her terribly,"

Everyone stared at her in stunned surprise. Finally, Luty once again broke the now tense silence. "You don't have a choice, Hepzibah, you gotta ask her. It won't be the easiest conversation you've had with the woman, but this could be what she was screamin' at Dearman about."

"And we know that John Sutcliffe lied

about the time he left London," Hatchet added gently.

"But you don't understand." Mrs. Jeffries sighed heavily. "I spoke to Fiona today, and during our conversation, she made it quite clear that she'd rather face the hangman than talk about her argument with Dearman. She claimed it wasn't her secret to tell. So if this is what he had on her, if he threatened to blackmail her, she'll never admit it."

"Did you find out anythin' else from her?" Mrs. Goodge looked at the clock again.

"A little." She told them about the rest of her conversation with Fiona. "So now we know that the Meadows' coming to London had nothing to do with Sutcliffe Manufacturing," she finished.

"I do wish Wiggins would get here," the cook muttered. "It's past five now."

"If everyone else is finished, I'll tell my bit," Phyllis offered. "It's not much, but I had an interesting chat with Mrs. Meadows' housemaid." She told them everything she'd heard from Blanche Keating.

"Good gracious, I'm not surprised someone murdered him," the cook said when Phyllis had finished. "Imagine sneakin' about and lookin' into a dyin' man's sickroom. That's disgustin'."

"I think the fact that the two widow ladies are planning on traveling is interesting," Ruth said thoughtfully. "But then again, perhaps it isn't so very unusual, especially as neither marriage seems to have been a happy one."

Fred suddenly leapt up and raced out of the room. A second later they heard several sharp taps on the back door. Mrs. Jeffries started to rise, but Phyllis waved her back into her chair. "I'll go see who it is."

"Surely it's not Wiggins," Hatchet said. "He'd not bother to knock."

They heard the door open, then the murmur of voices and the clatter of footsteps in the back hall. Phyllis returned, followed by two young lads, both of them rather ragged looking. The taller of the two, a redheaded boy, carried a gray flat cap in his hand.

"This young man has a message for you," Phyllis said to the housekeeper.

Mrs. Jeffries smiled in recognition. "I know you. We spoke on the street yesterday."

"That's right, Mrs. Jeffries, but this time, I'm bringin' a message for you. It's from Mr. Wiggins and he asked us to tell ya not to worry, that's he's on the hunt and he'll be home later tonight."

"Did he say where he was goin'?" Mrs. Goodge demanded.

"Liverpool Street Station," the shorter, dark-haired boy said. "He said he's got to meet a train and then do some followin'. Are you Mrs. Goodge?"

"I am."

"Then he'd like you to kindly keep his dinner in the warmin' oven," the boy replied, "as he'll be hungry as a bear when he gets in."

Mrs. Jeffries was in the foyer when the inspector came home. "You look very tired, sir," she said as she reached for his heavy overcoat and hung it on the peg.

"I am." He handed her his bowler. "Playing catch-up on a murder case is very time consuming. We've been all over London and I'm exhausted."

"Of course you are, sir." She hung his hat on the next coat tree peg. "But dinner won't be for another fifteen minutes. Would you like to have a sherry and relax?"

"Only if you'll have one with me," he replied.

A few moments later they were settled in their respective spots in the drawing room, sipping Harvey's Bristol Cream. Witherspoon put his glass down on the table. "It was such a busy day, and then to top it off, I had to go back to the station to read

Nivens' reports."

"Did you see the postmortem report?"

He nodded. "The doctor is of the opinion from the size of the bullet hole that the gun used in the murder is a small one, possibly a derringer or perhaps even an Enfield. But small or not, the shot was fatal and the victim died quickly." He reached for his glass and took a sip. "But according to all of the witnesses we've spoken to thus far, no one heard the shot."

"That's a very busy part of London, sir," she reminded him. "Nonetheless, a gunshot, even from a small weapon, is such a distinctive sound that I'm surprised that no one heard it. Surely there were people on the street and perhaps even some still in the building."

"There were," he agreed. "According to Nivens' report, there were clerks working late in an office on the top floor, but the constables that interviewed them wrote that they'd heard nothing. I didn't have a chance to speak to them myself, but I'm going to as soon as possible."

"You can't do everything on the first day, sir."

"No, and we didn't get there till late in the morning. We started off with a visit to the victim's home, and Mrs. Dearman was rather put out that she had to be interviewed again. She wasn't overly cooperative."

"Was she trying to hide something, sir?"

"I don't think so," he replied as he shook his head. "She simply seemed to be busy and didn't wish to be bothered with having to speak to the police. The vicar was coming to go over the funeral details. Her friend, Mrs. Meadows. was present and refused to leave, so I've decided to wait until after the service to interview Mrs. Dearman again."

"Will you be interviewing Mrs. Meadows as well?" Mrs. Jeffries asked.

"Of course, she was part of the victim's circle of friends." He grinned. "I think Mrs. Meadows' high-handed attitude annoyed Constable Barnes. Just as we were leaving, he suddenly asked her where she had been between six and seven on the evening of the murder. It was obvious the question annoyed her, but to her credit, she answered and told us she was home. Mrs. Dearman was a bit miffed at the constable as well."

"Constable Barnes doesn't like people to take advantage of your good nature, sir. Did anything else transpire when you were there?"

He told her about the rest of his interview with the widow. "But as I said, we didn't stay very long. After that, we went to the

Sutcliffe offices and had a word with the staff. I spoke with both John Sutcliffe and Henry Anson. That was quite interesting. Anson admitted there was a great deal of tension between himself and the victim."

Mrs. Jeffries forced herself to listen, but it was difficult. She kept wondering what Wiggins was doing. When Witherspoon finished speaking, she said, "Anson told you that when he was hired, he'd been given the definite impression that Dearman was getting the sack?"

"Absolutely." Witherspoon drank the rest of his sherry. "But when we spoke to Mr. Sutcliffe, he most certainly didn't confirm anything of the sort."

"What did he say?"

"He claimed that Henry Anson had been unduly sensitive about the matter and that as he'd not cut Dearman's salary, he'd accepted the loss of responsibility. He said he put Anson in charge of the plant operations because the company had grown so much they needed someone well educated handling the job and that he wanted to ease Dearman toward retirement. Dearman's performance was still acceptable, but he was starting to show his age, you know, a bit of memory loss, that sort of thing. Sutcliffe claims he never considered sacking him."

Mrs. Jeffries wished she could just tell the inspector what she knew about Anson and Sutcliffe's relationship. But that was impossible. The only thing to do would be to tell Constable Barnes and leave it up to him. "Are you going to confirm the time Henry Anson arrived at his fiancée's home? Oh dear, don't answer that, how silly of me to even ask such a question." She laughed self-consciously. "Of course you are. It's standard procedure."

He smiled indulgently. "We'll be having a word with his fiancée, Miss Throckmorton, tomorrow. Apparently, I'm going to have another very busy day. But that wasn't all that happened. I had the most interesting interview with the typewriter girl. You've heard of them, haven't you?"

"Yes, sir, I have. They're becoming increasingly common."

He nodded. "She was a very nice young lady, but she had no love for Ronald Dearman." He told her about his interview with Anna Blackburn.

Mrs. Jeffries only half listened as she tried to sort out who Wiggins was meeting at Liverpool Street Station and why he would think it necessary to follow them.

"The letter she'd typed for him was to a law firm in Sydney, about an estate for a

Mr. . . . Hinshaw, no, no, that's not it," Witherspoon said. "It was Grimshaw. Eldon Grimshaw."

That got Mrs. Jeffries' attention. "The typewriter girl prepared a letter to Australia?" she asked.

"She did, even though it was against company rules. Then, apparently, two days after he'd forced her to do his private correspondence, Dearman tried to sack her," he repeated, and this time, Mrs. Jeffries listened very carefully. "This young woman was lucky that Mr. Anson intervened on her behalf. Another employee from the accounts department, a young man named James Tremlett, was sacked ten days or so before the murder."

"I take it you'll be having a word with him?" She certainly hoped so; that way, Tremlett could tell Witherspoon about Dearman's hallway assignation with a mysterious stranger.

"Indeed. He's on my list of interviews for tomorrow." He glanced at his glass and noted that it was empty. "Do we have time for another one?"

"Of course, sir." She was already getting to her feet. She poured them both another sherry and took her seat again. "I'm glad you're on the case, sir. I have to admit, even though Fiona and I have been estranged for years, I was a bit alarmed when I found out that Inspector Nivens was in charge of the investigation."

"And you were right to be concerned." His good humor suddenly vanished. "One does hate to complain, but I must say, when I looked over Nivens' reports, I was somewhat appalled at the manner in which the initial investigation had been conducted. Nivens hadn't even bothered to have a constable interview Miss Blackburn. He'd decided they didn't need her statement because she was a woman. Can you believe that?"

"Actually, sir, I can."

"It is very important that anyone involved in the crime scene area be interviewed as soon as possible. The more time that passes, the harder it is to catch the culprit. Furthermore, I suspect the reason no one heard the fatal shot is because Nivens didn't send out enough constables to do the job properly. He didn't bother to get the names of the day laborers who'd come in for their pay packets from the office upstairs. One of them might have heard something. Nor did he send anyone to check for witnesses in the pub across the road or the surrounding buildings. That's the least he could have done, and what's more, it is standard procedure in all homicide investigations."

"I'm sure you'll rectify the situation, sir." She ducked her head to hide her amusement. It was rare for Witherspoon to criticize a fellow officer.

He sighed dramatically. "I suppose I shouldn't complain. Perhaps Inspector Nivens simply ran out of time."

She wasn't having that. "No, sir, I think you're right. Inspector Nivens simply isn't experienced enough to handle murder cases."

"You've had us worried," Mrs. Goodge chided as she put a huge plate of stew in front of Wiggins. "Now eat up, lad, you must be half starved."

"I'm sorry, Mrs. Goodge," Wiggins replied. "Especially as it all turned out to be a tempest in a teapot. But I was so sure she was up to somethin'. I just 'ad a feelin' about it." He picked up the spoon and tucked into the fragrant bowl of food.

"Don't apologize, Wiggins," Mrs. Jeffries said gently. "You did the right thing. Always trust your instincts."

The cook grabbed a loaf of bread and began cutting thick slices. "From what that maid told you, you had good reason to wonder about the widow Dearman. But what were you hopin' to see?"

"Dearman's travelin' bag," he said. "But the only thing the footman carried was a small trunk and a suitcase. I think the maid was right. Mrs. Dearman was probably lookin' for an old suit to bury him in. I followed her and the footman back to the house and watched him take it inside. I peeked in the window and everythin', but all I could see was them both goin' upstairs."

"The other servants weren't there?" Mrs. Jeffries asked.

"Nope." He nodded his thanks as the cook put a plate piled high with bread slices next to the stew. "Didn't see 'ide nor 'air of any of 'em. I waited a few minutes, and then I 'eard 'em comin' back down, so I 'ad to scarper. The footman come out right after and went 'ome, and not more than ten minutes later, all the downstairs lamps went out. Cor blimey, but it was a waste of my time."

"Do you think the maid was telling the truth?" Mrs. Jeffries asked curiously. "About the traveling bag and seeing Dearman putting money in it?"

"She'd no reason to lie," he pointed out. He reached for the butter pot.

"I think she was." Mrs. Goodge sat down next to Wiggins. "Dearman was a blackmailer. He had to keep his money somewhere. He probably used his little cottage as a nice hidin' spot. The bag could have been in the trunk the footman was carryin'."

"But we don't know that Lucretia Dearman knew of her husband's illicit business," Mrs. Jeffries protested. "And even if she did, that doesn't mean she murdered him to steal his ill-gotten gains."

The house was quiet as Mrs. Jeffries came down to the kitchen early the next morning. She hadn't slept well and finally had given up trying. Samson, Mrs. Goodge's ginger-colored tabby cat, was on his stool by the pine sideboard, washing his paws. He paused and gave her a malevolent glare. On one of their earlier cases, Wiggins had rescued the animal and he'd not been in the least bit grateful. He hated everyone save for Mrs. Goodge, whom he adored and who adored him. Mrs. Jeffries gave him a wide berth as she walked past and put her hand lantern down on the kitchen table. She'd not wanted to go to the trouble of lighting the gas lamps.

Pulling out her chair, she sat down and stared across the darkened room, letting her eyes adjust to the dimness as she gazed at the window over the sink. She let her mind wander as it would. Both Phyllis' and Wiggins' sources had said that Lucretia Dearman wasn't brokenhearted over losing her husband, but you could say the same of half the women in London, so that didn't necessarily mean she'd murdered him. On the other hand, she hadn't raised the alarm when he didn't come home, but then again, that could be explained. She and Dearman had separate rooms, and apparently it wasn't her habit to lie awake worrying about him until he was safely home.

Mrs. Jeffries blinked to refocus her eyes. Outside, a hansom cab went past, and she was vaguely aware of the jingle of the harness and the rattling of the wheels. Dearman was a blackmailer, and that was most likely the motive for his murder. As David used to say, the simplest solution was usually the correct solution. One of Dearman's victims had finally had enough. But she couldn't operate on that assumption alone; if they'd learned he was a blackmailer, the killer could have also found it out. Someone who wanted him dead would have realized that once the police found out about his illicit activities, they'd not look beyond that.

They'd assume the killer was one of his victims.

She sighed, got up, and grabbed the kettle. An image of David's face flashed through her mind and tears welled up in her eyes. It seemed disloyal to his memory to think that his sister might be capable of murder. But facts were facts. No matter how hard she looked at the situation, no matter what information they uncovered, more and more the signs of guilt pointed to Fiona. She'd do anything to protect her husband and her position in the community. Mrs. Jeffries brushed the sudden tears off her cheeks and went to the sink.

She stood at there and stared out the window into the darkened night. Again, she saw David's image, but this time it was his ravaged face as he sat drinking the evening he came back from meeting his sister after she'd become engaged.

Mrs. Jeffries forced herself to think back, to try to recall the details of that awful night. It had been one of the worst in their marriage, and she'd deliberately pushed it away, but now she had the feeling that there was something important he'd said, something that might help sort out this mess. She knew it was there. But for the life of her, she couldn't remember what it was.

CHAPTER 9

"You're up bright and early this morning," Mrs. Goodge said as she shuffled into the room. "It's not light out yet."

Mrs. Jeffries poured a second cup of tea from the pot she'd just put on the table and handed it to the cook. "I couldn't sleep and I finally got tired of tossing and turning, so I got up."

"Come to any conclusions?"

"One."

"What would that be?" The cook blew gently on the surface of her tea to cool it down.

"I'm behaving like an idiot," she said. "I've worried so much about whether or not Fiona is guilty that it's all I can think about. I even had a nice little crying jag earlier, and I've not done that in years."

"You're not an idiot, you're just tryin' to defend your family, and though you don't much like her, Fiona Sutcliffe is family. Of course you'd be overly worried, anyone would, so stop bein' so hard on yourself."

"Thank you." Mrs. Jeffries reached across the table and patted her on the hand. "You're a good friend, and you've made me feel much better."

"You're a good friend as well, Hepzibah, and I've faith in you. I've faith in all of us."

"So do I." She smiled self-consciously. "Last night, or early this morning, I should say, I made myself face my demons. I realized that what was really scaring me wasn't whether we could solve Dearman's murder, it was that deep inside, I knew that Fiona is quite capable of murder. I was terrified that I'd betray my husband's memory if my efforts sent his sister to the gallows."

"And that made you feel better?"

Mrs. Jeffries laughed. "Yes, oddly enough it did. The moment I faced that fear, I suddenly realized that I was foolish. The best way to help Fiona is for us to figure out who killed Ronald Dearman."

"You don't think she's guilty?" Mrs. Goodge asked.

"I don't. As I said, she's capable of it, but then again, so are most of us. The evidence is pointing at her, but there's something else in the picture, something I'm not seeing with my rational mind."

"Then stop thinkin' about it," she suggested. "Just let your mind wander where it will and see what you come up with. You do your best thinkin' when you've got some nice dull chore to do, so why don't you polish the silver. That's not been done in ages. Dearman's funeral is today, so I don't think we'll have much luck learnin' anythin'. Everyone involved in the case will be at his service."

"Excellent sug—" She broke off as someone pounded frantically on the back door. Alarmed, she looked at the cook and then got up, Mrs. Goodge shoved back in her chair and go to her feet. "Let me get Wiggins. We don't know who's out there."

The pounding came again, louder.

"We've no time for that." She took off for the back of the house. "I'll be careful. I'll ask who it is."

Mrs. Goodge whirled toward the cooker and grabbed the cast-iron skillet. "Wait for me." She hurried after her.

Mrs. Jeffries threw the bolt at the top of the door, grabbed the key from the hook on the wall, and inserted it into the lock. The knock came again. "Who is there?"

"It's me," a woman's voice said.

Mrs. Goodge, breathing heavily, came up behind the housekeeper and lifted the frying pan over her head in a defensive stance. "Go ahead and open it, I'm ready."

"Do be careful, I'm in the line of fire," Mrs. Jeffries said as she twisted the key and pulled open the door a crack. "Fiona? What on earth are you doing here at this time of day?"

The cook lowered her weapon and leaned back against the wall for support.

"Can I come in, please? I must talk to you," Fiona said. "It's urgent."

The housekeeper stepped back and waved her in. "You'll have to hurry. The inspector will be up soon and he mustn't find you here."

"Constable Barnes comes early as well," Mrs. Goodge hissed softly as their unwelcome guest stepped inside.

All three of them moved quietly as they went into the kitchen. Mrs. Goodge went to the pine sideboard and got down another mug. Mrs. Jeffries pointed at the empty spot next to her as she took her seat. "Sit down and tell me what this is all about, Fiona."

She pulled out her chair and glanced at the cook, her expression uncertain.

"This is Mrs. Goodge," the housekeeper said quickly, "and you can speak freely in front of her. She's as much a part of this as I am."

"Forgive me, Mrs. Goodge, I didn't mean to be rude, and I'm very pleased to make your acquaintance." Fiona eased into her chair. "I'm Fiona Sutcliffe."

"Nice to meet you, ma'am. No offense was taken. Let me pour you some tea; you look half frozen." She served their unwelcome guest and then took her place on the other side of the table.

Fiona looked down at the top of her cup. "I'm sorry to have barged in like this," she murmured. "I was going to wait until later, but then I saw the lights on down here and I need to get back, so I thought it best to come in before someone saw me in the garden and wondered what I was doing there."

"Fiona," Mrs. Jeffries said sharply. "Stop nattering on and tell us what you're doing here. What has happened? We've not much time. Constable Barnes will be here soon."

She looked up, her face ravaged with fear. "Alright, I'm sorry. I'll get to the reason I've come. The gun is gone."

"What do you mean, it's gone?" Mrs. Jeffries demanded. "Don't you keep it locked up?"

Fiona shook her head. "No, there was no reason to do so. We've no children in the house, and John wanted me to be able to get to it quickly. It was kept in the back of a drawer."

"Was it loaded?" Mrs. Goodge asked.

"Yes, I've a bit of arthritis in my right hand, which made handling the bullets difficult," she explained. "So we left it loaded."

"When did you discover this?"

"Last night. I kept remembering that you'd asked me about it when I saw you. I told myself not to be foolish, that it was still there, but I couldn't stop thinking about it. So I looked and it was gone." She gave a short, hard sob. "Oh my God, Hepzibah, what am I going to do? The police know I threatened Ronald, and once they find out the gun is gone, I'll be arrested."

Mrs. Jeffries' mind worked furiously, trying to come up with a solution that didn't involve lying to Witherspoon but that would keep her sister-in-law out of jail. But before she could gather her thoughts, Mrs. Goodge said, "That's not necessarily true. Does anyone else know where the gun was kept?"

Fiona finally looked up, her expression hopeful. "Yes, several people knew about it."

"Who?" Mrs. Jeffries asked.

She put a hand on each side of her head. "Just a moment, let me think. The servants knew, of course. John gave them all strict

instructions about it. He didn't want someone accidentally shooting themselves."

"Anyone else?" Mrs. Jeffries pressed. She
didn't think it likely that one of the Sutcliffe
staff had taken the weapon. "Anyone from
amongst your social acquaintances or the
company?"

"Maybe Ronald Dearman stole it," Mrs.
Goodge blurted. "He was always snoopin'
in drawers."

"He did know about it," Fiona replied.
"And so did Henry Anson and his fiancée,
Amy Throckmorton. John showed it to
them. It was just a few months ago, after
Henry got engaged. The Dearmans were
there, too, and Antonia Meadows. That's
right, it's all coming back to me now. It was
just after Thaddeus Meadows died, and
Miss Throckmorton asked Antonia if she
was frightened about living without a man
on the premises." She took a sip of tea. "I
can't recall exactly what Antonia replied,
but it was something to the effect that she
was nervous now that she was a widow. John
said she ought to get a gun and keep it by
her bedside."

"When did he show it to them?" The cook
glanced at the clock and grimaced.

"After we'd finished luncheon, John took
everyone up to his sitting room and showed

them the gun. He told Antonia that now that she was alone, she ought to get one for protection. Miss Throckmorton asked if there were bullets in it. John said that we always kept it loaded, and everyone stepped back. It was a bit comical and everyone laughed. Then Antonia said she didn't know how to shoot, and John said it was easy, that he'd taught me."

"So five people outside of your household knew where the gun was kept and that it was ready to use," the housekeeper muttered. "And all of those very same people were at your house last Saturday night."

"Which means that any of them could have stolen the gun." Fiona's shoulders sagged in relief.

"Was his desk locked?" Mrs. Goodge asked.

"Yes, but he kept the key on a hook just inside the bookcase. All of us saw him take it down and unlock the desk. I'm so glad I came here. I haven't slept all night." She looked at Mrs. Jeffries. "What should I do now?"

"You'll have to tell the police. But I expect it can wait until after Dearman's funeral." She knew she ought to ask Fiona if she knew about her husband's illegitmate son, but she simply couldn't do it. Not now. She'd wait until they were alone.

"What, you mean she come here in the middle of the night?" Wiggins exclaimed. They were at their morning meeting.

"It wasn't the middle of the night, it was just early this morning," the cook replied. "The poor woman was beside herself when she got here. But she felt much better after she'd told us about the gun. Mind you, we did have to chuck her out the front door right quick when we heard Constable Barnes comin' in the back."

"You didn't want him to see her here?" Ruth asked curiously. "But why not, if you think she's innocent?"

"We didn't want to put him in an awkward position," Mrs. Jeffries explained. "I know he helps us, but reading a few reports is one thing. Asking him to withhold evidence about the gun is something else. Besides, I think I know where that gun might be. But I'm getting ahead of myself. Constable Barnes told us a few things this morning. Dearman's office keys weren't on the evidence list nor have they been found anywhere on either the Sutcliffe premises or the surrounding area."

"So the killer likely took 'em," Luty muttered.

"Which means they are probably at the bottom of the Thames," Hatchet finished.

"Today is Dearman's funeral service and reception." Mrs. Jeffries looked at Wiggins. "And I'm going to ask you to do something, and if you would prefer not to do it, you must say so."

"Is it dangerous?" the cook demanded. In all the excitement of hustling Fiona out the front door while Constable Barnes had come in the back, they'd not had time for discussing plans, and she didn't want Wiggins put at risk.

"No, it's not dangerous, but it might be awkward for him if someone were to see him," she said. "Don't worry, Mrs. Goodge, I'd never put him in harm's way."

"What do you want me to do?" Wiggins asked eagerly.

"You'll need to go to Essex, to Ronald Dearman's old cottage."

He stared at her in confusion. "But we don't even know the name of the village, let alone the address."

"Yes we do," Mrs. Goodge said. "That's the other thing that Constable Barnes told us today. It's in Roxwell. It's called End Cottage, and it's the last place on the far side of the footbridge."

Wiggins nodded. "Right then, we already know it's run-down and uninhabited, so it should be easy to find." He looked at Mrs. Jeffries. "What do I do when I get there?"

She winced slightly. "See if you can get inside, and if you can, search the place."

"What am I lookin' for?" He got to his feet.

"The gun that killed Ronald Dearman."

"We'd best be going, sir, if we're going to get to the funeral service," Barnes said to Witherspoon.

The inspector shoved his chair away from the desk and started to rise. There was a short, sharp knock on the door, and a second later, a young constable entered. "We've just had this letter delivered for you, sir." The constable handed him an envelope. "A street lad brought it in and laid it on the front desk."

Witherspoon opened it and pulled out a piece of folded, plain white notepaper. He frowned as he read it.

"What is it, sir?" Barnes asked. The other constable, curious as well, hovered by the door.

"It says, *'If you want to find the key to the Dearman murder, have a good look around*

Fiona Sutcliffe's morning room.' Good gracious, this is most unusual." He looked at the constable. "You say it was a street lad?" he asked.

"It was, sir," the constable replied. "But not one of the regulars from the area. Both Sergeant Beckman and I were in the front when the lad came in, but neither of us recognized him, and we know most of the boys that work this patch. He walked up, slapped it on the counter, and left."

"When did it arrive?" Barnes asked.

"Just a few moments ago. I brought it right in when I saw that it was for the inspector." Curiosity satisfied, the constable nodded politely and went back out front.

Barnes pulled out his pocket watch and frowned. "If we're going to make the service, we'll have to hurry. Even if we take a hansom, it's a bit of a drive to St. Mary Abbots."

Witherspoon nodded, yanked open the deep bottom drawer, and stacked Nivens' reports inside. He slammed it shut and grabbed his coat off the back of the chair. "Right, let's be off, then, but right after the service and the reception, we'll go to the Sutcliffe house."

"You're taking the note seriously." Barnes reached for the door and pulled it open.

"You think there's something to it?"

"Someone bothered to send it and to hire a street boy to deliver it." He went through the door and into the hall. "It wouldn't be the first time an anonymous note or tip led us to the culprit."

It was almost noon by the time Wiggins arrived in Roxwell. He'd taken the train to Chelmsford and from there, hired a dog cart for the last four miles into the village. Once there, it took another twenty minutes before he'd found Dearman's cottage; he'd not wanted to draw attention to himself by asking at any of the local spots where the place might be.

He stood outside and looked around. A light misty rain had started, so there wasn't any foot traffic either on the bridge or farther up by the inn. He opened the gate and went inside. The property was surrounded by a tall, unkempt hedge that shielded him from prying eyes, but nonetheless, he hurried up the pathway, stumbling where the stones were missing, to the front door. The cottage was a single-story square building that had once been white but hadn't been painted in so long it was now a patchy, ugly gray color. One narrow window overlooked the front. Wiggins tried the door handle. It didn't budge. He looked at the window and realized he couldn't get in that way. Glancing over his shoulder, he hurried around to the back, passing a tiny flower bed, which was barren save for the muddy brown remains of last year's weeds.

The rear was nothing more than a small courtyard with a fringe of lawn surrounded by unkempt hedges. The cobblestones had once been red but were now faded, dirty, and cracked. An old iron heating stove and stack of firewood rested against the back wall. Wiggins scanned the property, looking for a way inside. There was no back door, just a slightly larger window than the one in the front. He walked over and studied the frame. It was a simple sash window, so he wedged his fingertips into the groove and tried lifting; the window moved enough for him to slip his hands farther in, allowing him to increase the pressure and edge the window upward inch by inch. It took ten minutes to get it open far enough for him to get inside, and he accomplished that feat only by pulling the heating stove over and climbing on it to give himself enough leverage.

Panting from the exertion, he stood and surveyed the small cottage. The inside was just as miserable as the outside. A faded green oval rug covered the scarred wooden floor, the once white walls were a dirty gray, and the bits and pieces of furniture were either deeply soiled or missing their cushions entirely. There was a door next to the fireplace, so he went toward it. It opened easily enough. The room beyond contained a single bed with a rusted metal frame and a tall wardrobe with two long, flat drawers at the bottom and double mirrored doors. The doors were wide open.

Wiggins knew the widow had already been to the cottage, but she'd looked to him like a lady who didn't want to get her hands dirty. A bit of grime and a few cobwebs didn't scare him, though. If there was a gun here, he was blooming well going to find it. He walked over the wardrobe, dropped to his knees, and pulled out the lower drawer.

Mrs. Jeffries had taken the silver upstairs to the dining room so that Mrs. Goodge could entertain her sources in the privacy of the kitchen. Phyllis declared she was going to the Meadows' neighborhood to see if she could pick up something useful there, Luty was going to have another go at prying financial information from her sources in the city, Hatchet wouldn't say what he was up to, and Ruth had gone to a committee meeting for one of her women's rights groups.

She hummed softly as she pulled out her chair and wondered whether she ought to have told the others that they needn't bother to go out at all. Once Wiggins got back from Roxwell, she'd have the last piece of the puzzle neatly in place. But she'd held her tongue. She'd not wanted to spoil their enthusiasm, and there was always the chance one of them might come across some additional worthwhile information. She took her seat and set to work. Everything she needed was spread out on the side of the table so she could sit facing the window. She reached for the knives, plucked the batch out of the case, and fanned them out on the old tablecloth she'd put down to cover the wood. She grabbed her polishing rag, dipped it in the open tin, and picked up the heavy utensil.

She stroked the paste on evenly and efficiently while at the same time thinking about the case. She hoped that Wiggins didn't run into any problems getting into the cottage, but he was a clever lad and would back away from the situation if it appeared that there was even the slightest chance he'd be caught. Having to explain why the footman had been caught breaking into an empty cottage would be embarrassing, to say the least. She cringed slightly at the thought that what she'd asked him to do was illegal, but honestly, there was no other way. The only way to prove the identity of the culprit was to find that gun. She'd told Wiggins to make sure it was at the cottage and then come home immediately.

She put the rag down on the stack of newspapers she'd brought up, grabbed the cotton polishing cloth, and rubbed furiously at the paste. She held up the knife and smiled as she saw her face reflected in the silver.

She started actin' strange, sellin' off all the master's things, you know, his watch, his desk, cuff links, and even his clothes . . . Now why on earth did that pop into my head? Mrs. Jeffries asked herself. It took her a moment to remember that the words had been spoken by Phyllis at their afternoon meeting a couple of days ago when she'd repeated what she'd heard from the Meadows' housemaid. She shook herself and picked up another knife and snatched up the polishing rag. This time, she wasn't quite as efficient as she slathered the paste over the surface. What on earth was wrong with her? She wasn't going to begin having doubts now; she was certain she was right. *Seems to me a dead body in a pony cart is worth mentionin'.*

She went still. What was happening to her? Once she was sure of the killer's identity, the pieces always fell right into place. She'd figured it out and it had all worked together into a nice, neat pattern that fit the facts. She dropped the rag, snatched up the polishing cloth, and mindlessly began rubbing. *It's about Henry Anson. He's John Sutcliffe's illegitimate son.* Blimpey's words echoed in her head, but before she could understand what her inner mind was trying to tell her, another phrase flew into her head and the inspector's voice was clear as a bell. *The letter she'd typed for him was to a law firm in Sydney . . . Apparently, two days after he'd forced her to do his private correspondence, he tried to sack her.*

Mrs. Jeffries finished her task and put the polished utensils back into the case. She got up and went to the window. "I was so sure I was right," she murmured to her reflection. She stared at the cold, gray day. She stood there for a long time and then cried out softly as she heard the voice of her long dead love. From down below came the sound of the back door slamming as someone either went out or came in. She went to the table and began tidying up. The silver could wait a bit longer; she'd finally remembered what David had told her on that night long ago.

"Surely you're jesting, Inspector." John Sutcliffe stared at Witherspoon and Barnes with an expression of disbelief on his face. Fiona Sutcliffe, still wearing her dark gray cloak and black hat, stood by his side. "We've just come from my brother-in-law's funeral reception. Can't this wait until tomorrow?"

They four of them were standing in the foyer of the Sutcliffe home. The two policemen had followed Fiona and John Sutcliffe inside the moment they got out of the hansom.

"I'm sorry, sir, but as I said, we've received information that evidence pertaining to Mr. Dearman's murder is in your wife's morning room. You are within your rights to refuse to allow us to search —"

"Let them do it, John." Fiona clasped her husband's arm. "We've nothing to hide, and I want this wretched business behind us. The sooner they search, the sooner they'll be out of here."

"Fiona, dear, surely it can wait. We've just buried my sister's husband. We're in mourning, and that needs to be respected."

"The best way to respect Ronald is to find his killer." She smiled at him. "Why don't you go back to Lucretia's. I'm sure she'd like your company. I'll stay here with these gentlemen."

"No, I'm not having that. I'll stay as well." He glared at the two policemen. "Lucretia doesn't need me. Antonia is staying with her for the next few days. I'll not leave you alone while our home is ransacked."

"I assure you, sir, we'll be very careful," Witherspoon said.

Sutcliffe nodded sullenly and strode down the corridor. "Follow me," he ordered. He led them to a door at the end, opened it, and stepped back so they could enter. "If you don't mind, I'll stand right here."

"That is your right, sir," Witherspoon said as he went past him into the room.

Barnes didn't have to ask where to start the search. He headed straight for the rose and green striped sofa while the inspector went to secretary in the corner. He looked at Sutcliffe. "May I open this?"

"I've already given permission for you to search," he snapped. "So get on with it, man."

Witherspoon noticed that Fiona Sutcliffe had now joined him. Trying to ignore the watching eyes, he opened the top panel

313

gently, taking care not to put undue pressure on the hinges. Inside, three rows of small cubbyholes ran the length of the wood. On the base below was an ink pot, a sheaf of cream-colored writing paper, and a small straw basket filled with cards, notes, and letters.

At the sofa, Barnes lifted the satin bolster tucked into the arm and ran his fingers along the bottom rim of the upholstery, then gently pulled the sofa out from the corner and scanned the floor. He did the same to the rest of the piece and then turned his attention to the pink velvet tufted formal armchair by the secretary. By this time Witherspoon had finished with the desk and moved to the small marble mantelpiece. He took care to avoid bumping the fire screen, a tall contraption with an elaborate black metal frame. A carved wooden table box with a lid of entwined birds held pride of place in the center. He wedged in closer and lifted the lid. Inside was silver key ring holding two keys. "Are these your keys, ma'am?" He picked them up and held them out toward the Sutcliffes.

She shoved past her husband, her expression confused as she crossed the room. "No, I've never seen them before. I've no idea who they belong to," she told Witherspoon.

"Is it possible one of your servants found them and put them here?" He nodded at the mantelpiece.

"No, the servants would have taken anything they found to our housekeeper," she said.

The inspector noticed that Fiona Sutcliffe had gone pale. He suspected he knew why. He was fairly certain he knew who owned the keys.

"Let me have a look." Sutcliffe came up behind his wife and took the keys. He recognized them instantly. "For God's sake, what on earth are these doing here?" he exclaimed.

"You know who they belong to?" Witherspoon asked.

"Why of course, these are Ronald's keys . . ." His voice trailed off as he realized what he'd said. "Oh my God." He stared at the two policemen. "You can't possibly think that either of us murdered Ronald."

"Do you have any idea as to how his keys got here?" Barnes asked.

"Obviously, someone put them here," Sutcliffe snapped. "I know what you must be thinking, but I assure you, we've had dozens of people in and out of here since Ronald was murdered. Any of them could have put them here." He handed them back to Witherspoon.

"Mr. Sutcliffe, do you own a gun?" Barnes asked.

"Wiggins, you're back, thank goodness. We were starting to get worried," Mrs. Jeffries exclaimed. "Gracious, what's wrong? You look so glum."

"You're goin' to be disappointed, Mrs. Jeffries. I searched every bloomin' inch of that cottage, and I didn't find the gun," he admitted. He took off his cap and jacket, hung it on the coat tree, and joined the others at the table.

"You found nothing?" Mrs. Goodge asked.

"I found somethin', but I'm not sure what it means." He pulled a little brown notebook, a duplicate of the one that Constable Barnes used, out of his pocket and flipped it open. "I found two lap desks under the floorboards in the bedroom; one of them was just a plain wooden box, but the other would 'ave been right nice if it'd been cleaned up a bit. It 'ad a picture of a butterfly painted on the top. The plain one was locked up tight, but I pried it open with an old knife I found in the kitchen. It didn't 'ave anythin' in it but another old box."

"Another lap desk?" Phyllis asked.

He shook his head and nodded his thanks

as Mrs. Goodge handed him a cup of tea. "No, it was a fancy little carryin' box. It was lined with red cloth and had the name 'Grimshaw' etched along the top."

"Grimshaw," Mrs. Jeffries repeated.

"That's right." He took a quick sip of his tea.

"What was in the other box?" Hatchet asked.

"That one wasn't locked, so it were right easy to open. It 'ad a ledger book, but not a big one like they 'ave in offices. It was smaller, about the size of a half sheet of paper. I think it was Dearman's accounts book for his blackmailin' business, but I can't be sure. All it 'ad was first names listed in one column and then a number listed in the next column and then an amount in the last column. I thought about it as I come 'ome on the train, and I think he was usin' a code of some sort just in case someone found it."

"That sounds logical," Ruth said.

"Was that the only thing in the box?" Phyllis asked.

"Nah, there was lots of little bits; there were two letters addressed to John Sutcliffe — they were both from a Mrs. G. Anson." He shrugged in embarrassment and looked back down at his notes. "The first one was

317

dated June 1 of last year, tellin' him he had a son, and the second one was dated July 7 and it was askin' him to give the boy, Henry, a position." He paused and took a breath.

Mrs. Goodge handed him a plate with a buttered scone. "Go on," she ordered. "Tell us the rest."

"The box also had a full bottle of laudanum and a sealed bottle of quinine grains. Both bottles 'ad 'Meadows' written in pencil on the label and were dated July 10 of this past year. There was also a yellow scarf with the initials 'E. L.,' and a set of love letters between a Donald and a Eugenia."

"No last names on the letters?" Luty asked.

He shook his head and helped himself to the scone. "Sorry I wasn't able to find the gun, but I looked everywhere and it just weren't there."

"That's because it isn't there," Mrs. Jeffries said. "I thought I knew who committed this murder, but I was wrong. There's something else going on, something that is right under my nose, but I'm just not seeing it and I'm not sure what to do next."

"Don't be so hard on yourself," Ruth said. "There's still time for everything to fall into place."

"That's just it," she cried. "I've got a terrible feeling that we're running out of time, that I'm not seeing the forest for the trees. Oh, I don't know what I mean! Having a family member, even one that I'm not particularly fond of, facing the hangman has ruined my ability to think clearly. One moment I'm certain I understand who the clues point to, and the next, I realize I've been dead wrong. Everything seems to be all jumbled together, both the past and the present, and I'm at my wit's end."

There was a short, shocked silence. Fred lifted his head and stared at her with a puzzled expression, and even Samson, who was perched on his stool, stopped licking his paw and stared at the humans.

"No, you're not," Mrs. Goodge said firmly. "You're just worried, but there is nothing wrong with your thinkin' abilities. Fiona Sutcliffe hasn't been arrested yet, and if you're sure she didn't do it, we need to get on with our meetin' so that we can keep it from happenin' to her."

Mrs. Jeffries exhaled heavily and then straightened her spine. For a split second, she felt foolish, embarrassed to have succumbed to panic. "You're right, of course. Now, who would like to go next?"

"I will," Phyllis chimed in. "I went to the

Meadows house. With the mistress gone to the funeral, I thought that Blanche Keating would nip out for a bit of time to herself and I was right." She didn't mention that she'd waited for the maid in the pub. "Blanche didn't have much to say, mostly she just went on and on about how scared she was of losing her position. I know I told you that before, but she seemed more sure that it was going to happen. She said Mrs. Meadows had already started spending all her time with Lucretia Dearman. She had Blanche bring down the small trunk from the attic, packed it up, and left for the Dearman house yesterday."

"Didn't she tell her staff when she'd return?" Ruth asked.

"She just said she'd be back in a few days, but you don't need a trunk, even a small one, if you're only going to be gone a short time."

"If I was the maid, I would start lookin' for a new job," Wiggins said.

"Blanche also told me that the only time Ronald Dearman ever accompanied his wife to the Meadows house was the day the poor man was dying."

"Ronald Dearman visited Thaddeus Meadows as he lay dying?" Mrs. Jeffries clarified. Laudanum and quinine were both

320

in Dearman's hidden box. Why? What could two bottles of old medicine prove to a black-mailer?

"The very same day he passed away," she replied.

"If you're done, I'll go next," Luty said to the maid. She waited for Phyllis to nod and then plunged right in. "My day wasn't as excitin' as Wiggins', but I found out a little somethin' about Henry Anson and Antonia Meadows." She grinned. "One of my sources told me that Antonia Meadows inherited her late husband's shares in Sutcliffe Manufacturin', the house, his income, and a nice-sized life insurance policy."

"How much was the policy?" Mrs. Jeffries asked.

"The biggest there is," Luty grinned. "Ten thousand pounds."

Once again, Mrs. Jeffries felt a tug at the back of her mind, but like the other ideas that had flashed there recently, she couldn't grab the wretched little beast and make it tell her what it all meant. "What about Henry Anson?"

"He's going to inherit plenty, too," Luty said. "But not until both the Sutcliffes are dead. My source told me that once Fiona Sutcliffe is gone, Henry Anson is going to be the sole heir."

"Good gracious, madam, how did you find that out?" Hatchet demanded.

"I'm not revealin' my sources," she said indignantly. "I didn't stick a gun to anyone's head and make 'em talk." Instead, she'd stuck a wad of pound notes into a junior clerk's hand at Sutcliffe's solicitor's office. That worked real well. "I don't ask you how you get your information, and I'll thank you to mind your own beeswax when it comes to mine."

"Really, madam, there's no need to resort to unkind remarks."

"You started it," she shot back.

"I'll go next," Mrs. Jeffries interrupted. "I remembered what it was that David said that night after he'd seen Fiona." She smiled self-consciously. "As I told you, he went to see her after he'd learned of her engagement to John Sutcliffe. He came in, took the whiskey bottle out of the cupboard, and began to drink. He wouldn't tell me what was wrong, and I didn't want to press him. I got ready to retire, and then I came out to check on him. I was very worried; I'd never seen him like this. He was sitting in front of the fire, the bottle was half empty, and he looked at me and said, *'My sister's a fool. She'll never find happiness with a man she's forced into marriage.'* At the time, I thought he meant that she'd . . . she'd . . ."

"Used the oldest trick in the book to get the ring on her finger," Ruth said. "You thought she'd told Sutcliffe she was expecting a child, right?"

Mrs. Jeffries nodded. "But she never had a baby. Nor do I recall her ever being bedridden or indisposed. That first six months they were married, she was out and about every day."

"I don't understand." Wiggins put another scone on his plate. "What's bein' bedridden or indisposed got to do with havin' a baby?"

"It means there was no evidence that she had been pregnant and then lost the child," Ruth explained.

Wiggins gaped in surprise and then looked down at his plate. "Sorry, I didn't mean to be indelicate."

"Don't be silly, boy, you were just curious." Luty looked at Mrs. Jeffries. "Well, if she wasn't expectin', how did she force someone like John Sutcliffe to marry her?"

"As a matter of fact, I do," Sutcliffe replied.

"What kind of weapon is it?" Barnes asked.

"A derringer."

Witherspoon and Barnes exchanged a

glance, both of them realizing a derringer was small enough to fit the description of the likely murder weapon that Bosworth had added to the postmortem report.

"May we see it, please?" Witherspoon asked.

Sutcliffe's eyes narrowed and his mouth flattened into a thin line. "No, you may not."

Barnes whipped out his notebook and pencil, flipped it open, and looked Sutcliffe directly in the eye. "Mr. Sutcliffe, are you refusing to show us the weapon you've already admitted that you own?" The constable was using an old tactic he'd learned when he patrolled the streets: Make a pompous announcement and make it look official by writing down the suspect's answer. He didn't know if it would work in this instance, but it was worth a try.

"I am." Sutcliffe stared contemptuously at the notebook. "So write down whatever you like, Constable. You've no right to barge in here and make unreasonable demands. This is my house and I've let you search this room, but I don't have to let you disturb us further. This is a house in mourning, and I'd like you both to leave."

"As you wish, sir." Witherspoon, who'd been holding the key ring, put it into his pocket. "We'll be taking Mr. Dearman's keys with us. They are evidence."

"You don't know they are Ronald's keys," Sutcliffe snapped irritably. "As a matter of fact, now that I think of it, they're mine" — he stuck out his hand — "and I'd like them back."

"Don't be absurd, John." Fiona gently pushed her husband's hand down. "These men are only doing their job."

"Fiona, please be quiet and let me handle this," he ordered.

She shook her head and looked at the two policemen. "My sister-in-law tells me you've never sent an innocent person to the dock, is that correct?"

Witherspoon glanced uneasily at Barnes and then back to her. "I like to think so," he replied. "We do our very best to ensure we don't make that kind of mistake."

"Then I'll have to trust that Hepzibah is justified in her faith in the two of you and have faith that you'll not make a mistake in this case," she said.

John grabbed her arm. "Fiona, what are you doing?"

She shook him off, keeping her gaze on Witherspoon. "The gun was upstairs in John's sitting room. But it's not there now. Someone has stolen it."

CHAPTER 10

Witherspoon smiled wearily at Mrs. Jeffries. "It's been a very long day." He handed her his bowler and began unbuttoning his coat.

"You look exhausted, sir. Would you care for a glass of sherry? Dinner won't be ready for another twenty minutes." She put his hat on the top peg of the coat tree.

He hesitated. On the way home, he'd worried about whether he ought to discuss the latest developments in this case. He wasn't concerned that Mrs. Jeffries would be angry; she knew he was simply doing his job, and in any case, she was far too fair minded a woman for that sort of nonsense. But he was anxious that the situation might make her uneasy. Though she and Fiona Sutcliffe had been estranged for years, Fiona was still her late husband's sister, while he was both her employer and more important, her friend. He knew better than most how divided loyalties could make one utterly miserable. He handed her his overcoat. "A sherry sounds lovely, and I'd like you to have one with me, but only if it won't make you uncomfortable. We always discuss my work, but in this instance I'll understand if you prefer we not mention it."

She took the garment and turned away, hanging it on the peg beneath his hat. She was touched by his efforts to spare her feelings, but it was quite unnecessary. "Quite the contrary," she said briskly. "I'd like to know what is happening. I have absolute faith in your integrity, Inspector, and if my sister-in-law is guilty, she should be arrested. If not, then I'm sure you'll find the true murderer and she's nothing to fear. But I appreciate your kindness. Come along, sir, let's have a nice glass of Harvey's."

Relieved, he followed her down the hall, and a few moments later, he was in his favorite chair relaxing while she poured their drinks. He'd hoped this situation wouldn't change their long-established habit. The truth was, he rather relied on his chats with Mrs. Jeffries. Talking to her gave him the opportunity to clarify his thoughts and often led him to understand the significance of a seemingly innocent remark. Her questions and comments helped him organize the facts he obtained during the course of the day into a useful collection of clues. "Thank you, Mrs. Jeffries." He took the glass she handed him.

"You're welcome, sir." She sat down. "Now, tell me about your day. Just pretend that Fiona Sutcliffe is a stranger to me. I don't want you censoring yourself because of our familial relationship. I do so look forward to hearing about your cases, and it would be a shame to treat this one any differently."

The matter fully settled, Witherspoon plunged ahead. "Dearman's funeral was today, and as all the suspects were in attendance, we went to the station and went over the reports."

"But I thought you'd gone through all Nivens' reports," she said.

"We have. I'm referring to the reports from the constables I'd sent to interview the witnesses Nivens had ignored."

"Oh yes, there might have been day laborers from the employment agency on the top floor," she replied.

"That's right. There were three men who had collected pay packets between six and seven on the night of the murder, but unfortunately, none of them saw or heard anything. It was the same with the regulars at the pub across the road, but the owner of the newsagent's stated he'd seen a woman standing opposite the Sutcliffe building several times in the days before the murder."

"Was he able to give you a description of her?"

Witherspoon gave a negative shake of his head. "He couldn't see her face clearly. She wore one of those old-fashioned oversized bonnets that have a wide brim."

"If he couldn't see her face, how did he know it was the same woman each time?"

"Her clothes — she had on the same long coat and hat each time," he said. "That's why he noticed her, but he wasn't able to confirm how many times he'd seen her. So it could well be she had a reason for being there that had nothing to do with the murder."

"Was he able to give you any other details?"

"Not many, only that the time or two he noticed her, she arrived before six and left about half an hour later. I'd like to find her if I can, so I've asked the local constable patrolling the area to keep an eye out and if he sees her, to take a statement."

"She just stood there and stared at the building?" Mrs. Jeffries asked. Again, there was a gentle tug at the back of her mind, and again, it disappeared as quickly as it had come.

"That's right. There wasn't much else in the statements. I instructed Constable Griffiths to reinterview the Dearman servants, and his report was there. It confirmed the statement that Nivens had taken from Mrs. Dearman. There had been nothing unusual in Dearman's movements in the days before his death. He'd worked half day Saturday, come home, and gone to the Sutcliffes' for dinner. On Sunday morning, he'd gone to his cottage in Essex, which he did most Sundays, but had come home in time for Sunday dinner that night and then stayed in all evening. Monday morning he'd gone to work as usual." He sighed. "So there was nothing there to help us. We'd just finished the reports when we received a note and" — he looked at her — "it sent us to the Sutcliffe house."

A wave of fear washed over her, but she refused to give in to it. "Who was the note from and what did it say?"

"It said, *'If you want to find the key to the Dearman murder, have a good look around Fiona Sutcliffe's morning room.'*" He smiled self-consciously. "The note wasn't signed. A street lad brought it in and laid it on the front desk." He drained his glass.

Her mind worked furiously, and to give

330

herself a moment to think, she got up and said, "Another one, sir?"

He handed her his glass. "Only if you'll have one with me."

"Of course." She went to the cabinet. An anonymous note. That was a trick she'd used more than once to get the inspector looking in a specific direction. But now she was in no mood to appreciate the irony of the situation. "What happened at the Sutcliffe house, sir?" If a street lad took the note to the station, perhaps she could find him, perhaps he could give her a description of who had given him the note.

"At first I didn't think Mr. Sutcliffe was going to allow us to conduct a search, but Mrs. Sutcliffe intervened and we went ahead with it. We found Ronald Dearman's keys," he said softly. "The one the killer must have used to lock his office door."

She sucked in her breath and closed her eyes. It was bad news, but it wasn't a catastrophe. Not yet. "Did either of the Sutcliffes have an explanation as to how his keys might have come into their possession?"

"Not really, but Mr. Sutcliffe pointed out that since the murder, a half a dozen people had been in and out of their home. Mrs. Meadows and Mrs. Dearman were there early this morning — they rode in the funeral carriage with the Sutcliffes to the church. Henry Anson had been in the house twice. Even the typewriter girl had come by to give Sutcliffe a contract to be signed. All of them, apparently, had either been in the morning room or had used the facilities and could easily have gone into the room if they were of the mind to plant evidence."

Mrs. Jeffries poured the sherry and picked up the glasses. "Here you are, sir. When was the last time that anyone had looked in the box where the keys were found?"

"No one can remember. It's an intricately carved wooden box, which is displayed for its beauty, not its usefulness. Nothing was kept inside it. The downstairs maid dusts the thing twice a week, but she claims she never opens it."

"So you've no idea when the keys were actually put there?" She sank down in her chair.

"It must have been after Dearman was killed. He used them on Monday morning to unlock his office. When John Sutcliffe realized what finding the keys implied, he then tried to say they were his, that he'd been wrong when he first identified them as belonging to the victim. Mrs. Sutcliffe intervened." He looked at her, his expression curious. "Did you tell her that Constable Barnes and I had never sent an innocent person to the dock?"

"I did, sir, because it's true," she stated simply. "She was quite concerned about this whole matter, and I wanted to reassure her that if she was innocent, she had nothing to fear from the two of you."

He smiled, pleased that she had such faith in his and the constable's integrity. "Thank you, Mrs. Jeffries, she obviously took your words to heart. She said that as you trusted us, she was going to trust us as well. Constable Barnes had asked Mr. Sutcliffe if he had a gun, and he admitted he did, but he refused to show it to us. That's when his wife intervened. She said that the gun, which is a derringer, had been stolen. This morning, she'd discovered the case empty, and the gun was nowhere to be found."

It was half past three in the morning when Mrs. Jeffries finally gave up on trying to get any sleep. She got up, dressed, and went downstairs to the kitchen. Outside, it was cold but dry, so she put on her heavy cloak, lighted an oil lamp, and slipped out the back door. Holding the light high, she made her way across the small terrace to the stairs leading into the communal garden.

Her feet crunched on the gravel path as she moved silently toward the center and the bench under the oak tree. A gust of wind slammed into her, making the lamp flame waver, but it didn't go out. She wasn't frightened of the dark; it often helped her think.

She came to the center, stepped off the path, and crossed over to the bench. She sat down and put the lantern beside her. For once, she stopped thinking about the case; she simply lifted her chin and stared off into the distance, letting her eyes focus on the bare limbs of the trees on the other side of path. The gray bank of clouds clustered overhead reflected enough light so that the branches formed black patterns against the sky. For a few minutes, she saw shapes and pictures in the patterns the limbs formed, and then for what seemed a long time, her mind went completely blank. Then little by little, snatches of conversation and other bits and pieces drifted into her thoughts. *There's been gossip about their marriage, so I thought it perfectly possible that he'd decided not to come home for reasons of his own,* Fiona's cultured voice said. A few seconds later, another voice spoke to her; it was Ruth, repeating a tidbit she'd overheard: *She was lucky because if the tinker had been a minute later, I'd not have been home. It was our executive committee meeting.*

Mrs. Jeffries angled her head the other way, causing the distinct shapes of the branches to shift and form completely different patterns. The jingle of a harness and the sound of carriage wheels came from the surrounding streets before fading into the stillness of the night. She continued gazing off in the distance, letting the voices of the others float in and out of her consciousness. *I didn't find the gun,* Wiggins said. A second later, it was Luty's strong American accent ringing in her ears. *If she wasn't expectin', how did she force someone like John Sutcliffe to marry her?* Mrs. Jeffries blinked to clear her vision. *What's always seemed strange to me is that the gear was the only thing that Sutcliffe invented.*

Her mouth dropped open, and if there'd been anyone in the garden to see her expression, she'd have felt a right fool. "Oh my gracious, that's it," she murmured. She leapt to her feet, blew out the lamp, and stepped over to the path. Her eyes had adjusted enough for her to see her way. But she didn't turn toward the house, she walked in the other direction. The path forked into two directions, one that went directly across the garden to the center and one that went around the perimeter in a large oval. Wanting to think, she kept to the edge and walked for what seemed hours, thinking it through. By the time she picked up her lamp and headed for the back door, she knew exactly what had happened.

Mrs. Jeffries put the lamp down on the table and rushed upstairs. Once in her room, she changed into her good shoes, made sure her hair was decent, and scribbled a quick note to Mrs. Goodge. Back down in the kitchen, she put on her outer garments, dropped the note on the table, and left.

Even though it had just gone six in the morning, she was able to find a hansom cab on Holland Road. "Number seventeen, Whipple Road in Mayfair," she told the driver as she climbed inside.

Twenty minutes later, the vehicle pulled up in front of the Sutcliffe house. Mrs. Jeffries paid the driver and started up the side walkway to the stairs leading down to the servants' entrance. There was a faint, pale light on in the kitchen. She knocked on the door, and in the stillness it sounded loud enough to wake the dead. She had just raised her hand to knock again when she heard hurried footsteps on the other side, then the sound of a bolt being thrown, and a young maid stuck her head out.

"Who are you and what do you want this time of the mornin'?" the girl demanded. She looked Mrs. Jeffries up and down, her eyes widening as she took in the well-cut cloak and expensive gloves.

Mrs. Jeffries smiled politely. "My name is Hepzibah Jeffries, and I do apologize for intruding this early in the day. However, my business is urgent. Can you please go and tell your mistress that Mrs. Jeffries is here to see her."

"I don't care how urgent your business is, I'm not wakin' her up at this time of the morning. You'll have to come back at a decent hour." She tried to close the door, but Mrs. Jeffries slapped her hand against it and shoved hard, sending the girl flying backward. She let out a scream.

"Mrs. Sutcliffe is my sister-in-law." Mrs. Jeffries pushed into the house. "And I don't like to be rude, but the matter is quite literally one of life or death. Now, either you go upstairs and tell her to get down here immediately or I'll go myself."

The girl, her eyes now wide with fright, bobbed her head and raced down the hall. Mrs. Jeffries closed the door and leaned against it. She hated being a bully, and she felt bad that she'd frightened the girl. The poor lass didn't look more than fourteen and was no doubt terrified of waking up her mistress at such an early hour. But the deserted kitchen and the ungodly hour were precisely the reasons Mrs. Jeffries was here at the crack of dawn. She needed to see Fiona, and if possible, she needed her to be alone. She trusted in the fact that even if John woke up, Fiona would find a way to keep him from coming downstairs. She was also counting on the maid being the only one up, and she'd been right. Formal households had a very strict pecking order: The youngest scullery maid got up at the crack of dawn and started the fire, did numerous other chores, and then made tea for the cook.

A few minutes later, Mrs. Jeffries heard footsteps hurrying down the stairs. She straightened away from the door just as Fiona appeared. She wore a pink woolen dressing gown and slippers. Her hair hung in a long braid that she'd pulled over her shoulder. "Hepzibah, what on earth are you doing here?"

"I need to speak with you," she replied. "It's urgent. Is there someplace we can speak privately?"

"We can go up to my morning room." She motioned for her to follow, turned, and went back the way she'd come.

Moving quietly, they went upstairs. Once inside, Mrs. Jeffries sat down on the chair by the secretary, and Fiona sat down on the end of the sofa. "What is so urgent?" Fiona asked softly. "John hasn't been sleeping well, and I'm worried about him. He almost woke up when the maid came to get me."

"I know why Ronald Dearman was trying to blackmail you."

Fiona drew back slightly. "You do?"

"Yes. Your husband didn't invent the gear that's made Sutcliffe's rich for the last thirty years. It was invented by an engineer from Australia, a man named Eldon Grimshaw."

Her face drained of color, and her hands curled into tight balls. "That's absurd," she whispered with trembling lips.

"Eldon Grimshaw was found dead in a pony and trap just outside the Sutcliffe country house on the very day John announced his engagement to you," she continued. "That's how you got him to marry you, isn't it? Something happened that day with Mr. Grimshaw, and somehow you turned it to your advantage. Tell me, Fiona, did you and John kill that poor man and make it look like an accident?" She'd been guessing about some of what must have happened on that day, but her sister-in-law's reaction proved she'd guessed correctly.

"We did nothing of the kind." Fiona's eyes filled with tears. "We had nothing to do with his death. Grimshaw was talking to John, asking him to look at his invention, when all of a sudden he clutched his heart and fell over. Dear Lord, we both tried to help him, but it was too late. He was dead."

Mrs. Jeffries stared at her skeptically.

Fiona jumped up and began pacing the small room. "For God's sake, Hepzibah, you've got to believe me. I'm David's sister. We were raised in the same house and shared the same beliefs. We went to church every Sunday. I may have been more ambitious than my brother, but I'm not a monster. I wouldn't be a party to murder just to further my social ambitions." She stopped in front of the fire screen and stared into the empty fireplace.

"But Grimshaw's death is how you got John to marry you, isn't it?" Mrs. Jeffries said. "He was getting ready to propose to Antonia, but that day at the village fete, he suddenly announced he was marrying you."

Fiona whirled around. "So what if it was the reason. He didn't love Antonia. He was only going to marry her to save the family business. The Whitleys had money, but I loved him."

"But did he love you?"

"I most certainly did." John Sutcliffe stepped into the room and closed the door behind him. "And I've never regretted for one moment that she agreed to be my wife."

"Oh, John." Fiona rushed to him. "You weren't meant to hear any of this."

He pulled her close and kissed her gently on the lips. "You should have woken me. This is something we need to face together. Come, dearest, let's sit down. I'd like to tell your sister-in-law what really happened that day." They sat down close together, and he turned to Mrs. Jeffries.

"You're right, I was going to ask Antonia to marry me," he began. "I'd just taken over the company and discovered the finances were a mess. That day, we'd gone to our country house outside York for the village fete."

"Was Ronald Dearman there?"

"He was Lucretia's guest. I didn't care for the man, but he was from a good family and he seemed to care for her, so I couldn't object. Antonia and her family were there as well, but they weren't staying with us. Everyone in the village was at the fete. I'd planned on asking Antonia for her hand after the picnic luncheon and then making the announcement at the afternoon tea in the parish hall, but before luncheon was served I went back to the house. I can't remember exactly why, but when I got there, a pony cart pulled up and this stranger got down. He was carrying a brown leather bag. He asked if I was John Sutcliffe and introduced himself as Eldon Grimshaw. He asked if I'd gotten his letter and I said I hadn't. He asked if he could have a few minutes of my time and said he'd come all the way from Sydney to see me. It was still early and the fete was boring, so I agreed. We went inside and chatted for a few minutes. He told me a little about himself and said he was an inventor. Then he asked if I'd be interested in manufacturing a gear he'd invented. The moment I saw it, I knew it was an amazing piece of equipment. He'd come prepared; he'd brought his drawings and notes and showed me those as well. I immediately agreed to produce it and asked if we could discuss it the next day, which he said would be fine, he'd go get a room in the village. As I accompanied him to the door, I asked why he came to England to get it made, and he said he'd no family in Australia and wanted to start a new life here. I made some comment about it being such a wonderful piece of engineering that I was sure his colleagues must be green with envy, and he said no one but me had seen it." He paused and took a deep breath. "That's when he clutched his chest and keeled over."

"Lucretia had sent me to the house to get her a fan," Fiona interjected. "I heard Grimshaw talking to John and wasn't sure what to do. When Grimshaw collapsed, I ran in to see if I could help. But he was gone. John was going to call the doctor, but I stopped him. I told him that he should keep the gear and manufacture it for himself. Grimshaw had just said he had no family, no heir, and from the way he spoke, he didn't even have any friends."

"What happened then?" Mrs. Jeffries asked.

"John argued with me, he said it wasn't right, but I pointed out that we were cheating no one and that by the time any rightful heirs were found and John could buy the device from them, Sutcliffe's would be out of business."

"The poor fellow was all alone in the world — I made sure of that before I put the gear into production. I engaged a private inquiry agent to ensure we weren't cheating any of Grimshaw's heirs." He glanced at his wife, who stared at him in surprise. "I'm sorry, my dear. I never told you." He looked back at Mrs. Jeffries. "But if I had found someone who was morally or legally entitled to that device, I would have handed it over right away."

She smiled at him. She liked this man and was sorry they'd never had the chance to get to know one another. "I believe you, but what happened then? What did you do with Grimshaw's body?"

Fiona clasped her husband's hand. "We put him back in the pony cart, and John walked it down the road a piece."

"Weren't you frightened you'd be seen?"

"Everyone was at the fete. It was customary for the Sutcliffes to provide a very luxurious picnic luncheon, and no one wanted to miss that. I told John to make sure he turned the pony cart around so that when it was found, it would be facing toward the house," she said.

"Giving everyone the impression that Grimshaw was coming from the train station but hadn't actually arrived at the Sutcliffe residence," Mrs. Jeffries said.

"That's right, so if anyone is to blame for this, it's me, not my husband," she declared. "But we made a mistake, and that mistake led Ronald to the truth. He found the wooden box that housed the gear. Grimshaw had etched his name on the top. We didn't even realize it was gone, but Ronald had come in looking for John and found it. He kept it all these years."

"So the name etched on the box led him to send inquiries to Sydney," Mrs. Jeffries surmised.

"Yes. He found out Grimshaw wasn't just a mechanical engineer, but an inventor," John said. "It didn't take him long to figure out the rest. He knew I wasn't talented enough to invent such a brilliant device."

"Why did he wait so many years to black-mail you?"

John frowned thoughtfully. "He was quite content with working at the firm until I brought Anson into the company," he said.

Mrs. Jeffries looked at Fiona. "There's only one reason you'd take a human life," she began.

"To protect my husband." Fiona smiled bitterly. "Yes, I'm capable of that, but in this instance I wouldn't have had to. You see, I was going to give Ronald what he wanted. I was going to pay him off."

"Really?"

"After he'd told me he had Grimshaw's box and I'd foolishly shouted that I was go-ing to murder him, we both calmed down. That's when he told me he'd found and contacted Grimshaw's solicitor in Sydney and his papers were being shipped to him."

"And you were afraid the papers would prove beyond a shadow of a doubt that Sutcliffe's hadn't invented the gear," Mrs. Jeffries finished.

Fiona nodded in agreement. "I told him he'd won and that I'd pay his price. I asked him how much he wanted. He laughed and said he'd let me know. But he said he'd make it a reasonable amount. If you don't believe me, you can ask Mr. Bodian. He's a very discreet jeweler with a shop just off Regent Street. I took my diamond necklace to him for an appraisal. He offered me quite a good price for it."

"Fiona," John gasped. "How could you even consider doing such a thing!"

"Because Ronald was going to ruin us," she replied evenly. "You didn't see his face that night. He was positively glorying in the fact that he had the power to destroy not only you and me, but the company as well."

"Why would he do that? It would destroy Lucretia," John cried. "Their marriage wasn't perfect, but surely he loved her."

"Don't be naive, John. He hated Lucretia and he hated you," Fiona said.

"I always tried to do right by him," he whispered.

"I know," she said softly. She turned to

Mrs. Jeffries. "As God is my witness, I didn't kill him. I may be capable of such an action, but because one is capable doesn't mean one chooses to do evil."

"I know you didn't kill him," Mrs. Jeffries stated. "And neither did your husband."

Fiona's eyes widened. But before she could speak, Mrs. Jeffries continued. "That's what you were really frightened of, isn't it?"

"But I was in Birmingham," he protested.

"True, but you were on the nine o'clock train, not the five forty-five," she said. "And your wife knew it." She was guessing about that, but she was certain she was right.

"Hilda Laidlaw saw you getting out of a hansom at the station just before nine on Monday evening," Fiona said to him.

"And she mentioned it to you." His shoulders sagged. "I'm sorry, my dear, I didn't want to lie to you, but there was another matter I needed to attend to before I left. It's a rather delicate situation, and I only kept it from you to avoid causing you pain."

"You mean Henry Anson." She smiled sadly. "He's your son. I've known since the first time I saw him. He looks like you. I'm surprised no one else has noticed the resemblance."

"Oh, my darling, I'm so very sorry." His face was a mask of misery. "I'd not hurt you for the world."

"I know that." She sighed. "But we'll talk about it another time. Right now, we've got to decide what to do." She looked at Mrs. Jeffries. "Should I hire a solicitor? I've a very strong feeling that your employer is coming back today to ask me to accompany him to stations."

"I don't know that we're at that point yet, but I'm sure he'll be back with more questions."

"I won't tell him about Grimshaw," Fiona declared.

"There's no reason you should. Except for the fact that Dearman tried to blackmail you over it, it's got nothing to do with his murder. You weren't his only victim. He'd been blackmailing people for years."

Both of them looked at one another, their expressions stunned. "I don't know what to say," John finally said. "I paid him a decent salary . . ."

"That has nothing to do with it," Mrs. Jeffries said. In the distance she heard the chiming of a clock. "It's about power and greed. For people like Ronald Dearman, there's never enough of either."

Fiona eyed her speculatively. "You know who the killer is, don't you?"

"I'm fairly certain I do, but it's going to

take some very clever manipulating to make it obvious to Inspector Witherspoon, and I'll need help from the two of you."

"Of course, we'll do anything you say," John said.

Mrs. Jeffries had the hansom drop her at the other end of the street, in front of Ruth's house. She hurried up the steps, hoping that her friend was an early riser. There was one last thing she needed to confirm before she set the remainder of her plan in motion.

She knocked on the door, and a few moments later, the butler appeared. "Mrs. Jeffries?"

"Good morning, is Lady Cannonberry up? I must speak to her."

The butler nodded politely and opened the door wide. He was under strict instructions that any person from Inspector Witherspoon's household was to be admitted immediately. "Yes, madam, she's having coffee in the drawing room." He closed the door and led her down the hall.

"Mrs. Jeffries is here to see you," he announced as she raced into the room. Ruth dropped her newspaper, a look of alarm on her face. "What's wrong? Has something happened to Gerald?"

"Oh dear, I am sorry, I didn't mean to

frighten you," Mrs. Jeffries apologized. "Everything is fine. But I had to speak to you. I think I may have found a way to unmask our killer."

Ruth sagged in relief. "Thank goodness. Please bring another cup," she told the butler.

"That won't be necessary," Mrs. Jeffries said quickly. "I'm only staying a moment."

"Very well, madam." He closed the double oak doors as he withdrew.

"What do you need from me?" Ruth asked eagerly.

"What day does the executive committee meet?" she asked.

"The executive committee?" Ruth looked puzzled. "You mean from my women's group? It meets on the Monday before the Wednesday general meeting."

"And the meeting is always at six o'clock?"

"That's right. Why?"

"I don't have time to explain now. I want you to do something, something I'm hoping will bring this case to a close. If I'm wrong, it could end up being a wild-goose chase."

Ruth waved impatiently. "Don't worry about that."

"You'll need to get Luty and Hatchet. It's going to take the three of you to cover the area in the time we've got left."

"If we're pressed for time, I'll take a hansom instead of my carriage, it's faster. Now, what do you want us to do?"

"You and Hatchet need to go to Cannon Street Station," she explained. "But Luty needs to go to the newsagent by the Southwark Bridge."

"Stop frettin', Mrs. Goodge." Wiggins covered his mouth as he yawned. "Mrs. Jeffries knows what she's about."

The cook had gotten him and Phyllis up earlier than usual, and now the three of them were sitting at the table, waiting for the housekeeper's return.

The kettle boiled, and Phyllis got up, grabbed a pot holder, and took it off the cooker. She poured the boiling water into the big brown teapot. "I hope she gets here soon. I'm all excited wondering what's what."

"The note didn't say," Mrs. Goodge said, her tone irritable. "It just said for me to wake the two of you and have you at the ready and for me to ensure that Constable Barnes stayed put in the kitchen until she got back. It didn't even say where she'd gone."

Phyllis put the pot on the table next to the cream pitcher and the sugar bowl. She went to the sideboard, opened the cupboard, and pulled out the mugs. They heard the back door open, and she reached in and grabbed another one.

"It's about time," the cook exclaimed as Mrs. Jeffries raced into the room. "Where have you been?"

She untied her bonnet strings as she walked. "To the Sutcliffe house and then to see Ruth. I think I know who murdered Dearman, but in order to prove it, we're going to need everyone's, including Constable Barnes', help. Oh dear, he's not here yet."

"He doesn't come this early," Mrs. Goodge reminded her. "Sit down and have your tea. You can tell us what's happenin', and more important, what you're to be wantin' us to do."

She nodded and hung up her outer garments. By the time she joined them at the table, Mrs. Goodge had poured the tea and passed everyone their mugs. "Now, what's goin' on?" she asked.

Mrs. Jeffries wasn't sure where to begin. She thought she knew who the killer was, but she wasn't one hundred percent sure. There were so many unknown elements in the situation, and it was possible that any of three people could be the culprit. The idea she'd come up with would eliminate two of the suspects, and if two were absolutely out of the running, then it followed that the killer had to be the third person. At least she hoped that was how it would work out.

"Well," the cook demanded. "We're waitin'."

"Yes, yes, give me a moment to put it into some coherent sequence," she pleaded. "It's complicated. Oh blast, there simply isn't time to tell you my suspicions. We must take action now if this is going to work."

"What about our morning meeting?" Phyllis asked.

"We won't be having one. I've sent the others to Cannon Street Station and the Southwark Bridge." She looked at Wiggins. "You know the lads that hang around the Shepherds Bush Station, the street boys who take messages and run errands?"

"I know who you mean, them young boys that was 'ere the other day," he replied. "What about 'em?"

"Most street boys have a patch they work, don't they?"

"Yup, and they can get right nasty if another boy tries to work their territory." He took a quick drink of tea.

"I want you to find which boy it was who took a note for Inspector Witherspoon into the station and left it on the counter yesterday afternoon. Once you find that person, there's two things you'll need to make certain of before you come back here. One, can the boy identify who it was that gave him the note, and two, that he's willing to hang about in front of the station until Constable Barnes comes and gets him."

"I can manage that, but what if none of the Shepherds Bush lads did it? There's street boys in every neighborhood, and most likely, whoever sent the message would 'ave used someone from their own area to make the delivery."

"I know." She turned to Phyllis. "That's why I'm going to have you go to the Notting Hill Station and do the same thing as Wiggins. If my theory about the murder is correct, then a boy from Kensington, Notting Hill, or Shepherds Bush stations took that note into the police station. We have to find the person who gave the boy the note. Do you think you can do it?"

Phyllis gave her an uncertain smile. "I'll try."

"You're not wantin' me to go to the Kensington High Street Station?" Mrs. Goodge asked, her expression alarmed.

"Of course not. I'm going to ask Wiggins to do it."

"But I'll be at Shepherds Bush," he exclaimed.

"Only until you know one way or another if anyone there did it," she explained. "If no one there admits to it, go on to Kensington and have a go at those boys. If this works out the way I'm hoping it will, Constable Barnes will be able to get to all three stations sometime this morning. It's important that the lad who took the message be available to go with him." She got up and went to the sideboard. Opening the top drawer, she pulled out a large handful of coins. She scooped half of them into her other hand and held them out to the footman. "Here, this ought to help. When you find the lad that did it, give him a shilling to stay by the entrance to the station and promise him another shilling once this is over." She gave the rest of the coins to Phyllis. "You'll have a more difficult time. The lads at Shepherds Bush know us, but the boys at Notting Hill don't, so you'll have to be a bit clever."

"Maybe I ought to go to Notting Hill," Wiggins offered.

"No, I want Phyllis to do it." She smiled at the maid. "I think she'll be good at convincing the boys to trust her. Besides, you might need to get to Kensington as well."

"I'll do my best," Phyllis promised as she

put the money in her pocket.

"I'm sure you will." Mrs. Jeffries gave her an encouraging smile and turned to the footman. "Wiggins, come right back if it's one of the lads at Shepherds Bush. If we get lucky, maybe the constable will still be here and I can let him know."

"And I'll come right back once I know one way or another," Phyllis said as she followed the footman to the coat tree.

As soon as they were out the back door, Mrs. Goodge tilted her head to the side. "Are you sure about this?"

"Not as sure as I'd like to be," she admitted.

Constable Barnes hoped that Mrs. Jeffries knew what in the blazes she was doing, because it sounded as if it were the sort of plan that could easily go wrong. For one thing, though her theory about both the planning and the commission of the crime sounded right, that didn't mean it had actually happened that way. Second, the odds of the others finding just the right street lad at any of the four locations weren't good, and third, he was going to have to do some very fast talking to convince the inspector. But Mrs. Jeffries had a knack for being right, and if the worst happened, he'd just look like a fool. He could live with that.

He waited till he and the inspector were out the front door before he opened his mouth. "Excuse me, sir," he began as they reached the pavement. "But are we going to the station this morning?"

"Yes, I want to go over all the witness statements." Witherspoon turned toward the corner where they usually grabbed a hansom.

"Are you looking for anything in particular?" Barnes asked. He hung back a bit, trying to slow them down.

"I'm not certain." The inspector sighed heavily. "That's not true, I tell a lie. I want to go back over all the statements and see if there is anything I might have missed. I shouldn't admit this, but I suppose I'm looking again just in case there's evidence pointing to someone other than Mrs. Jeffries' sister-in-law. I know they're not close and that Mrs. Jeffries would want me to arrest the guilty party no matter who they were, but I feel wretched about the whole matter. The only real evidence we've got points directly at Fiona Sutcliffe."

"It could equally point to her husband," Barnes said. "We only have his word he was on the five forty-five train to Birmingham." In fact, he knew that Sutcliffe had actually been on the nine o'clock train. "But now that you've mentioned it, sir, there's something you said that set me to thinking."

Witherspoon stopped and looked at him, his expression hopeful. "Really, what was it?"

Barnes knew he had to phrase this carefully. "It was your comment about that note we received yesterday. I heard you mumbling under your breath that the only person that could have given it to the street lad was the killer."

Witherspoon looked genuinely surprised. "I said that?"

"You did, sir. It was when we walked out into the hall. I don't think you were even aware that you said anything out loud." Barnes looked his superior directly in the eye. One part of him felt guilty about lying to a man who was both his superior officer and his friend, but another knew that if the inspector arrested the wrong person, he'd never forgive himself, especially as that person was part of his housekeeper's family.

"Gracious, I didn't realize I talked to myself."

"You usually don't, sir." Barnes hastened to reassure him. "I think you were so deep in thought you just mumbled it instinctively."

The inspector stopped and tapped one finger against his chin. He was in deep thought. He knew that sometimes, his "inner voice" as Mrs. Jeffries liked to call it, led him intuitively to see the connections between obscure clues and hence to apprehending the guilty party. Could it be that this inner voice was trying to tell him something and he simply was too busy to listen properly? Perhaps that's why he'd spoken out loud, perhaps his own mind was trying to get his attention, albeit in a rather roundabout way. "That's good to hear."

"But I think you were right and there is a good chance that it was the killer that sent us that message. It was a bit too convenient, if you know what I'm saying."

"It's bothered me as well. Fiona Sutcliffe didn't strike me as a stupid woman. If she'd taken Dearman's keys, I suspect she'd have had the brains to get rid of them."

"And the gun, sir," Barnes added. "If she was going to murder Dearman, especially after she knew she'd been overheard threatening him, why use her husband's own weapon? She'd know that all we'd have to do is ask her servants if there was a gun on premises. In which case, the intelligent course of action would have been to leave it where it was, so that when we asked to see it, it would be sitting there right as rain and we'd start looking elsewhere for the killer. She's plenty of money; she could have bought one and then tossed it in the river." He was talking fast, trying to cover everything before Witherspoon could think of an objection. "Even if Mrs. Sutcliffe didn't want to be seen purchasing it herself, she could have found someone to get it for her; there's always men hanging about willing to do that sort of errand if the price is right."

"You think the guilty party was deliberately trying to point us in the wrong direction?" Witherspoon asked. He had great respect for the constable's experience; he'd patrolled some of the worst streets in the city in his years on the force. The inspector also trusted his judgment.

"I do, sir, and I'd like to propose something. Instead of me going to the station with you, I'd like to go and have a look for that street lad."

"But surely that's the sort of work we can assign to another constable," Witherspoon protested.

"It is, sir, but I've got a few sources I can tap in that regard," he said. "I think I can do it faster than the other constables. Some of the older street boys owe me a favor or two, if you know what I mean, sir."

"If you think that's best, Constable," he said, but he didn't look convinced. "I'll go on to the station, then. Perhaps I'll see something in the reports to give me a different perspective on this matter. What time do you think you'll be back?"

This was the crux of the matter, and Barnes knew he had to be persuasive. "It'll not take long, sir. If someone is deliberately trying to frame Mrs. Sutcliffe, perhaps she'd have some idea of who it might be. Women are good at that sort of thing, sir, if you know what I mean."

Witherspoon didn't but wasn't sure he wanted to admit it. "You think she might know who this person could be? Then why didn't she tell us yesterday? We gave her plenty of opportunity."

"I'm not saying she knows who is trying to point us in her direction, but mark my words, she'll know who hates her enough to *want* to do such a thing, and that would be a starting point."

"I suppose the least we can do is ask her." Witherspoon started walking again. "Meet me at the Sutcliffe house at one o'clock. That should give us both enough time to complete our tasks."

CHAPTER 11

They could hear Luty laughing as she, Ruth, and Hatchet came through the back door of Upper Edmonton Gardens. Wiggins, Mrs. Goodge, and Mrs. Jeffries looked up expectantly as the three of them entered the room.

Luty burst in ahead of the others, her purple veil streaming behind her as she raced to the table. She was grinning broadly. "I found him, I found our boy."

"Madam, please, slow down," Hatchet shouted. "You're going to hurt yourself."

She just laughed and tossed her muff onto her chair. "Pish-posh, I'm too excited to let that happen." She started undoing the big brass buttons on her long mauve cape. "You'll not believe it, but I found the kid right away. He was working the bridge, and I spotted him as soon as I got out of the hansom." She slipped the garment off her shoulders.

Hatchet caught it and took it to the coat tree. "And you've been crowing about it ever since," he said as he hung it on the peg.

"She has good reason to crow," Ruth said. She slipped off her mantle and nodded a thanks as Hatchet took the garment and hung it up. "Where's Phyllis?" she asked as she took her place at the table. The maid's chair was empty.

"She's not back yet," Mrs. Jeffries said. "But I'm sure she'll be here any minute."

"I think you shoulda let me go to Notting Hill." Wiggins glanced anxiously toward the back door. "Cor blimey, what if she run into trouble?"

Hatchet slipped into the seat next to Luty. "Should one of us go and look for her?" he asked.

"I can do it," the footman said quickly.

"Don't be daft, she's perfectly alright." Mrs. Goodge began pouring tea. "You're actin' like she's a half-wit. Give her a chance. She's probably late for a reason. In the meantime, why don't we hear what this lot" — she jerked her head in Luty's direction — "has to say."

"That's an excellent suggestion," Mrs. Jeffries agreed. But like Wiggins, she was beginning to worry. "Tell us what happened, Luty?"

Luty chuckled and gave Hatchet a wink. "We was just finishin' breakfast when Ruth showed up and told us what you needed us to do this mornin'. So we grabbed our coats and went lickety-split toward Cannon Street."

"I kept the hansom waiting while I went in to get them," Ruth added.

"There was plenty of traffic, but the driver was a sharp one and he got us there right quick." Luty reached for the cup of tea Mrs. Goodge passed to her.

"Yes, madam, that generally happens when you offer to pay them double," Hatchet said.

"It worked, didn't it? They let me off first at the newsagent's across from the Sutcliffe offices, and they went on to the station. I had a good look around the area, trying to suss out where I'd plant myself if I wanted to spy on the comings and goings of the building, and I found a right nice little hidey-hole between the pub and the bank."

"Yes, yes, madam, we know how clever you are," Hatchet complained. "Now get on with it."

"You're just jealous that I found him first." Luty made a face at him. "Anyways, once I found the spot, I started huntin' for the local street lads. I figured that most of them probably were at one of the train station doors, but then I saw this young'un at the bridge. He weren't larkin' about, if you know what I mean, he was watchin' the people walkin' across from the other side. Suddenly, he darted out to give this well-dressed businessman a piece of paper. I waited till he'd finished his business, and then I raised my hand and yelled for him. He came over and I asked if this was his patch and he said it was. We got to talkin' and it turns out the boy is right there 'bout every evening. He'd noticed a woman standin' in the hidey-hole for a good ten days before the murder. Said the only time he ever saw her move was when a passin' ferryboat blasted its horn."

"Can he identify her?" Mrs. Jeffries asked.

"Yup, he said he got a right good look at her face when she shooed him away." Luty grinned. "Smart boy, he'd gone over to ask her if she needed him to run any errands."

"So what happens now?" Mrs. Goodge demanded. "Do we just wait —" She broke off as the back door slammed.

A few seconds later, Phyllis ran into the room. Her cheeks were flushed, and she was panting heavily. "I'm sorry to be so late" — she paused and gasped for air — "but I stayed with him until Constable . . . B . . ."

"Sit down and catch your breath," Mrs. Jeffries ordered. "We can wait thirty seconds to hear what you've got to say. In the meantime, Luty can finish."

"Not much more to tell," Luty said as Phyllis sank into her chair without bothering to take off her coat. "The boy, his name is Samuel Bassington, was right pleased to do business with me. He's a smart boy, and he understood everything I told him. We went to the main door of Cannon Street Station, and he agreed to stay there until Constable Barnes come to fetch him. I gave him a pound for his trouble and promised him another one once the constable told us he'd kept his word."

"You gave him a pound!" Phyllis exclaimed. "Oh no, I only gave Martin a shilling, and I didn't promise him anything for afterward. Was I supposed to do that?"

"You found the boy who took the note to the station?" Mrs. Jeffries asked.

Phyllis nodded and took a sip from the mug the cook had just handed her. "Yes and he's a nice lad. I explained that he had to tell the truth when he pointed out the person that gave him the note but that he wasn't to mention me. He was to say that Constable Barnes had found him. That's why I'm so tardy for the meeting. I waited with him until the constable arrived. It seemed the best way to make sure everything worked out properly. Then I rushed back here."

"But the constable did come and get him?" Mrs. Jeffries was more relieved than she cared to admit. But she wasn't completely out of the woods yet. There were still a number of things that could go wrong.

"They were getting in a hansom when I left," Phyllis replied.

Hatchet eyed Luty speculatively. "When exactly did you offer this young ruffian you found a pound for his services?"

Luty pursed her lips. "You think I was born yesterday? I didn't mention money until I knew for sure he was the one. Sam's a good boy. Just because he's a street lad don't mean he'd lie about what he saw."

"Sorry, madam, I wasn't casting aspersions on the young man's character, but occasionally, people do take advantage of your good nature and your pocketbook."

"Are you goin' to tell us what's what now?" the cook asked Mrs. Jeffries. "Who is the killer?"

But the housekeeper shook her head. "I don't have time to explain it. Not yet. There's still one more thing to be done." She waved her hand around the table.

"Wiggins, Phyllis, and Hatchet need to go back out. They've got to keep watch on the Sutcliffe house, and there are three ways in and out of the place."

Phyllis giggled in delight. "I'm glad I didn't take off my coat." She pushed back from the table and rose to her feet. Hatchet and Wiggins got up as well. The three of them looked at the housekeeper.

"Wiggins, you take the front door. But before you find a hiding place, have a look in the neighborhood and make sure you know where the nearest policeman is patrolling. You may need to get him if things go badly." She turned to Hatchet. "There's a small entrance on the left side of the house. It's off the main study and John uses it occasionally, so the door is in working order." Finally, she looked at Phyllis. The girl's eyes sparkled with excitement. "You take the back. The servants' entrance is accessible from both the front and the back of the house. Wiggins will be able to see the front, but we need someone to guard the back. There's a mews that delivery vans and locals use, so be careful."

"Who am I watching for?" she asked.

"If anyone, other than a servant, comes out that way, get help," Mrs. Jeffries told her. "Especially if that person appears to be fleeing. Wiggins is at the front and can get Hatchet. They know what to do."

"Why do they get to go?" Luty grumbled. "I know what to do, too. One of us keeps 'em in sight while the other gets Constable Barnes."

"You think the murderer might make a run for it?" Mrs. Goodge asked.

"The killer is desperate," Mrs. Jeffries said. "And if I'm correct, that person knows that neighborhood well enough to give our inspector the slip if they can get out of the house fast enough."

"Good day, Inspector." Fiona smiled brightly and got up from her chair. "We didn't expect to see you here again."

"Good day, Mrs. Sutcliffe." Witherspoon stood in the doorway and surveyed the room. There were people everywhere. John Sutcliffe stood by the fireplace. He gave the inspector a friendly smile. Henry Anson and a lovely brown-haired young woman sat close together on a love seat. Opposite them Lucretia Dearman and Antonia Meadows occupied the sofa.

This wasn't what he'd wanted or expected. For that matter, he'd also expected to find something in the reports that might prove useful, and he'd expected his constable would be here by now. "I'm sorry to barge in on you like this, but I had a few more questions to ask you."

Fiona knew what to do. Mrs. Jeffries had been very clear about how they must behave. "Come in and sit down, Inspector Witherspoon. I believe you know everyone here."

"I've not had the pleasure of meeting that young lady." He smiled at the woman next to Anson.

"This is my fiancée, Miss Throckmorton," Anson said proudly.

Witherspoon bowed in her direction. "I'm very pleased to meet you."

She smiled. "Likewise, Inspector."

"We're just having coffee," Fiona continued. "I'll pour you a cup." A silver coffee service was on a trolley next to the chair she'd just vacated. Without waiting for his answer, she reached for the pot.

"I hardly think this a social occasion," Lucretia Dearman snapped. She glared at the inspector. "If he wants to ask you his questions, he can wait until you're free."

Fiona smiled graciously as she continued with her task. "Oh, that won't be necessary. I'm willing to speak to the police at any time. Besides, I'm sure the inspector has questions for you as well."

Surprised, Lucretia's jaw dropped. "For me? Don't be ridiculous. I've already talked to the police."

"That's absurd." Antonia Meadows stood up. "She's been through enough. She just buried her husband."

Witherspoon had no idea what was going on; why were the Sutcliffes treating him like a guest? Where was Barnes and why in the blazes wasn't he here? But in truth, he did have some questions for Mrs. Dearman. He ignored Mrs. Meadows and took the cup of coffee that John Sutcliffe, who'd moved away from the fireplace, handed him. "Thank you."

"Sit down, Inspector." Fiona had gone back to her chair. She glanced at the sofa. "You'll be quite comfortable there."

"Really, Fiona." Lucretia gave her a disapproving frown. "What on earth is wrong with you? This man isn't a guest, and I don't want him sitting next to me." She glanced up. "You're hovering, Antonia. Do sit down."

Witherspoon, who'd started toward the sofa, stopped abruptly. He noticed that John Sutcliffe was now standing by the double doors and that Henry Anson and his fiancée were exchanging confused glances.

"The inspector is quite welcome in my

home," Fiona said.

"Thank you." He took a quick sip of coffee and tried to avoid making a face. He hated coffee, but it would have been ungracious to refuse, especially under these very bizarre circumstances. He put the cup down on the ornate side table and looked at Lucretia Dearman. "I'm terribly sorry for your loss, ma'am, but I'd like to know where you were last Monday evening."

Antonia Meadows gasped, but Lucretia said nothing; she merely stared at him.

"Lucretia, you're being rude," John said. "Answer the man's question. This whole matter has caused Fiona and me a great deal of misery and I want it over and done with."

Lucretia looked at her brother and then back at Witherspoon. "As I told that other policeman, I was home that evening. If you people bothered to speak to one another, you'd know that."

"We do speak to one another and to many other people as well," he replied. "What time did you come home that day?"

"John, do something," Antonia cried. "You're the master of the house, tell him" — she jerked her thumb toward the inspector — "to leave."

The doors opened and Constable Barnes

stepped into the room; a young black-haired boy wearing a faded green jacket and scuffed shoes trailed behind him. He nodded politely to Sutcliffe. "Good day, sir. Sorry to come in like this, but it's rather urgent that I see the inspector."

"What's the meaning of this?" Lucretia got up. "John, I'm sorry you and Fiona have been inconvenienced by my husband's death, but I demand that you do something about this. They've no right to come storming in here and badgering people without so much as a by-your-leave."

"I don't think they've badgered anyone," Sutcliffe said quietly. "Don't you want to know who murdered your husband?" He turned his attention to the new arrivals. "Come in, Constable, and bring the lad with you."

Barnes gave the boy an encouraging smile, and they stepped farther into the room. "That's Inspector Witherspoon. I want you to tell him exactly what you told me."

"If you'll excuse me, I'm going to leave." Antonia started for the door. "I've a dreadful headache."

John Sutcliffe stepped over and blocked the now-closed door. "I'll have the butler bring you a powder."

"Go ahead, young man," the inspector

said to the boy. "Tell me what you told the constable."

But the lad wasn't really listening. He was staring at Antonia Meadows. "She's the one," he said, pointing to her. "She's the one that give me the note. She told me to make sure I took it to the Ladbroke Road Police Station."

Antonia's eyes widened. "For God's sake, what is that creature talking about? I did no such thing."

"You bloomin' well did," the boy charged. "You come up to me in front of the Notting Hill Station and give me a sixpence to do it. I weren't the only one who saw ya, my mate was there, too."

"You're the one that sent the anonymous note to the police?" John Sutcliffe said. He stared at her coldly.

"Ma'am, would you care to explain yourself?" Witherspoon moved toward her. "How did you know that Mr. Dearman's keys were in Mrs. Sutcliffe's morning room?"

"I saw her put them there." Antonia pointed at Fiona. "And I'm not ashamed of what I did. She murdered Ronald, and I knew she was going to get away with it if I did nothing."

"Exactly when did you see this happen?"

the inspector asked. He knew she was lying, but for the life of him, he couldn't think of a way to prove it.

"When I was here on Tuesday with Lucretia. We stopped in late that afternoon. Lucretia wanted to discuss something with John." She swallowed heavily. "I saw Fiona go into the morning room, and I went down there to visit with her while I waited. The door was open a crack, and I saw her put the keys into that box."

"You're lying," Fiona stated. "I wasn't in the morning room that afternoon."

"Stay right here," Barnes instructed the boy. He went to the door again, opened it, and stuck his head out. A second later, another boy, this one brown haired and wearing even scruffier clothes, stepped inside. "Do you see the woman in the room?" Barnes asked him.

Again, Witherspoon wasn't sure what was going on. The constable was supposed to bring one boy back, the one who'd taken the note, not two. But he trusted Barnes and so he kept his expression serene, as if he knew exactly what was going to happen next. "Yes, if you do, please point her out to us."

The boy gazed from one woman to the next, smiling a little as his eyes landed on the very lovely Miss Throckmorton. He moved on, his expression sobering. "That's her." He pointed to Antonia. "She's the one. She stood there starin' at that buildin' for days, and the only time she ever moved was to look at her timepiece whenever the ferry blasted its ruddy horn. Don't know why she kept checkin' it. That horn blows every day at the same time."

"Dear God, Antonia, what have you done?" Lucretia stared at her friend, her expression stricken, her face pale.

Antonia held out her hands and moved across the room toward her friend. "Dearest, don't be alarmed. I've done nothing. They can't prove anything. This is all a tempest in a teapot."

Lucretia's arms went up, and she flattened her hands toward Antonia as though to ward her off. "Stay away from me. Oh dear Lord, what have you done, what have you done?"

Antonia stopped abruptly, and her odd, dreamlike expression was gone. Her lips curved down and her eyes grew hard. "What have I done?" she repeated. "I've set you free, you stupid woman. I've done what you didn't have the nerve to do. I've put a bullet in his damned head. It's a bit late to be acting like the grieving widow. You hated him and he hated you."

"I didn't hate him," Lucretia shouted. "We had our differences and I know he wasn't a good man, but he didn't deserve to be murdered."

Antonia's face changed again; this time, she looked frightened, confused. "But I thought that's what you wanted. Remember all those times when we were together, how we'd talk about both of us being free and traveling the world. I was free and I wanted you to be free as well."

"Is that why you killed him?" Fiona asked archly. "To free your friend?"

Antonia whirled to face her. "I killed the bastard because he was bleeding me dry," she snapped. "Just like he was going to bleed you dry, but you know what the best part was? It wasn't putting a bullet between his miserable eyes; it was arranging it so the police would think you'd done it. It would have worked, too, if those nasty little creatures had kept their mouths shut." She jerked her chin in the direction of the two boys.

"Maybe I woulda if you'd given me more than a sixpence," the black-haired lad yelled.

Barnes caught Witherspoon's eye, and both men edged closer to Antonia. Neither of them wanted to do anything that would shut her up; there was nothing better for a conviction than someone confessing in a room full of witnesses. Henry Anson and Miss Throckmorton were both staring in fascination at the spectacle.

"I know you always blamed me for taking John away from you, but this is monstrous," Fiona said softly. John had come to stand next to her; his arm encircled her waist.

Antonia's lip curled. "It was no more monstrous than you ruining my life. Good God, are you stupid? Because of you snatching him away" — she pointed at John — "I endured a miserable thirty years with Thaddeus Meadows."

"But you were free of him," Lucretia said.

"Yes, and for a few months I was happy." She gave a short, mirthless laugh. "I had money and freedom. But then Ronald showed up on my doorstep. He had Thaddeus' medicine bottles with him. He said that if I didn't pay him every month, he'd tell everyone I murdered him, that I'd withheld his medicine and that was why he'd died."

"He couldn't have proved such a thing," Lucretia said. "You were a fool to believe him."

"But he could," she admitted. She looked at the policemen. "But I'm not going to tell you how. If you want to hang me for his murder as well, you'll have to prove it."

The room went quiet; even the usual noise of the household seemed suspended as everyone stared at her in stunned disbelief.

"Bloomin' Ada," the brown-haired boy said. "She don't look like a killer, does she. Just goes to show, me mam is right: You can't tell anythin' about a person just by lookin' at 'em."

Once again, the inspector and Barnes locked eyes, and the two men moved toward her. "Antonia Meadows," Witherspoon said, "you're under arrest for the murder of Ronald Dearman."

"I was hoping she'd make a run for it," Phyllis announced as she took her seat. "But she didn't. Mind you, it was exciting when they brought her out of the house. We had to scarper about a bit to avoid being spotted by the inspector and the two street lads."

"Alright." Mrs. Goodge looked at the housekeeper. "You've kept us in suspense long enough. How did you figure out it was her?"

Ruth, Luty, and Mrs. Goodge hadn't even tried to get her tell them her theory as they knew it would be useless, and in the sense of fairness, they wanted to wait until everyone was together. While they waited, Ruth had gone home to write some letters (she was the correspondence secretary for her women's suffrage group), Luty had taken Fred out for a walk, Mrs. Jeffries paced the downstairs hall, and Mrs. Goodge got the roast and vegetables for the inspector's dinner into the oven.

But they were back now, and to Mrs. Jeffries' utter delight, everything had gone well. "I didn't realize who it was until the wee hours of this morning," she admitted. "And even then, I wasn't quite certain whether it was Antonia Meadows or Lucretia Dearman that had done it."

"Ain't you glad it wasn't your sister-in-law?" Luty said to her. "I mean, I know you ain't friends but still, it musta been hard wonderin' if she was goin' to be arrested."

"It was, but the most difficult part was that at one point, I thought she might be guilty." She laughed. "But that turned out not to be the case, and if I'd been thinking clearly from the beginning, I'd have seen who the real culprit was much earlier. There were numerous clues that pointed directly to Antonia."

"Yeah, she left a trail a mile wide." Luty nodded, her expression glum. "But we didn't see it till it was almost too late."

"Go on, Mrs. Jeffries, tell us how you sorted it out." Wiggins, who, like Phyllis, had missed both breakfast and lunch, reached for one of the sandwiches from the plate in front of them.

"It was the way Dearman tried to sack people that got me to thinking about what he was really up to," she began. She had to be careful here; she'd already decided that it wouldn't be fair to Fiona and John Sutcliffe to make their story public, and she knew that in the telling of how she'd figured it out, there were several pertinent clues she couldn't explain. "He sacked James Tremlett for no apparent reason."

"He'd seen Dearman by the back stairs getting an envelope," Phyllis added eagerly. "So Dearman had to get rid of him so he could keep his secret about what he was up to."

"Correct." She nodded encouragingly. "I think we'll make a detective out of you yet!"

"But who else did he try to sack?"

Mrs. Jeffries was ready for that one. "The typewriter girl. Dearman had bullied her into typing a private letter for him."

"And it was probably to one of his victims," Wiggins added, not to be outdone by Phyllis.

"That's my suspicion, but luckily for her,

she went right to Henry Anson and he saved her position. When we got confirmation that Dearman was a blackmailer, it opened up the floodgates, and all of a sudden, I began to look at some of the other information we'd learned differently."

"Yes, but that could have pointed the finger of guilt at any of our suspects," Mrs. Goodge said. "Look at Henry Anson, for instance. He said himself that he was sure Sutcliffe had hired him with the intent of forcin' Dearman out of the company and that he'd even seen him goin' through Sutcliffe's desk. Seems to me that's pretty strong evidence that Dearman was even tryin' to blackmail Sutcliffe. I think that's why he was kept on at the firm."

"I agree," Mrs. Jeffries said quickly. "I don't think it was out-and-out blackmail for money. I imagine he hinted to Sutcliffe that he knew Anson was his illegitimate son, and whatever plans were in the works to force him out went out the door. At Dearman's cottage, Wiggins found the letters that Anson's mother had written to Sutcliffe. I suspect that Dearman had found them in Sutcliffe's desk and used them to keep his position in the company."

"Why would Sutcliffe keep something so

private in his office desk?" Phyllis murmured.

"He wouldn't risk keeping them at home,"
Ruth answered. "He'd not want his wife or
one of the servants finding them."

"And he didn't know Dearman was a
blackmailer," Hatchet said. "He probably
had no idea that the fellow regularly went
through his desk."

"What caused you to realize it was Antonia
Meadows?" Phyllis reached for another
sandwich. It was her third. "There seemed
to be so many people who hated him."

"A number of things," she replied. "I kept
thinking about how Blanche Keating had
told you that right before Thaddeus Meadows died, she'd seen Dearman skulking
about outside the house, and I wondered
why. He didn't approve of his wife's friendship with Antonia, so why should he have
been so interested in her husband's passing? Then when Wiggins found the two
unopened medicine bottles in Dearman's
cottage, it began to make sense. Thanks to
you and your conversation with the maid, I
was able to understand his actions."

Phyllis grinned broadly. "Blanche also said
that when Meadows first died, Antonia
Meadows stopped making her and the cook
pay for their own tea and sugar and that she

was more generous with their food, like she had plenty of money. But then she started selling off all his things."

"Maybe she just wanted to get rid of everythin' that reminded her of 'im," Wiggins suggested.

"No." Mrs. Jeffries shook her head. "She suddenly started selling his things because it was just about then that Dearman began blackmailing her and money became scarce again. He'd found the unopened bottles, and he'd been at the house when Meadows died. I suspect there's a good chance that he'd seen something."

"Seen somethin'," Luty repeated. "You mean like her holdin' a pillow over his face?"

"Really, madam, that's a bit far-fetched," Hatchet chided.

"Don't you believe it," she shot back. "There's been more than one miserable marriage that ended when the sick one was laid up and too weak to fight back. Meadows died of pneumonia, so the doctor wouldn't have been able to tell that she'd smothered him. He might have been a cheap, miserable miser of a feller, but no one deserves to die like that."

"We're only speculating here," Mrs. Jeffries said. "But I think Luty is right. Whatever Dearman had on her, it was enough to make her begin making payments to him."

"That's probably when she decided he had to die," Ruth said. "She'd been unhappy in her marriage and was finally free. I imagine that the moment he told her what he'd seen and that she had to pay him to keep quiet, he signed his own death warrant."

Mrs. Jeffries nodded in agreement. "But because she was so much in the background, I didn't think of her as a potential suspect. Then last night, I remembered what your friend from your women's meeting had told you."

Ruth nodded. "That's right, Edwina Hawkins. She lives next door to the Meadows. Is that why you asked me about our executive committee meeting?"

"When you confirmed that it was Monday, the day that Dearman was killed, I was fairly sure I was right."

"What does that have to do with it?" Mrs. Goodge asked.

"Antonia Meadows told Constable Barnes she was home that evening, but she couldn't have been. She'd given a door-to-door tinker her umbrella to fix, and he tried to return it that night. He knocked and knocked, but she never answered. He took the umbrella next door and gave it to Mrs.

Hawkins, who was on her way out to an executive committee meeting, which start promptly at six fifteen. Which means she wasn't home when Dearman was murdered. When I was outside last night, I also remembered that she had begun letting her two servants off every afternoon."

"She gave them the time off so she could slip out of the house," Phyllis guessed. "She wanted to watch the building."

"That's right. When the inspector mentioned that the newsagent had noticed a woman staring at the Sutcliffe building, I remembered the discussion we'd had on how the assailant had known Dearman was going to be alone in the office."

"That's why she went there," Wiggins said excitedly. "She 'ad to make sure the office was empty, and the only way to know that was by watchin' who came in and out every day. That way, she'd know everyone and she'd be able to tell who might be still inside."

"But why not just ask Lucretia Dearman how many people worked there?" Mrs. Goodge asked.

"She wouldn't have known," Mrs. Jeffries explained. "She had no interest in the company, and Antonia didn't want to draw attention to herself by asking questions about Sutcliffe's. That was the heart of her plan, and it almost worked. Besides, she had to know who came out of the building, not how many worked for the company. She memorized faces. If someone she'd seen leaving at six o'clock didn't walk out that front door, she wouldn't go ahead with her plan. She knew she had only a short time between when the office emptied out and the porter arrived."

Ruth added, "It was also common knowledge that it was either Henry Anson or Dearman who locked up at night, so once she saw Anson come out, if Dearman was still inside, she could go ahead with it, providing of course, she'd seen the other familiar faces from the building come out. It still seems like a very odd way to plan a murder." She reached for the teapot and poured herself another cup

"Odd, perhaps, but effective," Hatchet said. "Watch the place till you're familiar with the comings and goings, make sure your victim is alone inside, walk in, do the deed, lock the door, walk out free and clear. She must have stood there with that gun for several days before the circumstances were right."

"She took a big risk." Ruth stirred her tea. "She must have stolen the gun days ago.

What if someone had noticed it was missing?"

"That weren't likely," Luty said. "How often do ya check to see if somethin' is where it's supposed to be?"

"True." Ruth took a sip. "Lord Cannonberry had an Enfield revolver. It's in one of the drawers of his old desk in the study, but I've not looked at it in ages."

"The smartest part of her plan was no one findin' the body till the next morning," Luty said. "It gave her plenty of time to figure out how she was goin' to frame Fiona Sutcliffe. She needed Dearman's keys to lock his office, but she could have chucked 'em in the river on her way home; instead, she planted them at the Sutcliffe house."

"In Mrs. Sutcliffe's morning room," Phyllis added eagerly. "She wanted her to be arrested for the murder. She must have hated her."

"She did," Mrs. Jeffries said with certainty. "She blamed Fiona for all the years she was in that miserable marriage to Thaddeus Meadows. She probably never forgave her the humiliation of losing John Sutcliffe, either."

"She almost got away with it." Mrs. Goodge pushed the almost empty sandwich plate toward Wiggins. There was only one left. "Take the last one. These don't keep well, and we don't want it goin' to waste."

"Ta, Mrs. Goodge." He scooped up the food. "Guess Mrs. Meadows didn't count on bein' noticed by anyone. But cor blimey, she must 'ave known the street boy she used to deliver the message to the police station would remember her."

"She was counting on Mrs. Sutcliffe being arrested," Mrs. Jeffries pointed out. "Once that happened, the police wouldn't bother to keep looking for witnesses."

"In other words, if it hadn't been for us, your sister-in-law would be facin' the dock." Luty chuckled. "Dang, we're good."

"What about all the money that Dearman had been collecting?" Phyllis asked. "What happened to that? It wasn't in his cottage."

"Some of it might have been, and some of it might have been in the house somewhere," Mrs. Jeffries said. "He was seen by one of the maids putting money in a traveling bag. I think he had a hiding place somewhere in the house, and I think his widow found it as soon as she knew he was dead. I suspect he kept the rest of it at the cottage. That's the reason Lucretia Dearman went out there the day before the funeral. She wanted to have a good hunt for any valuables she could lay her hands on."

"But she didn't find the lap desks with the ledger and the other bits." Wiggins picked up a piece of roast beef that had fallen onto his plate and popped it into his mouth.

"We don't know that," Mrs. Goodge said. "She might have just left them there. From what we've heard of her, she wasn't interested in blackmailin' anyone, she just wanted to travel and see the world."

They discussed the case until they heard a hansom draw up outside. Luty, Hatchet, and Ruth all left by the back door before the inspector came in the front.

Mrs. Jeffries dashed upstairs and met him in the foyer. "Did you have a successful day, sir?"

He nodded cheerfully. "Absolutely. We made an arrest in the Dearman murder, and I'm delighted to tell you that it wasn't Mrs. Sutcliffe. It was Antonia Meadows."

She pretended to be surprised. "Really, sir? You must tell me all about it. Are we going to have a sherry before dinner?"

"Of course." He handed her his hat and coat. "She confessed everything. Apparently, Ronald Dearman was blackmailing her over the death of her husband. He had evidence that she'd murdered the poor fellow."

"How did you know to look at her for the

crime?" Mrs. Jeffries hung up his garments on the pegs.

He grinned boyishly. "One doesn't like to blow one's own horn, but I will say that it was my 'inner voice' as you call it that moved the case in the right direction. Come along, let's go have that drink and I'll tell you all the details."

"Have you heard from your sister-in-law?" Mrs. Goodge asked. She and Mrs. Jeffries were alone in the kitchen.

"No," she replied. "But there's no reason why I should. The case is closed and we had very little to do with one another before the murder, so there's no need for her to contact me now that it is over and done with."

Two weeks had passed since the arrest and life had returned to normal. Mrs. Jeffries had been gratified to find out from the inspector that her ideas about the case had been proved correct. Antonia Meadows was going to stand trial, and their efforts had kept an innocent person out of the dock. Lucretia Dearman was quietly making plans to go abroad, Henry Anson had taken over the running of the office, and Sutcliffe Manufacturing hadn't been harmed by the scandal of murder.

She'd been relieved that she'd been able to keep John and Fiona's secret from thirty years ago, but it hadn't set well on her conscience. Eldon Grimshaw may not have had any family, but he deserved more than a quiet burial in what to him was a foreign land. Still, what good would come of making it public? Sutcliffe's could very well end up mired in legal issues if one of Grimshaw's long lost relatives turned up, and that would mean that hundreds of people both here and in Yorkshire could be out of work if things went badly in court. So despite her misgivings, she'd kept silent.

"She should have at least sent you a thank-you of some kind," Mrs. Goodge exclaimed. "If it hadn't been for you —"

"If it hadn't been for *us*," Mrs. Jeffries corrected. "Everyone helped. It wasn't just me."

From upstairs, they heard the mail drop into the basket on the front door. Mrs. Jeffries wanted an excuse to avoid this conversation. "I'll go get the post. Maybe there's a letter for us from Canada."

She went up the back stairs. The truth was, she *was* annoyed that she'd not heard a word from Fiona. But she wasn't going to dwell on it; she didn't want a relationship with her anyway. Yet, still, it would have been nice if Fiona had acknowledged they'd all worked hard to keep her out of jail. She snorted delicately and stomped down the hall to the front door.

There were two letters in the post basket. She opened the latch and pulled them out. One letter was for Inspector Witherspoon, and the second was for her. The heavy, cream-colored envelope, clearly of expensive stationary stock, displayed her name in bold, elegant strokes above the address. She ripped it open and yanked out the enclosed paper.

It was from Fiona. She scanned the contents and laughed out loud.

She ran back downstairs. "Mrs. Goodge," she called as she hurried into the kitchen. "We've all been invited to the Sutcliffe house."

"What?" Mrs. Goodge looked quite alarmed. "What do you mean, we've been invited to the Sutcliffe house?"

"Fiona and John want us all to come for a thank-you luncheon." She held out the letter. "Take a look."

Mrs. Goodge took the paper, read it, and then looked up. "Well, what do you know about that. It's considerate of her to make it a luncheon and not a dinner. She said here that she didn't want to put us in the awkward position of mentionin' it to the inspector."

"That was thoughtful of her," Mrs. Jeffries said.

Mrs. Goodge smiled tightly. "It sounds like she not only wants to thank us for our help, but also to establish a better relationship with you." She handed the letter back. "That's nice. You're family. You should be part of one another's lives."

Mrs. Jeffries took it and eyed her friend curiously. "Was there something in this that offended you?"

"No, no don't be silly. It is a lovely letter, and I'm glad she wants you to come to tea once a week. Now that you've gotten to know each other, you can be family."

She'd expected the cook to be delighted by the invitation. But she could tell by the strained smile and the false note of cheer in her voice that she was upset. It took Mrs. Jeffries a moment before she understood what was happening. Mrs. Goodge had spent her life as an outsider, always in someone else's home, cooking for someone else's children, and living at the mercy of others. Until she'd come here. They'd forged a family together, and Mrs. Goodge was worried that a new face in the mix might change that. But it wasn't going to happen.

"Don't be silly, Mrs. Goodge," she said softly. "My real family is right here at Upper Edmonton Gardens. I love and cherish all of you. Fiona Sutcliffe is part of my late husband's family, and all she'll ever be to me is an in-law. The people in this household will always come first with me."

Mrs. Goodge looked at her for a long moment and then a real smile spread across her face. "Just as you'll always come first with me."